THE JACK NOBLE SERIES

For paperback purchase links, visit:
https://ltryan.com/pb

End Game (Jack Noble #12)
Noble Ultimatum (Jack Noble #13)

For paperback purchase links, visit:
https://ltryan.com/pb

1

THE WOMAN EMERGED FROM A PACK OF PEDESTRIANS. THEY
parted as she passed. They stared at her in awe. I imagined them asking each
other, "Who is that woman?" She drew attention in part because of her
beauty. In part due to her confidence.

Surrounding her were six men.

Dressed in black.

All armed.

Not a sight you see every day on the outskirts of London.

Yet people didn't notice them. She made them look invisible.

I presumed the men had training on a level close to my own.

The woman and the men continued their approach down the street. Her
black hair was parted down the middle. It splashed across her shoulders. The
breeze lifted it at the edges and it danced in the wind.

They stopped in front of Cataldi's. The restaurant had a wood burning
stove. The cooks had started it a few minutes ago. The exhaust fan spit
flavored smoke into the sky. It passed by me. My stomach ached with anticipation. As much for the meal as for the job.

The woman and her bodyguards continued on. They'd stopped in front
of the restaurant the previous three days. They never went in. Three doors

down sat the cafe. If the woman were as much a creature of habit as I thought, and counted on, they'd go in there again this morning.

The roof offered a view of the entire street. The downside to that was that I could be seen from the street from both directions. With the woman and her security team close by, I retreated. No big deal. Their plans weren't secret.

I touched the button on the device connected to my ear. Steady static ensued. "I've got visual confirmation. Heading inside now." I tapped the button again. The static faded away.

Noise crawled along the building's two hundred year old facade. The chatter of those passing, a moped racing by, the steady thud of the body-guards' hard-soled shoes, and the woman's stilettos attacking the sidewalk.

They stood out from the rest.

Staying low, I crossed the rooftop, coming to a stop in front of the building access. Nothing in the surrounding environment had changed. I pulled the door open, kicked the prop out of the way and hit the stairs, taking them two at a time.

The lobby door crashed open. Heavy steps hit the stairs. The person ran up. Their heavy breaths indicated that they had been running even before they entered the building.

I froze in place, pulled my Beretta and leaned back against someone's door.

A mother scolded her child. The little kid raced through the apartment behind me. A door slammed. The mother let out a frustrated sound.

The footsteps kept coming toward me. Had they spotted me? I moved away from the wall and toward the stairs. The person stopped. I held my breath. They let out theirs. Then they took a deep breath and exhaled again.

"Good run," they said, followed by a door opening and closing.

Shaking my head, I reflected on how close I'd come to killing an innocent bystander. No time to dwell. I continued my descent.

Sasha's voice filled my ear. "She's in front of the cafe, Jack."

I didn't stop to reply. Five steps separated me from the lobby. I'd see for myself in a few moments.

Black and white checkered tile led to the front of the room where double doors swayed back and forth a few inches. I ran up to them, stopped, scanned the street in front of me. I couldn't see her. The two men positioned behind her were too tall and too wide.

Where'd they find these guys? The pro wrestling circuit? They sure as hell weren't former Special Forces.

I drove my shoulder into the door, pushed it open and stepped onto the sidewalk. Down here, the smell of the grill was stronger. It combined with that of the pastry shop next door. It was almost enough to throw me off.

I turned left and started walking, using the windows next to me to watch the scene on the other side of the street. One of her security detail studied me. He was mammoth in size. He stayed outside along with another big guy, while the other four accompanied the woman into the cafe.

"They're heading inside, Jack."

I reached up and activated the speaker. "Are we set up?"

"We never got inside."

"Say again?"

"They had two waiting."

"So she's got eight bodyguards today?"

"The threat was high. You knew this. You said you were prepared for it."

Three elderly women approached. I said nothing with them in earshot. One of the women smiled at me. Bright red lipstick coated her lips, as well as skin above and below. Even her teeth were shades of red. I smiled back and nodded at her.

"Jack? Do you want me to call everyone back and abort?"

I looked over my shoulder. The woman was no longer in sight. Two men stood in the doorway. The elderly women crossed the street. One of them skipped a step. Must be one good cup of coffee inside.

The older women approached the two behemoths standing guard. The guards demanded that the ladies open up their purses so they could search them. They tossed items on the ground. One of the women protested loudly. The guy said something to the effect of, "Don't like it? Get lost."

"Jack?" she yelled.

"Call them off," I said.

"You're giving up?"

"They weren't doing this yesterday."

"What?"

"I'll see you in an hour."

"Jack, what are you going to do?"

I pulled the device off my ear, tossed it into the trash, continued on another half block. I reached behind my back and drew my Beretta. It went into the trash, too. I stepped off the curb, paused for a white Fiat that honked at me as it passed, then crossed the street. A group of teenagers told me to go back to America. I ignored them.

Ahead, the last of the elderly women stepped inside the cafe. The guard closest to me turned his head in my direction. He watched as I approached.

I stopped in front of the cafe. Placed my foot on the first step.

The guy stuck his thick hand out. He wagged his finger in front of me. When he spoke, his accent was Irish, thick, like he was from Cork. "I saw you exit the apartment building and head up the street."

I nodded. "Had a coffee date with a woman. She called it off. Kind of happy, actually. This place has the best brew in town. First time I've seen security here, though. What's going on? Did the Queen stop by today?"

The men glanced at each other. They looked like two defensive linemen about to converge on the quarterback at the same time.

"Come up here," the guy on the right said. He was local.

I stepped up, held my arms out to the side.

"Turn around," Cork said.

I faced the apartment building. A kid walking by looked up at me. I stuck my tongue out at him and crossed my eyes. He smiled. The guy behind me patted me down, stuck his hands in my pocket, and cupped me somewhere he shouldn't have. I rose up on my tiptoes.

"You gonna buy me a pastry now?" I said.

"Shut up," Cork said.

"Go on in," the other said.

Neither held the door for me. I felt cheated after how close we'd become.

I used the hard toe of my right shoe against the door's kick plate and nudged it open. The aroma of dark roast met me. My mouth watered. It was necessary to stay focused, so I scanned the room, breaking it down into quadrants.

The woman sat in the corner, surrounded by guys smaller than the two at the front door. These were the pros. The other two were meatheads whose only purpose was to scare the store's patrons. I kept my eyes moving. Didn't want to linger on her too long. Or on the men.

There were three people behind the counter. The day before there had only been two, and those two weren't present today. I figure most people would assume that the biggest one would be the plant, if there was one. Not me. And not the skinny guy with red hair and acne either. I pegged it as the cute girl with the dimples. She smiled and winked and put my mind at ease.

Not an easy thing to do.

I ordered a Cafe Americano and took a seat at a table fifteen feet away from the woman.

Her name was Marcia Stanton. The name meant nothing to me. I'd been told Marcia was an up and comer in politics. She had gained relevance by attacking and bringing down some powerful people. A grassroots movement built, and next thing she knew, people encouraged her to run for office.

At first, she declined. The offers didn't stop. So when a heavy hitter stepped in and told her she owed it to her country, she agreed.

And that opened a Pandora's Box of hell for her. Death threats came. Bodyguards were hired. Three attempts on her life had resulted in the hiring of three more bodyguards to replace her core four.

All of that led to me being seated in that cafe, mid-morning, hungry, tired, unarmed and uncaffeinated. At least one condition was close to being remedied.

"Sir?"

I glanced up at the cute girl with the dimples. She threw a pale elbow on the counter and held out my mug with the other hand. I rose, stole a glance at Marcia and her bodyguards, and walked to the counter. The girl watched me the whole way. One hand wrapped around the mug. The other dropped a tip on the glass top.

"Cream or sugar?" she asked.

I shook my head. "Black is fine. The rest of the stuff gets in the way."

She shrugged. "Anything else?"

Behind her, the big guy glared at me. I noticed a swastika tattooed on his wrist. We engaged in a stare-off. He looked away first.

"Sir?" the girl said.

"I'm fine," I said.

She turned around, rolling her eyes. I was just another schmuck to her, and that was OK. I returned to the same table, sat in a different seat. This one allowed me to see the counter and Marcia's booth. The downside to that was that the table created an obstacle that I had to go around in order to do my job.

One of the bodyguards rose. He headed toward the hallway that led to the restrooms.

Hand Tattoo passed through a beaded curtain. I figured he went into the kitchen. Dimples glanced around the cafe. Her gaze came to a stop on Marcia's table. A minute later, the girl joined the guy in back, leaving the skinny red-head all alone.

I stood, walked to the counter and leaned against it.

Skinny Red said, "Help you?"

"I'm good," I said.

Skinny Red seemed too calm, relaxed, confident. If there was a plant, it had to be him.

The front door opened. A man stepped inside. A sheet of sweat coated his forehead. His breathing was erratic. His eyes shifted side to side. They never settled on anything. He looked at me, Skinny Red, the beaded curtain, and at Marcia. And when he saw her, he bent over and reached for his ankle.

2

ONE HAND REACHED TO MY EAR, AND THE OTHER AROUND MY BACK. Neither found what they were looking for. I'd thrown away the ear piece and pistol a few minutes ago. I hoped to recover them soon. Making it out alive became priority number one. There was no backup now. I had no idea who was and wasn't trustworthy in the cafe.

The nervous man caught the attention of Marcia's table. One of her men rose. He strolled over to the guy. This left Marcia with two bodyguards. One next to her, and one across the table.

The guy who'd stood up now blocked the path of the nervous man, who was bent over with two fingers in his sock. The man lifted his head three inches. His gaze followed along. His eyes angled inward. They focused on the barrel of the pistol aimed at his forehead. The expression on his face took a few moments to change.

"Don't move." The bodyguard's accent wasn't easy to place. South Africa, maybe? Perhaps New Zealand. I get those mixed up quite often.

The nervous man let out a sound I'd once heard a dying squirrel make. A couple seconds later, drips of water hit the floor. It wasn't water though. A puddle formed at his feet.

"Disgusting," the bodyguard said. He jabbed the end of his pistol into the nervous guy's chest.

Around the cafe, patrons stared in horror at the scene unfolding. It seemed everyone was enthralled by the event. All except for one of the elderly women. She bit into her pastry and refused to put it down.

I remained still, watched the scene play out.

"Get up, slowly," the bodyguard said.

The nervous man shook. He came up halfway, convulsed, then straightened his body. The front of his shorts were wet. His *weapon* shook in his hand. The bodyguard swatted at it. Two five-pound notes drifted to the floor.

The bodyguard looked over his shoulder. He laughed, and said, "You believe this?"

The other two members of Marcia's security detail laughed. One held up his hands and shrugged.

I heard footsteps behind me. The fourth bodyguard, presumably, returning from the bathroom.

I was wrong.

Dimple's perfume hit me before she passed on my left. Hand Tattoo's body odor eradicated her sweet smell. He had a gun dangling from his right hand. He lifted his arm and aimed at the bodyguard who stood in the middle of the cafe.

The bodyguard's training forced him into action. Already armed with an M40, he spun. He drove his shoulder into the nervous guy's chest. The man flew backward, sprawled out, skidded to the door. Hand Tattoo fired first. He caught the bodyguard in the gut. A crimson bloom formed near the man's navel. He fell backward, landed on the nervous guy's legs. Feeble attempts to lift his sidearm failed.

I heard another shot, glanced toward Marcia's table. One of her men lay face down on top of it. Unfocused eyes stared toward the display cabinet. Above them, blood flowed from a hole in his forehead. The bullet he took ended his life.

I grabbed a mug off the counter. It felt thick, heavy. I whipped my arm around and slammed the mug into the back of Hand Tattoo's head. His scalp split in two. The coffee cup shattered. The only thing left in my hand was the handle. Hand Tattoo fell to his knees. I struck him twice with each fist. He fell forward, unconscious.

The men out front tried to get back inside. One drove his shoulder into the front door. It dinged as it opened. It didn't get far, though. The nervous man and the bodyguard who took the gut shot blocked the door's arc, preventing it from opening all the way. That didn't stop the two men outside from driving it open repeatedly. The nervous man took the brunt of the door's steel frame. He screamed with every thrust.

I looked away after his arm broke. There were more pressing issues to deal with at that time.

With Hand Tattoo out of my way, I had a good view of Dimples. She fired a second shot. The live guard at the table covered Marcia Stanton. The bullet entered through his lower back. Dimples fired again. It hit the wall. A plaster cloud loomed in the air. Dimples cursed.

I glanced over the counter and located Skinny Red. He lay on the floor, hands over his head. I felt disappointed in being wrong about the guy.

Dimples retracted then extended her arm. The trigger clicked. The bullet didn't fire. She turned the gun sideways. Her head lowered an inch. She shook the weapon and tried again. Nothing happened. The pistol had jammed.

Already moving forward, I reached inside my pocket and pulled out a pen. Dimples looked over her shoulder. Her eyes grew wide. Her right shoulder ducked. She turned on the ball of her left foot. Four feet separated me and my pen from her and her gun.

She reached out and screamed and squeezed the trigger.

I cocked my left arm back, and twisted and jumped.

Her pistol roared. The muzzle flash was bright and instantaneous. The bullet sliced past me and smashed into the plaster wall. A chunk fell to the floor.

She looked pissed. Her mouth contorted. She turned and reset her aim.

I swung my left arm and drove the pen into the side of her neck. I wasn't going for her jugular, or even a kill shot. The pen did damage in a different way. My only job was to insert the tip. The fluid inside the hollow body did the rest. I watched and waited. She brought her hand up to her neck, wrapped it around the pen. Her twisted expression told me that the fluid coursed through her system.

Quickly.

Dimples dropped to one knee. She fell sideways against the display case. Her lips smeared against the glass as she slid down it on her way to the floor.

"What just happened?" Marcia Stanton said.

I pushed myself off the floor, got to one knee, and said, "You're OK now. It's safe."

The front door burst open. The two men came in shouting.

"Just stay there," Marcia told them.

Like well-trained dogs, they remained in place.

With one foot off the ground, a pen in one hand, and Dimple's Glock in the other, I rose. The adrenaline letdown had begun, and delayed my reaction to the footsteps behind me.

Marcia's hands went out and she shook her head side to side. I think she might have said, "No, no, no," but I can't be sure.

Something smashed against the back of my head. I fell forward, catching the side of my face against Marcia's table, inches from the dead bodyguard's blood. Might have slid into it. Maybe not. Hard to tell, because that was about the time that I blacked out.

3

BRIGHT RED.

THAT WAS WHAT I saw, even though my eyes were closed. I heard voices around me. They were muffled and deep. My face felt hot. My body felt detached. It was almost like I'd spent a day buried up to my neck in sand at the beach.

I forced my eyes open. A bright light hovered above me. I brought my hand to my face. Metal joints creaked. The light swung away. It cast its insidious glare toward the corner of the room. The retinal burn faded, bright to dark to faint then gone. I looked around the room. There was a woman standing next to the bed. I recognized her.

"Jesus, are you OK, Jack?" Sasha asked.

I nodded. My neck felt stiff. "Yeah, I'm all right."

"What the hell happened in there?"

Glimpses of the attempt on Marcia's life played in my mind.

"I'm not quite sure." Slipping my hand between my head and the pillow, I massaged the base of my skull and glanced around. It wasn't a normal hospital room. "Where am I?"

"Where do you think?"

"I wouldn't ask if I had a clue."

"You're in the basement of my facility. One of our guys, you know, the ones you sent away, he heard gunshots. By the time he got to the cafe, you were face down in a pool of someone else's blood. We found multiple others on the floor."

"Not all of them were my fault."

"The people in the cafe told us that you took two of them out, but one of them had taken out the dead guy on the table."

"And the guard who stood in the middle of the restaurant."

"And another guard at the table is paralyzed from the waist down."

"And some innocent guy got battered by the front door."

She nodded.

"And Marcia Stanton?" I asked.

"She's fine. We got her out along with the member of her security detail that took you out. In all, she left behind one dead guard and the blood of two others. I hope, at least. Both men that were shot are in critical condition at this time."

I checked my facts against hers in my head. She sounded like she had a pretty good idea of what happened. Guess she figured I could fill in some holes.

I shook my head. "So she made it through unscathed."

Sasha nodded.

"And it was one of her guys that took me out?"

She nodded.

I reached for a glass of water perched on the nightstand next to the bed. It had red lipstick on the rim. I spun it around and took a sip. "And what about the two I neutralized?"

She said, "What about them?"

I said, "You didn't let them go, did you?"

She said, "We've got them in custody. Thank you for confirming that you're responsible for them."

I nodded. "They came out of nowhere. I took the guy out first, Dimples second."

"Dimples?"

"She had dimples. They stood out."

Sasha said nothing.

"You didn't notify anyone, did you?"

"Who would I notify?"

"You know who."

"No, I didn't tell Erin." She looked away. Bringing up Erin around the woman always produced this result.

When I had agreed to remain in London and help Sasha, she had asked me to leave Erin with the impression that I had left the country. I didn't. Even though things had long since quieted between Erin and me, she was the mother of my child. A child I hadn't known about until recently. My time away from the job was spent with Mia, and in turn, Erin.

"It's best that you didn't," I said. "I don't want to worry Mia."

"And Erin."

"You sound jealous."

"Maybe I am." She could have burned me with her stare.

I smiled. She looked away.

"You feel well enough to get dressed?" she said.

"Bit of a headache, but I'll manage," I said.

"OK. There's a shower in the bathroom. Get yourself cleaned up, changed, and then come up to my office."

I watched Sasha walk away. Her dark hair was pulled back in a ponytail. It swung to the side. Every step revealed a bit of her neck. She exited into the hallway and pulled the door shut.

I swung my feet over the bed and stood. My head spun. Perhaps I had risen too fast. The edge of my vision darkened for a second or two. A hand on the bed steadied my body. The sensation passed. I breathed in through my nose, held it, and exhaled through my mouth.

"OK," I said. "That was fun."

I stepped into the bathroom. A folded towel, washcloth, and unopened bar of soap waited for me on the toilet seat. I reached past the thin shower curtain and turned the shower faucet. Ice-cold water dribbled from the shower head. It'd warm up, I supposed.

I looked at my reflection in the mirror that hung over the sink. Blood caked my forehead. I parted my hair in a dozen spots but found no wound. I recalled the pool of blood on the table in the cafe. It had spread. Or I had moved. Same result either way.

My fingertips skated along my scalp. They met in the back. There I felt a line of stitches. Twelve by my count. They hadn't bandaged the wound, so I figured it wasn't too bad.

My headache dissipated. The blow had rendered me unconscious, but I didn't feel too many aftereffects. That didn't mean a concussion didn't exist. I had a feeling that Sasha would insist I stay in the infirmary all night. It was that or the city hospital. At least the building offered safety.

The mirror fogged up. I wiped it with my palm, leaving behind thin streaks of condensation. The gaps filled back in.

I stepped into the shower. Red-tinted water pooled below my feet. My blood or someone else's? Ignoring it, I washed my body three times just to make sure I'd removed it all. The minutes passed and the water turned clear.

I cut the faucet off, dried myself and went back into the room. Sasha had left a change of clothes for me. She'd set my wallet and cell phone next to them. I put on the khaki pants and an off-white polo. They fit just right. Had she been creeping around my closet? I grabbed my cell and the wallet, inspected both, and stuffed them in opposite front pockets.

My shoes must've taken a beating in the cafe, because she'd left a new pair for me. Brown, leather, steel toed and hard soled. Another perfect fit.

I grabbed the glass of water she'd left behind. The condensation on the outside of the cup felt cold against the skin of my palm, which was still hot from the shower. I emptied the glass, sat it down, walked to the door, and stepped out of the room. My head started to spin again. I stopped, placed my hand on the wall, waited for it to pass.

It didn't take long, and it wasn't as bad as the first spell.

A nurse witnessed the event. "You OK?"

I nodded. "I'm fine."

She said, "Positive?"

I closed my eyes, dropped my head back, turned my palms up and walked on a line. "Would I be able to do this if I was lying?"

"You better come back down here after you're done with your meeting."

I got the distinct feeling that Sasha had to override the nurse to get me out of the room. I resumed walking like a normal person.

She shook her head.

I nodded and smiled as I passed her.

She said, "I'm serious, Jack."

This was the second time she had treated me. Last time had been off-site. I felt bad that I couldn't remember her name. I glanced toward the tag on her lapel, but she'd already turned back to her paperwork.

"I know you are," I said. "That's why I always refer to you as Nurse Serious. Best of the bunch."

"Get out of here," she said, laughing.

I stopped in front of the elevator. There were no buttons, only a card reader. I retrieved my wallet and found my access card inside. I waved it in front of the device on the wall. The steel doors parted and I stepped inside the mirrored lift.

Sasha's office was on the top. That correlated to the button labeled four on the elevator's panel. I pressed it. The doors shut. The elevator dropped a foot, then darted upward. It took a second for my stomach to catch up. I braced myself for another dizzy spell, but it didn't happen.

The lift came to a stop. The door didn't open. They wouldn't on their own. Sasha worked on a restricted access floor. I still held my access card in my hand. I swiped it through the reader above the buttons. A light switched from red to green. The doors opened. A guard straightened up. He placed his hand on his sidearm and stared me down.

I walked toward him. "At ease, mate."

He rolled his eyes at me. I never tired of it. They did.

He reached across his body and pressed a button. The double doors in front of me clicked and hissed. I reached out, turned the handle on the right and pushed the door open.

This section of the building was gray. No other way to put it. Gray floors, gray cubicles, gray doors on the offices. Even the windows were covered with gray blinds. Half the people looked gray. Not their hair, their skin. Perhaps someone that paid too much money for the work they did figured the dodgy look of the floor made the workers more productive.

It depressed the hell out of me, and I'd only been inside a few seconds.

I glanced into the cubicles as I passed. Most occupants ignored me. The ones that didn't glared at me. They all did anything but work. I saw Facebook, Twitter, and a couple rounds of solitaire being played.

So much for the productivity theory.

A guard was positioned at the end of the cubicle-lined corridor. He stared me down. I looked anywhere but at him.

"You're supposed to have your ID clipped where I can see it," he said.

I ignored him.

"You there," he said. "You hear me?"

I glanced at him, nodded and angled my body in advance of turning to the right at the last cubicle in the line.

"I need to see your ID," he said.

I fished out my wallet and produced my identification card.

"Thank you."

"I wouldn't be in here if I didn't have it, you know."

"I know," he said.

Asshole.

I continued on until I reached Sasha's office. The gray door was closed. I knocked three times.

"Come in," she said.

I opened the door, and said, "Give a guy a badge and a gun and all of a sudden he's..." My words tapered off. I hadn't counted on another person being in the room.

4

SASHA AND ANOTHER WOMAN SAT IN CHAIRS POSITIONED IN FRONT of Sasha's bare desk. The view behind her empty high-back leather chair was of the Thames. Dark clouds gathered in the distance. The other woman faced the window.

"Jack," Sasha said. "You met Marcia Stanton earlier."

Marcia turned toward me. She smiled. She could have been a toothpaste model.

"Yes," I said. "We had a cup of coffee together."

"Right," Sasha said. "Forgive him," she added. "He's American."

The way she said it made me feel like I should apologize. Fortunately, that sensation passed quickly. I grabbed the empty chair and placed it three feet between and in front of the women. We formed a triangle.

"What's this about?" I asked.

"I wanted to thank you," Marcia said.

"Just doing my job," I said.

"You're too gracious," she said.

"Jack's one of the best operators I've ever met," Sasha said.

"I believe it," Marcia said. "I've never seen someone act so decisively."

"I froze," I said. "And while I enjoy having my horn tooted by two attractive women as much as the next guy, I can also tell when I'm being buttered up for something. So cut the crap and tell me what's going on."

The women looked at each other for a moment, then turned toward me.

Sasha said, "Marcia feels that—"

"Allow me," Marcia interrupted. "Mr. Noble—"

I held my hand up and looked at Sasha. "You told her my name?"

"It's OK, Jack. She checks out."

I shook my head. "Anyway, continue."

Marcia glanced toward Sasha, then back at me. She smiled. It wasn't the winning grin she had displayed a few minutes ago. The woman felt nervous now.

"I'm going to assume you know my story. Most of it, at least. What you don't know, Sasha will fill you in on after I've left." She uncrossed her legs and leaned forward. "I've pissed off a lot of people, Jack. Some of those people want me dead, as you are well aware. They are getting closer and closer to being successful. My concern grows larger day after day. I go to sleep wondering if I'll wake up. I wake up wondering if I'll live to go to sleep. I'm not sure how I even survived that scenario today."

"Neither am I," I said.

"What do you mean?" she asked.

"You go have coffee at the same place every day this week."

"I'm trying to reach out and become a part of this community so I can win the election."

"You hire amateurs for your security detail."

She straightened up and crossed her wrists at her waist. "They came highly recommended. I was told they were the best in the business."

"Then you were duped. Those two guys out in front of the cafe, they were goons, Marcia. They harassed old ladies, for Christ's sake. You got a guy that gets up and goes to the bathroom. Another leaves the table and bullies a man who was already shaken by the thugs out front. That leaves you with two bodyguards, and that's after two-thirds of the staff behind the counter disappears. Frankly, Marcia, I'm not sure how either of us is alive right now."

The woman said nothing. An awkward silence ensued. Sasha tried to break it.

"What Jack is trying to say is—"

"There's no trying. I said what needed to be said. And I'm going to add to it. You're stupid for following through with this whole election. You're going to end up dead. Maybe not this week, or the next. Hell, you might make it to and through the election. You might even make it through a term or two. But the longer you're in, unless you go the way of most other politicians, you're going to keep pissing off the wrong people and one day it's going to come back to bite you on the ass."

Marcia narrowed her eyes. Her hands rose into the air and became animated. "I know the dangers. I saw what happened to the Prime Minister."

I glanced at Sasha. "She doesn't know?"

Sasha shook her head.

A few months prior there had been an incident that brought Sasha, Prime Minister Alex Parkin, and me together. In order to save the man's life, I had to shoot him in the shoulder. It worked out in the end. I didn't go to prison. We caught the bad guy, the bad girl, and Parkin became a hero.

"He's lucky he's not dead," I said. "Anyway, did you really bring me in here to talk about Alex Parkin?"

"I'll get right to it, Jack. I know my security has been bad."

"I exaggerated," I said.

"No, you didn't. I need the best." She glanced at Sasha, then back at me. "That's why I want to hire you."

"What?" I looked at Sasha. She shrugged.

"Money is not an object," Marcia said. "You can name your price. I can provide every resource you need. If you want to bring in your own men, I can accommodate that."

I leaned back in my chair and crossed my left leg over my right knee. Marcia's stare never left mine. She looked serious, and perhaps scared. The attempt today had left her shaken. Understandable, I thought. She sat motionless. It was up to me to respond. She was not going to break the silence.

"Listen, I'm not sure what Sasha told you, or what your people might have said about me, but I'm not in the body guarding business. It works against my natural instincts."

"I saw you in the cafe. You knew the two people behind the counter didn't belong there."

"No," I said. "I knew the girl didn't, but then I figured the skinny kid was the plant. You know what happened to him? He ended up wetting himself on the floor. I was just as wrong as the men you hired."

Marcia said nothing. She leveled me with her dark eyes. Half of me said to take the job. The other half said to run away.

"Sasha, tell her I'm not the right guy for this."

Sasha put her hands in the air. "I don't want to lose you, Jack, not for any amount of time. But if you agree, I have no qualms about you going. I don't want to see anything happen to Marcia."

"Thanks, Sasha." I shook my head.

"Four weeks, a million dollars U.S."

"What?" I said.

"One point five," Marcia said.

I rose and walked past the women. The storm clouds to the north had thickened in the short time I'd been in the office.

"Two million dollars, Mr. Noble."

"You could buy a full team of pros for a quarter of that." I turned to face her. "I'll give you the number of a guy. He'll have four men here by midnight. They're specialists. They can keep you safer than I can."

"I don't want them," Marcia said. "I want you."

"This is crazy. I'm not a bodyguard."

"I'm not leaving this office until you say yes."

"Hope you brought a change of clothes then." My cell buzzed against my thigh. I held my finger out as I reached for it. "Hold on." I glanced at the screen. "I've got to take this."

Sasha glanced over at me. "Erin?"

"No, someone from the States." I walked past them, turned when I got to the door. "Let it go, Sasha."

5

I STEPPED INTO THE HALL WITH THE PHONE BUZZING IN MY HAND. No one seemed to notice or care. I answered the call before it diverted to voicemail.

"Jack?"

I hesitated a minute. It'd been over a year since I heard a voice that sounded like my own.

"Sean?" I said.

"How's my baby brother doing?"

"I'm doing OK. How... How'd you get this number?"

"I've got my sources."

"Who?"

"Is this how you start a conversation after going a year without talking to me?"

"No. You're right. Sorry, Sean. What's going on? Is everything OK? Is Dad OK? Did something happen?"

"Dad's all right. Crazier than a hoot owl, but he's doing fine. Deborah and Kelly are fine, too. No need to worry about them."

I glanced at a clock mounted above an office door. I performed a quick time conversion. It was mid-day back home. I couldn't shake the feeling that something had happened. Sean was a lawyer and a busy guy. He wouldn't call in the middle of the day for nothing.

"You didn't call just to chat, Sean. I know you better than that. I mean, unless I blacked out and it's Christmas already. Just get to the point."

The door opened behind me. Sasha mouthed, "What's going on?"

I shook my head and walked away from her. An overhead light was out. The corridor between cubicles and offices grew dim.

"I don't know how to put this, so I'll just say it." He paused. It sounded like he took a drink. "They found Jessie dead last night."

It felt like a blast wave hit me. "Jessie? Jessie Kline? My old fiancé?"

"That's the one." Sean paused a beat. "She's Jessie Staley now. Or, she was."

"Jesus." I felt the blood drain and my knees went weak. I found a wall to lean against for support. "What happened?"

"I don't know all the details yet, Jack, but I'm hearing suicide."

"That doesn't make sense. Jessie had always been a positive, strong woman."

"When did you last see her?"

I thought about it. "Over ten years, I guess. Well, I saw her at Mom's funeral. We said hi, but that was it."

"Things change, Jack. I heard rumors that she wasn't happy. I spotted her husband at the bar a couple times. He was with other women. I never made much of it. He wasn't all over any of them or anything. Maybe there was more to it than I realized."

"When's the funeral?"

"Three days. You thinking of coming?"

I looked toward Sasha's office. "I don't know if that's possible right now, Sean."

"I'm sure Jessie's family would appreciate it. Deb'd like to see you, I know that. Kelly doesn't even remember you. She knows your picture, but nothing other than that. I'm sure it's the same way with you and her." Sean paused. The emotional impact of his words set in. "And I wouldn't mind a couple days catching up with my baby brother."

"I…" I couldn't say yes, and I couldn't say no.

"Look, think about it for a bit. Talk to whoever you need to talk with. I'll call you in a bit. You've got my number now. If you come to a decision before I get back to you, hit me up."

"Will do." I ended the call.

"Jack?" Sasha said.

I walked away from her, found an empty office and went inside. The chair behind the desk was a replica of Sasha's. I sat down. The chair glided in a half-circle. I looked out over the Thames. An eight-person scull floated by. They worked in unison with the exception of the coxswain who commanded their pace. Nothing in my life worked as fluidly as that team.

Jessie had been a part of my life since I was a kid. We hated each other when we were little. I tormented her from first grade through sixth. Dirt and earthworms turned into signs pinned on her back and crude jokes. One summer I grew up, sort of, and so did she, a lot. Then I fell in love with her. It took three or four years to convince her to give me a shot. I left for the Marines at the age of eighteen. From that point we were on-again off-again for a few years. Eventually we went our separate ways.

Eleven years ago I wound up in a sticky situation outside of D.C. My partner Bear took a bullet. I knew Jessie lived nearby. She was a trauma nurse at the time. I thought the two of us might make a go of it then. It didn't turn out that way. I almost got her killed. I did get her and her parents threatened by someone high up and out of my reach. We had busted a three-star Army General by the name of Keller. Some folks didn't respond well to that.

Last time I saw her was at Dulles Airport. She went one way, I went the other. I took a few months off after that. Spent it down in the Keys. She had an open invitation. Never showed. She'd moved on. I did the same.

A rap at the door interrupted my thoughts. I swung around in the chair. Sasha had already opened the door and entered the office.

"What's going on, Jack?"

"Just got some news from back home."

"Another job offer?"

"No. I mean back home as in where I'm from."

"Oh." Her gaze drifted to my right. I pictured another scull racing by, this one a single or a double.

"There's been a death. Someone close to me. I know the timing's not right, but I think I should go back for her funeral."

I expected her to protest, throw a fit, and demand that I stay.

Instead, she said, "Let's go get a drink."

I placed my hands on the desk and stood. "What about Marcia?"

"I sent her home with a couple of our guys. Told her you needed a day to think it over."

"What's to think over? I'm not doing it."

"Don't rush to a decision like that yet, Jack. That's a lot of money."

I shrugged. "It's not always about the money."

"She's a good woman. She deserves the best protection out there."

I rounded the desk and came to a stop in front of Sasha. She stood a few inches shorter than me and had to look up to make eye contact. She inched forward until we were almost touching. Her perfume mixed with her natural scent. The combination was intoxicating.

"She does," I said. "And we should arrange it for her. It just can't be me."

Sasha sighed and shook her head and put her hands on her hips. She took a step back, brushing against a fake ficus. "Come on, Jack. I'll drive."

We exited the office. The artificial fluorescent light did little to enhance my mood. Sasha led the way to the main cubicle corridor and into the elevator lobby. I winked at the first security guard, ignored the second. Sasha swiped for the elevator. We got off at the parking garage.

"Nurse whatever-her-name-is wanted me to come back for the night," I said as we stepped into the muggy garage.

"You can come back if you're still feeling bad after we get some food."

"I'd prefer not to. And when did this turn into dinner?"

Sasha said nothing. She pulled out her keys and hit a button. An Audi beeped twice. Its brake lights and turn signals flashed three times each. The red and orange lights splashed across the concrete floor and ceiling. Sasha walked toward it. I followed her. Our footsteps echoed through the deserted garage.

"Borrowing from the fleet?" I asked.

She shook her head, and said, "Bought it last week."

"Not bad." I slid into the leather bucket seat. It smelled new inside. I couldn't find a smudge or a trace of dirt anywhere. "I'm starting to think you aren't paying me enough."

"Who says you're getting paid anything?" She pushed the ignition button. A hefty eight-cylinder engine roared approvingly. Sasha released the emergency brake and shifted into reverse. A minute later the car was in third gear and we were going fifty down the middle of the road.

The sky in front was seven shades of red and orange. Behind us, storm clouds loomed. Around us, commercial buildings gave way to row homes. Everything seemed so compact. I thought of the thousands of people who spent their days working away inside of a cramped building, only to go home and spend their nights inside a house sandwiched between two others.

This was no place for the claustrophobic to live.

Fortunately for them there were sunsets like the one tonight, and plenty of places to grab a pint.

Ten minutes passed without a word between Sasha and me. I broke the silence.

"Where are we headed?" I said.

"Just a place I know," she said.

"Why do I feel like I'm being set up?"

She laughed, didn't make eye contact. It didn't comfort me. Ten minutes later she pointed toward a pub. I didn't catch the name. We parked in back between two cars half the size of the Audi. The sleek new car made the other two look like garbage cans.

I opened my door. The smell of seared meat was strong. I headed for the street to walk around to the front entrance.

"We can go in back here," Sasha said.

I stopped and turned toward her. She walked toward the back door where two middle-aged men in aprons sat on the hood of a car smoking cigarettes. The guys looked at me, then her. I didn't think they were going to glance in my direction again.

I jogged across the parking lot and met her by the back door.

The two men returned to their conversation.

"Ready?" Sasha said.

"Sure," I said.

She pushed the door open and led me through the kitchen. A man behind the grill wearing an apron looked her way. He smiled and nodded. Sasha waved and continued on. I followed her lead. She stopped and turned and knocked on a door cut into the side wall. There was a small window, but I couldn't see inside.

An older man in his sixties with white hair on his face and head opened the door. He reached out, grabbed Sasha by the shoulders and pulled her toward him. He whispered something into her ear that I couldn't make out. She laughed. He turned his attention toward me.

"Who's this?" he said. The joy drained from his face.

"That's my partner, Jack. The one I told you about."

I felt confused. My expression probably showed it.

"Jack," she said. "This is my father."

I extended a hand. "Nice to meet you, sir."

"You keeping my daughter safe?" he said.

"Sure am."

"I can't say the same for him, though," she said. "He took a nasty one to the back of the head today, Daddy. Think you can spare a couple porter-houses for the two of us?"

"Of course." He stepped out of the office, grabbed an apron and headed toward the grill.

I caught a glimpse inside before he shut the door. Pictures of Sasha lined the wall, floor to ceiling. They looked to chronicle her life from the time she was an infant. There were newspaper clippings from as recently as a couple weeks ago, featuring Sasha. I saw myself in the background of a picture for one of the articles.

She caught me looking. I offered a consolatory grin. She rolled her eyes, shrugged.

Her father said, "Go get a drink and find a seat. I'll have these out to you in less than twenty minutes."

"I like mine medium rare," I said.

He waved me off. "You'll take it how I make it."

Sasha touched my elbow and nodded toward a cream-colored door. The bottom half of it was covered with scuff marks from the staff's shoes. A result of years of kicking it open.

I followed Sasha out of the kitchen. The bright lights gave way to an intimate setting. The room was dim and cool and soothing. We passed a dozen empty tables on our way to the bar.

"What do you want to drink?" she said.

"Beer is fine."

"OK," she said. "Go grab a table. I'll be there in a minute."

I glanced around the place. The floors were hardwood, solid and old, with the kind of imperfections that indicated character instead of a flaw in craftsmanship. The walls were decorated with the kind of kitsch you might find in any family-owned restaurant in any city. The tables looked like Sasha's grandfather might have bought them. The chairs had intricate designs, all hand carved. They were scattered throughout the dining room with no attention paid to their placement. It was anything but uniform. Maybe that's what her father wanted.

I walked over to a table close to the rear and sat with my back to the kitchen. While the majority of the tables were empty, more than half the barstools were occupied. Sasha was the youngest person up there by twenty years.

She turned around and scanned the room. She spotted me and raised two pints in the air over her head. One looked dark. The other amber. I couldn't know which was for me. She crossed the floor, eyes on me and avoiding the mismatched maze of tables like she'd walked across the room ten thousand times. She placed both mugs in the middle of the table. I reached for the dark one. She looked disappointed.

"I can take the other," I said.

"How about we share?" she said.

I nodded. She grabbed a chair, dragged it around and sat down next to me.

"Your father's going to think we're a couple," I said.

"Nah, he knows I can't sit with my back to the front door. He'll figure you can't either."

Four more barstools now had occupants. "Looks like the bar does good business."

She nodded. "Those men have been coming here since I was a girl. Four or five nights a week you'll find a familiar combination of locals littering the place. Daddy's always treated them right, and they do the same for him. And don't let the empty tables fool you. It'll fill up around the time we leave."

I tapped my finger in time with the song playing. An old Coltrane piece. Dark, sultry and rich.

"Told you before I got my love of jazz from him."

I smiled, said nothing. My thoughts had drifted back to Jessie. We used to lay on my bed as teenagers listening to my father's jazz collection. He'd get bent out of shape about it from time to time, but I knew he enjoyed the fact that we shared a love for the same kind of music.

"You're really going to go, aren't you?" Sasha said.

"Probably," I said.

She sighed, reached for her mug and took a drink. Foam coated her upper lip. She used the back of her sleeve to wipe it away. "There's nothing I can say to change your mind?"

"Most likely not."

The door to the kitchen opened. A waitress emerged carrying a small tray. She headed toward our table. I caught a whiff of the steaks on the grill. The waitress's perfume drowned it out. She smiled at Sasha, gave me a look, and dropped a basket of chips on the table.

Sasha grabbed the basket and placed it between us. I slid it away.

"You don't like chips?"

"They're fries. And they have too many carbs."

She laughed. "Americans."

I sipped on my carb-laden beer and said nothing.

"Marcia is going to keep insisting that you take over her security."

"You know how I feel about this."

"I do, Jack. At the same time, she had a point. You were the only one who knew. You were smart enough to call everyone off. If we'd all been in there, it could have been even worse."

"You call that smart?" I said. "I nearly died. One of her men did die. Another is paralyzed. Another took a shot to the gut. The only reason the guy in the bathroom didn't get hurt is because he's got a weak bladder. In fact, his need to piss is the reason the back of my head is stitched up." I looked away, took a moment to calm down. "If I'd have had one more person in there, it could have turned out differently and she wouldn't be going on and on trying to hire me."

Sasha said nothing. I didn't need a bunch of lights to know that her cheeks had turned red.

"And where's she getting this money? Offering me two million for four weeks? Is she crazy?"

"I'd say the answer to that lies in the fact that she keeps pushing on despite all these attempts on her life."

"That's another thing," I said. "There must be more to this than I know, because I don't see why they are going after her this hard."

Sasha's gaze drifted away. I followed it. A man stood in front of our table. He had slicked back white hair. Looked to be in his sixties, still in good shape, too.

"Yes?" Sasha said.

"Not you," the old man said. "Him." He aimed a knobby finger in my direction.

"What?" I said.

"You better sir me," he said.

I said nothing.

His cheeks turned red. "Stop yelling and start treating the girl with some respect."

I looked at Sasha. "Relative?"

She shrugged.

"OK," I said. "Now go back to your dinner."

The man wandered off to his table. He sat down facing us. He didn't take his eyes off of me after that.

"Anyway," Sasha said. "Look, Jack, I understand if you feel you need to go back. Just keep it short, OK? I can get you a private jet into D.C., New York, or Atlanta."

"Atlanta's closest."

"OK, that's settled then."

I didn't know if it was. Here she was applying pressure to get me to stay. At the same time she was willing to help me go. Part of me wondered if she planned to tell the pilot to circle around for five hours and land in London.

Sasha pulled out her cell phone. "Would you excuse me for a moment?"

"No need to get up. I'll grab some fresh air." I stood and walked to the front door. The hardwood floor felt springy under my steps. Did the place have a basement? What was down there? The questions lingered for a second or two as I pictured the space.

I stepped outside. The air felt cool against my warm cheeks. Thick clouds blocked the moonlight. What time would the storm start? Would it be bad enough to keep the plane from departing? The chances of that were slim.

A trace of cigarette smoke passed by. It had been months since I smoked. My first reaction had been to cough. An old desire popped up, though. Will power, I told myself.

I turned around and opened the door to the pub. The old man who gave me a talking to barreled through the door. He didn't back down. I stepped back and held the door for him. He puffed his chest with pride. There was no reason to disrupt his moment.

My eyes adjusted to the lighting in the pub after I stepped inside. Sasha waved at me from the table. Our food had been brought out. Steam rose from the thick cuts of steak.

"Eat up," she said. "You leave in two hours."

6

WE LEFT THE RESTAURANT AFTER EATING AND HAVING A FEW more beers. After navigating through the streets, Sasha got on the M4 heading west. I figured we were further east than I had estimated. I closed my eyes for a few minutes. The Audi's soft leather headrest felt better than most hotel pillows. Five minutes passed. I opened my eyes and saw we were still on the highway.

"Why are we headed toward the city?" I asked.

She glanced at me and gave me a look. "We're going to the airport."

"I know I'm not from around these parts, but isn't Heathrow behind us?"

"Who says you're leaving via Heathrow?"

I thought she would understand by now that I hate wasting breath. "Then where are we going?"

"London City Airport."

"Never been there."

"It's not the type of attraction a tourist would head to." She paused a moment, presumably to see if I would take the bait. I didn't. She continued. "It's all charters. Definitely easier for us to use in a case like this. You'll get out unnoticed, which is better for all of us. We don't need anyone over there to know that you've left the country."

"Do you have intel that says someone is watching me over here from there?"

She shook her head. "Don't need it. You'll always be watched, Jack. And as long as you work for me, it's in my best interest to keep them off your back."

I shrugged. "I can handle that."

She said nothing. She changed lanes without signaling. A car honked at us.

I glanced out the window. "So you're sneaking me out of England to deposit me into the busiest airport in the U.S.?"

"No, you aren't going to Hartsfield-Jackson. We've arranged to drop you off at Dobbins."

Sean couldn't get on base. This grew more complicated by the moment. "This isn't necessary, Sasha. I can fly under an alias. I've got a clean one no one knows about. Passport, credit cards, everything."

She wagged her hand at me. "Don't tell me things like that. Besides, someone, somewhere, knows this information, which means they might, too."

I resigned myself to the fact that she had an answer for everything. She always did. And I didn't mind. Last thing I wanted to do was worry about the details. It had been a hell of a day. My head ached, and so did my heart.

I called Sean as we passed through the center of London. He didn't answer. I left him a message telling him when I expected to land and that I'd work on getting a flight to Florida. I hung up and leaned back, letting my head fall to the side. My unfocused eyes watched lights pass by like laser beams.

"No luck reaching him?" Sasha said.

"No."

"You can call from the plane. It's only, what, around four there?"

"Something like that."

A few minutes later Sasha pointed toward a sign I didn't bother to read. "Almost there."

I nodded and emptied my head again. But a single thought brought me back.

"Dammit," I said under my breath.

"What is it?" she said.

"Mia."

"You want to say goodbye."

I nodded. I hadn't seen my daughter in ten days. I hated the thought of leaving without letting her know.

"We can stop by if you'd like."

I was surprised she offered. Didn't sound like something she would have thought of as a good idea. I contemplated it for a moment.

"Better not," I said. "It's late. And it'll just worry her and Erin. Besides, I'm only going to be gone a couple days."

"OK," she said. "That's that."

"That's that," I repeated.

We drove in silence until we reached the small airport. She pulled up to a gate manned by an armed guard. One look at her identification was all it took to get us past.

"That's it, right there." She extended her arm in front of me and aimed her finger at a passenger jet. She stopped the car fifty feet away.

I cracked my door. The smell of jet fuel overwhelmed me. My nostrils burned and my eyes itched. I took a moment to adjust, then stepped onto the pavement. My back and shoulders had stiffened during the hour-long ride over. I worked out the kinks before heading toward Sasha.

She stood at the back of her car. The trunk was open. She reached in and pulled out a small bag.

"Be careful," she said, handing the bag to me. "It's loaded."

I took it from her, unzipped it and looked inside. "M40?"

"I know it's not your favorite. Only untraceable one I had."

I pulled the sidearm out and tucked it behind me. "You can keep the bag." I tossed it into her trunk.

She shook her head.

"What?" I said. "It could be bugged."

"Whatever, Jack. There's a suitcase on board containing a couple changes of clothes. Not that you'll take it."

"Don't need it. I can borrow some of Sean's. We're the same size."

"You sure about that?" She attempted a joke by patting my stomach.

"No change on my part, Sasha. Looks the same as it did twenty years ago."

She rolled her eyes. "When was the last time you saw him?"

"I guess six years ago."

"And you don't think it's possible that he's put on a few pounds?"

"Sean? Doubtful."

"Take the clothes, Jack."

I wasn't going to get rid of her until I agreed, so I said, "OK."

She walked me to the jet. I glanced up. The lights and the clouds made it impossible to see the sky. We stopped in front of the stairs. She wrapped her arms around my neck. Beer and steak and perfume and her natural scent washed over me. I had the urge to kiss her. I didn't, though.

"Take care of yourself, Jack. Be safe, and be careful."

"I'm going home, Sasha. It's the safest place I know."

She pulled back far enough to look me in the eye. A small crinkle appeared in the middle of her forehead when she furrowed her brows. "Where exactly is home?"

"Only two people I know have that information, and I'm not about to make it three. If that got out, it wouldn't be the safest place anymore, would it?"

She kissed my cheek. Her lips felt soft and wet. She slowly released her grip, then took a couple steps back.

"You best get going." She looked up. "That storm is getting close."

I followed her gaze and glanced up again. The clouds were thick and gray. Too early for the remnants of a hurricane, I thought. I opened my mouth to ask, but Sasha had already closed her door. The Audi's brake lights lit up. The emergency brake clicked when she disengaged it. She raced toward the gate we had entered through.

I worried about her. She'd gotten too close. Her feelings went too far. I could tell that.

And I knew that left her vulnerable in too many ways.

She wasn't the only one though.

"We're ready to depart, sir."

I looked up at the man at the top of the stairs. He had short, dark hair and wore blue pants and a white polo shirt. He motioned for me to board. I climbed the steps and brushed past him. He didn't smell as good as Sasha.

"Sit anywhere you'd like," he said.

A leather couch stretched along the opposite wall. It was dark and deep and wide and broken in.

"Can I lay there?" I asked.

"After we take off, you can," he said. "Grab a seat and strap in and I'll let you know when you can move."

I grabbed a spot near the couch. It felt as soft as the couch looked. I strapped my seat belt over my lap and settled in for takeoff. Ten minutes later we were in the air. Twenty minutes after that I was on the phone with Sean.

"They're taking me to Dobbins."

"How long until you arrive?" Sean said.

"Four hours. Maybe five. Not exactly sure."

"So around seven or eight my time?"

"I guess. They said there will be a car waiting for me if I want to use it, but I'm leery of that. No telling if they want to try to track where I'm going."

"They don't know where you're from?"

"I hope not. Last thing I want to do is bring a bunch of my kind of people into town."

Sean exhaled into the phone. It sounded like a powerful gust of wind.

"I just messaged Deb. She's cool with me coming to get you. I'll probably be there around nine-thirty, though. Think you can find your way off base, maybe head over to a Waffle House or something?"

"It's Atlanta. I shouldn't have trouble finding a Waffle House."

"You know what I mean, Jack."

"Yeah, I'll get somewhere and meet you there."

"All right, baby brother."

"All right, old man winter."

"I'll see you in a few hours."

I kept the line open for a few seconds longer.

"You there?" Sean asked.

"Yeah," I said.

"What's up?" he said.

I paused a beat. I hadn't had anyone to talk to for a while now, and there was a lot I needed to work through. Sean had always been a good ear for me. He had things to do, though. I knew that. Perhaps on the ride home.

"Forget it. I'll see you soon."

7

I HUNG UP, LAY DOWN ON THE COUCH AND CLOSED MY EYES. MY MIND drifted and settled on Sasha for a few minutes. The woman had become a big part of my life over the past month or so. But the tension grew between us. It seemed to culminate tonight. If there's one thing that life had taught me, it was that two people in my line of business should never get involved. It always ended messy. What if one of us was captured? Tortured? I'd heard of spies giving up every ounce of intelligence they had to save a spouse or child. That's why I never let anything get far enough to be a detriment.

And that's why Mia threw such a wrench into my life. I was still trying to come to grips that I had a daughter. Only a few people knew. One of those people was Sasha, and that posed a problem.

This all factored into my decision to decline the offer from Marcia Stanton. The money she dangled in front of me almost got me to accept. Perhaps Jessie was still trying to save me, even from the grave.

With the vision of Mia in my mind's eye, I dozed off. The nap extended into a deep sleep. I never saw the Atlantic Ocean even though we flew into the sunset.

I felt a hand on my shoulder and opened my eyes. It wasn't the man who welcomed me on board. My right arm reached across my body and grabbed a hold of their wrist. The woman gasped. She dropped the water bottle she'd held in her other hand.

A second later I realized where I was and let go of her arm. She moved to the other side of the plane. She was out of breath and shaking.

"Sorry," I said. "You startled me."

She gave me a tepid smile. The water bottle rolled around on the floor. She chased it down.

"Are we close?" I said.

"Fifteen minutes," she said.

"That water for me?"

She nodded, held the bottle out.

I stood up and took it from her. After taking a sip, I said, "You familiar with Atlanta?"

She shook her head. "I could look some information up on my phone for you."

"That's OK." I returned to my original seat and buckled in.

The woman walked toward the front of the plane. She glanced back once, still scared. I didn't see her again.

The sun was still out. The horizon was orange and red and pink. The city looked like a painting of Tuscany. We passed downtown in a matter of seconds.

Our landing was smooth. The jet came to a halt in front of a large green hangar probably made from galvanized steel and large enough to fit a couple football fields inside.

The pilot stepped out from the cockpit. He tossed a look in my direction. The stairs banged against the side of the plane. The pilot opened the door and gestured for me to get up.

"You ready?" he said.

I nodded.

"There's a black automobile over there. I believe that is for you. See the man standing next to it for the keys."

"How do you know it's that one?"

"Because there aren't any others out there."

"Fair enough." I stepped past the man.

My footsteps echoed as I jogged down the steps. Heat rose off the black-top. Less than ten feet from the jet, the Georgia humidity swallowed me whole. My forehead grew damp. The thick air disagreed with my sinuses and lungs.

"You forgot your luggage," the pilot called out.

"You keep it," I said. "I don't need it."

He gave me a funny look, but didn't protest. They were used to eccentric people, I figured. The charter jet business had to be an interesting one.

I continued toward the Lincoln. A black man in a black suit stood next to it. However hot and muggy I felt, he had to feel ten times worse. The guy waved at me. I waved back. He dangled a set of keys and gave me a thumbs up and a big smile.

Nice fella, I thought.

He popped the trunk and opened the driver's door. The engine roared. The belts whined. I barely noticed the puff of exhaust from the tail pipe. He walked toward me, smiling.

"Luggage?" he said.

"Nah," I said.

"None?"

"Not a single bag."

His eyebrows lowered and his lips and nose rose up. He angled his head to the side and looked past me, toward the plane. The thought of no luggage must've perplexed him more than the pilot.

"It' a quick trip," I said. "I'm traveling light. They'll have what I need when I get where I'm going."

"Hey, if it works for you," he said.

"It does."

He turned and took a few steps toward the front of the car. I closed the trunk. By the time the lid latched, the man had opened the rear door.

"What's this?" I said.

"I suppose you can sit up front next to me if you'd like," he said. "Most folks don't," he added.

"I'd like to sit up front in the driver's seat. Car's for me, right?"

"Yes, sir. And I'm your driver."

"Driver?"

He rolled his eyes. "You ain't gonna call me your chauffeur, now, are you?"

"I think there's a misunderstanding. The car was supposed to be left for me. Me. Not you *and* me. Just me. All alone. I don't work any other way."

"No, sir. That's not how this works. Now pick a seat, front or back, and let's get you on your way."

"I don't think you're hearing me right."

He closed the door, took a step forward. "Look, man. We get off base, you do what you want. OK? But for right now, we both need to be in this car to get out of here. Those guys guarding this place with M16s ain't gonna take kindly to either of us walking around on the streets. Especially after dark. You got no idea what I had to go through just to get in here. So if you want to get out of here, get in the car."

I wasn't familiar with the layout of the base. I couldn't tell anyone how to get to the PX, or the Commissary. I didn't know whether the place had a movie theater or bowling alley. Getting out wouldn't be a problem. If I had the car. Wandering around looking like I did was sure to draw some attention, though.

"All right, man," I said.

He smiled wide. His teeth stood out against his dark lips and the black goatee that surrounded them.

I walked around the back of the vehicle. The jet had already taxied away. I double-checked the trunk. It remained latched. I shifted my pistol from the back to the front of my pants. No reason other than being cautious. The man didn't strike me as anything other than a glorified cab driver.

He waited in front of his seat. I got in, then he did. We were both sweaty. We both exhaled loudly when we sat down. He reached for the air conditioning control and turned it to max. Cold air shot out of the vents. I adjusted the two in front of me so the streams met at the middle of my face. The air smelled like used cigarette butts, but it felt good.

"So where we headed?" he asked as he shifted into drive.

"Off base," I said.

"Then where?"

"Wherever you want to get out, man."

He took his foot off the gas. The car slowed to a crawl. He let the car glide to the right. The wheels scraped the curb.

"This is my car," he said. "You aren't getting it. If you want to go somewhere in this car, I'll be driving."

I looked at him and smiled.

8

WE PASSED THROUGH WITH NO ISSUES. THE MP POSITIONED THERE glanced over his shoulder at us. That was it. The man drove west, away from Atlanta, toward the outskirts of Marietta.

I waited five minutes before asking where we were going.

"You didn't say anything," he said. "So I'm going home. There's a motel nearby. You can stay there."

At that moment I knew this guy wasn't affiliated with anybody or anything. He was just a driver. Sasha must've used the internet when she arranged for a car to meet me. All that trouble to sneak me into the country unannounced, only to put me in a vehicle with a random stranger. Didn't make sense. Of course, what did these days?

So I faced a dilemma. Let the guy drop me off somewhere, or flash my gun and steal his vehicle. With Sean on his way up, I didn't have to go far, so I didn't have a need for the man's Lincoln. Still, I had to make it look real. I spotted a rental car lot up ahead and knew that was the best option.

"Drop me off there," I said.

"OK," the guy said.

He pulled into the parking lot and stopped beside the front door. The thick air enveloped me before I placed one foot on the ground. The sedan pulled away after I got out. I turned and watched and waited until it disappeared from sight. Then I waited a few minutes more. Finally, I entered the air-conditioned building.

"Help you?" the guy behind the counter said.

I shook my head without looking back at him. I had no intention of renting a car that night. I pulled out my cell and called Sean.

"Where you at?" I said.

"Macon," he said. "What about you?"

"Somewhere in Marietta, I think." I looked over my shoulder at the guy behind the counter.

He nodded.

"Yeah, Marietta."

"That's about two hours away still," Sean said.

I held the phone to my chest. "Anywhere to eat around here?"

"Down the road a block or two," he said.

I put the phone to my ear. "I'm gonna grab a bite to eat. I'll let you know the address of the place after I get settled in."

"OK. Load up on coffee. I'm going to need you to drive home."

"Past your bedtime?"

He laughed. "I wish. Work's busy. I'm going to need to do a bit on the laptop on the way back."

We said goodbye and hung up. I glanced back at the man behind the counter. He'd taken a seat and his gaze was fixed on his computer monitor.

I had a walk of at least two blocks ahead of me. I hesitated to leave. By the time I got anywhere, my shirt would be clinging to my body. I couldn't wait inside the building for two hours, though. What if the driver had been instructed to double back and check up on me after he checked in?

The door dinged as I stepped back out into the humid air. I crossed the parking lot, slipped between two Ford Focuses and found a sidewalk. Sweat dripped. I hadn't felt humidity like this in a while.

To the west I saw a couple apartment buildings, a hotel, and the entrance to a neighborhood. Maybe that's where the driver headed off to. I glanced east. There I spotted a couple options for dining. Vehicles packed Applebee's parking lot. Sitting at the bar of a crowded restaurant held little appeal. Just as well, though. Across the street was a twenty-four hour Waffle House.

I stepped to the curb. Headlights came at me from both directions. I jogged across the street at the first break in traffic. An old lady and two teenage guys sat on a green bench waiting for the MARTA bus. The guys were too engrossed with their nude magazine to notice me. The old woman placed a second hand on her purse and pulled it into her torso. She glanced up at me. I shrugged and kept going.

The Waffle House's parking lot was deserted. It appeared that they enjoyed no overflow from Applebee's tonight. It didn't take long to figure out why. I took a seat at the counter. The middle-aged rail-thin man beside the grill didn't budge. He held a spatula in one hand, and a cell phone in the other. He stared at his phone's screen. His thumb worked overtime. He smiled a couple times. Laughed once. He glanced at me, exhaled, and went back to his message or his Tweet or his Facebook or whatever.

"Billy," a woman said. "We got a customer."

I glanced to my left. A woman three times the size and about the same age as Billy walked toward me. The door to the ladies room closed behind her. She had to pass me to get behind the counter. A trail of potpourri scent lingered for a few seconds after she did.

By the time she stood in front of me on the other side of the counter, she'd run out of breath. The potpourri scent had faded. Now she smelled like Johnny Walker and a pack of Camels. Her nametag said her name was Joan.

"What can I get for you?"

"Got pancakes tonight, Joan?"

She didn't smile at my attempt at humor. "This is the Waffle House, sir. You can get waffles, eggs, sausage—"

I threw up my hands in surrender. "Four eggs, over easy, and six pieces of sausage."

"Drink?"

"Coffee," I said. "Endless cup, please." I smiled.

She rolled her eyes. Must've been a long day. As she turned away, she said, "Billy, he wants—"

"I got it," Billy said. "I got it." He turned his back to both of us and squirted a fake butter substance on the flat top.

I spun around on my stool, leaned back against the counter, and pulled out my phone to check for messages. I didn't have any. The address of the place was stenciled on the outside of the front window. I deciphered it and texted it to Sean. Then I pulled up a web browser, checked the news and the weather.

Tomorrow's forecast called for hot and humid and thunderstorms to roll in during the afternoon. Typical for Florida in the summer.

By eight-thirty, I'd finished my meal and retreated to a booth in the corner with a fresh cup of coffee. The restaurant had filled up, and I figured Billy and Joan could use a couple fresh customers at the counter.

An hour and two mugs later, a new Mercedes pulled into the parking lot. It was black and had halogen headlights that looked blue. The car pulled into the parking spot on the other side of the window. The driver's door opened. The dome light cut on. I saw my brother for the first time in six years.

Sean nodded at me. I nodded back. He pointed at himself, then at me, then shrugged. I rose, dropped a twenty on the table and placed my half-filled mug on top of it. Sean met me outside, by the front door. It was awkward. We didn't know whether to shake or to hug. So we stuck our hands in our pockets and did neither.

"You look good," he said.

"Not as good as you, though," I said.

"That's a given."

"I take that back. You look old."

Sean laughed. "Take a look in the mirror recently?"

"I try to avoid it if at all possible. Some guy in his late thirties keeps showing up."

"Wait till you're forty." Sean took a step back and opened the driver's door and ushered me inside.

Sitting down felt like plopping onto a cloud. I thought Sasha's Audi was nice. It had nothing on the Mercedes. It had to be the most comfortable seat I ever felt. Then again, I might have been tired. The seat didn't need a single adjustment. It fit like a glove. Ever since the day I turned twelve, people always assumed Sean and I were identical twins. We were the same height, width, weight, but we didn't look exactly alike. Good for one of us, bad for the other. We each had our own opinion on the matter.

Sean opened the passenger door, got in and leaned back.

"This is nice," I said.

He held out his hands and shrugged. He didn't need me to tell him that, but it felt like the right thing to say.

"How do I get onto the highway from here?" I said.

He fiddled with the LCD screen built into the upper part of the dash. A female computer-generated voice came over the speaker system and guided me toward I-285 west.

"This'll loop us around the city to the south. We'll hook up with 75 in about thirty minutes."

"Sounds good." I fiddled with the radio until I found something both of us would like. "I'm glad to be heading home. I wish it were under different circumstances, but it's good to see you, Sean."

He said nothing.

I looked over. Sean had fallen asleep. The press of a button on the steering wheel changed the radio station again. Enough mashes against it returned a station playing smooth jazz. I lowered the volume. Even with the music barely audible, the Mercedes let almost zero road noise in the cabin. Impressive.

9

LEON BARBER SAT BEHIND THE WHEEL OF A BEAT UP EARLY NINETIES Tercel in an Applebee's parking lot. He'd been there for two hours, watching the man identified to him as Jack Noble. During that time, his target had moved from a stool at the counter to a booth in the corner. Leon noticed that Jack's eyes moved constantly, always scanning the crowd around him, the parking lot, and the street.

Leon didn't know who Jack was, but he could tell the man was dangerous.

After he'd dropped Noble off at the rental car place, Leon turned the corner and exchanged the Lincoln for the piece of crap he sat in now. He was stuck in the car, too. He had parked across the street and watched. When Jack stepped out and started walking, Leon did a double take. He had been prepared to follow the guy in a car, not on foot.

Fortunately for Leon, Jack didn't go far. Once the man settled, Leon cut across the street and settled into his current position.

He'd been in contact with his boss, Vera Ferrell, throughout the night. All she told him was to stay put and proceed with caution. She gave him no information on Noble, what he was doing in Marietta, Georgia, or what he was capable of. He didn't even know what to do if he encountered the man. Sit tight and wait, she had said. And so Leon did. For two long hours.

And now, it appeared that his wait was over.

A Mercedes pulled up and parked opposite Jack's booth. Noble got up, left the restaurant. A man stepped out of the sedan. When the two met on the sidewalk, they looked like mirror images of one another.

Leon placed another call to Vera.

"He's getting in a car with a guy that looks just like him."

Vera said, "I want you to stay with them. Hang back, though. You don't want to be spotted."

"Is the other guy his brother?"

Vera didn't answer.

"Vera?"

"Stay close and call me with updates."

She hung up. Leon placed his phone in the center console and fired up the whiny four-cylinder engine. He almost lost sight of the Mercedes. The man that drove had a heavy foot. He caught site of them taking the on-ramp for I-75.

Leon caught up and kept at least one car between himself and Noble.

The boring drive led his thoughts to wander. Who was this guy? What was so important about Jack Noble that Leon had to leave a card game in Charlotte to pick the man up at Dobbins AFB?

It wasn't unusual for Leon to be told nothing. In many ways, it made it easier. *Act the part of the good soldier,* he told himself. When the time was right, he'd be given the necessary information.

And then it would be time to pull the trigger.

Would Jack Noble be the target?

Or someone else?

10

SEAN SLEPT FOR THREE HOURS. HE'D SAID HE HAD WORK TO CATCH up on. I knew he didn't want to admit he was tired. I used the time to do a lot of thinking. Old friends crept into my thoughts. They always did, no matter how hard I tried to push them away.

It had been a couple months since I'd last seen Clarissa. She walked out of my life in D.C. on a spring morning and I hadn't heard from her since. I knew I would one day, though. It always worked that way with us.

I thought about Bear and Mandy. Where had they settled? The big man wanted her to have a normal life. He felt like they should go someplace where the past couldn't haunt her. I knew that meant a location far away from me, and it'd be best that I never visit. We decided it was best that I didn't know. For now, at least. Too much was left unsettled after what we went through with Alex Parkin in London. He'd been there, too. Things had been too close. I put the man's life at risk too often, and with another life to worry about, that risk was too great for him.

I envied him for it.

I blanked out for a bit and just drove. It didn't last, though. No matter how much I tried to avoid it, Jessie crossed my mind over and over. I questioned every decision I ever made regarding her, from leaving for bootcamp, to splitting up a few years later. I had one last chance back in '02 to make things right. I'd screwed that up too. If I hadn't let her get away from me that last time, both our lives would have turned out differently.

And she wouldn't be dead right now.

Sean woke up around the time we entered Valdosta, Georgia. Orange street lights lit up deserted shopping centers and restaurants. Sean yawned, stretched, rolled down his window, stuck his head out, rolled it back up and yawned again.

The blast of wind felt good and gave me a jolt, so I cranked my window down a notch for a second or two.

"Valdosta?" Sean glanced at the clock. "Already?"

I shrugged.

"You sure you want to get pulled over?" he said.

"You left your wallet in the console. Figure if I did, I'd just say I'm you."

"That's not gonna fly." He rubbed his eyes with his palms. "Slow down," he added.

"Sure thing, Dad." I slowed down to five over the generous seventy mile per hour speed limit. It felt like going in slow motion the first few minutes. There weren't many cars on the highway, but the ones that were out started passing me. I hated that.

"Only about two hours from here," Sean said.

"I remember."

"You do? I figured it'd be a bit hazy after six years." He grinned, slightly.

I saw it in time. I chose to skip the bait. Sean had always enjoyed bringing up how long it had been since my last trip home. He'd goad me along until the urge to defend myself arose. A tricky proposition, considering the line of work was always classified or illegal.

Usually the latter.

Until recently.

We crossed the Florida state line. Two groups of palm trees sat on either side of the road and a big sign welcomed us. A half-mile later, Sean gestured toward the rest area. I pulled into the exit lane.

The place was nothing special. Looked like most other rest stops. It had two parking lots, one for truckers and one for the rest of us. A building had been stuck in between the lots. There were enough streetlights to make one think it was daytime. Maybe that had been the point. Weary traveler? Stop here and trick your mind into thinking it's only two in the afternoon.

We both got out and headed toward the flat-roofed building. Sean went into the restroom. I bought two bottles of water out of a vending machine. They were two bucks a piece. Highway robbery. Literally. Coffee would have been nice, but I didn't see a machine. Even if I had, I wouldn't have purchased coffee from it. We could find a fresh pot at the next exit. And if not there, the next one.

I headed back to the car, tossed the water bottles on the front seat. I used the empty parking spot next to me to stretch. A woman walked two big dogs on the sidewalk. One barked at me. The other wagged his tail and ran up to me. I scratched his head and talked to him like he was a baby. The woman smiled, pulled her dog back and walked away.

Sean showed up a minute later. I got in on the passenger side as he approached.

He got in and held the water bottle up like it had come from a polluted river in Africa. "No coffee?"

"No machine." I didn't elaborate on what I would have done if there had been one. "We'll stop and grab some."

He looked at the clock, shrugged. "I think I can make it the rest of the way. If I drink caffeine now, I'll never get to sleep."

"Suit yourself. I'm good either way."

Ten miles passed in seven minutes. I didn't see any palm trees. Perhaps the tourism department had planted the ones at the rest area for travelers who needed another visual cue to let them know they'd reached the state.

"Tell me how Dad's really doing," I said.

"I told you on the phone, he's OK," Sean said.

"You were lying."

Sean chewed on the inside of his cheek. He'd done it since he was a kid. It meant he was trying to think of a way to say something to lessen the impact of his words. He exhaled through tightly pressed lips, creating a flapping sound.

"He's not doing well, Jack. His memory is, I don't know, fragile. Even more so than before. It seems like he deteriorates week by week now. One visit he knows me, the next he doesn't. Sometimes he calls me by your name, other times I'm his only kid. I honestly don't know how he's going to handle seeing you. He might think you're me."

"We should go together then."

Sean nodded. "We could. I don't know how he'll handle that. Last time he saw both of us was Mom's funeral." He took a drink of water. "And you know that didn't end well," he added.

I thought back to that day and the fight I had with my brother.

Mom had been the one to take care of Dad through his early days of dementia. He'd taken a bullet to the head in Vietnam. Of all the stories the old man told us, he never mentioned that one. We didn't find out until we were both in our late twenties, after he'd been diagnosed. The doctors had told him that the previous head trauma was the cause.

The first few years weren't bad. Then things got worse. He started having more trouble remembering. It was little things at first. Toothpaste and pain ointment, things like that. His cognitive functions started to deteriorate. His movements became uncoordinated. A few years before Mom passed, the doctors had said that the dementia had him in a death grip, and it would progress quickly. She took care of him as if her life depended on it.

In the end, it did her in.

Sean knew that he couldn't take over for her, so he arranged for Dad to be sent to a home. I argued up and down about it and told Sean he should take dad in. I even offered to pay for in-home care. It was selfish of me, and he let me know that. I'd never be around. Hell, I hadn't since I left for the Marines some thirteen or fourteen years earlier.

The argument escalated, as it always did. We started cutting at each other for various things. His wife said something to me. I said something I shouldn't have. Next thing I knew, Sean took a swing at me, caught me on the jaw. I hit him back. He went down. His friends jumped me. No one tried to help me out. In the end, four of them went to the hospital and I took the next flight out. Drove to Tampa that night, got on a plane to New York, and never looked back. It took about eighteen months before we spoke again.

In our case, I believe that time had healed the wounds. We seemed to get along fine. So far, at least.

"Anyway," Sean said. "I doubt he remembers that. Some days he asks when she's coming down for breakfast, or lunch, or dinner. The meal never coordinates with the time I'm there."

I said nothing as I bounced back and forth in time.

"He loves Kelly though. Hasn't once forgotten who she is, even though she wasn't even born when he was diagnosed."

I looked across at him and smiled. I thought about bringing Mia up, but decided against it. Perhaps in the morning.

We exited I-75 after passing Lake City. Our conversation stalled. It was two in the morning. Felt like eight to me. The fumes I'd been running on were gone.

I dozed on and off for the next hour or so until we reached Sean's house. He pulled into the driveway and parked in front of a two-story Spanish style home.

"I see the car wasn't your only upgrade," I said.

"Had it built three years ago," Sean said. "Five bedrooms, plenty of space, even has a courtyard in the middle with a small pool, and a big pool behind the house."

I got out and looked around. The area seemed deserted. I glanced up and saw a sky full of stars. "Best part appears to be no neighbors."

"There's a few around. Everyone keeps to themselves, which is fine with me. I'm too busy for all that rah-rah HOA crap these days."

I couldn't imagine having to adhere to rules telling me what color fence I had to put up, and who to have build it. So, in that sense, I felt proud of Sean for breaking free from the humdrum suburbanite zombified lifestyle.

"You still driving to Tampa every day?" I said.

"Nah," he said. "I've got fifteen lawyers in three offices in Tampa, St. Pete's, and Bradenton. I mostly manage it all from here. I'm down there two days a week at most. I don't go at all some weeks. Anyway, I'm going inside. You coming?"

"In a minute."

"Not gonna smoke, are you?"

"No. I quit some time ago. Just want a few moments under the stars."

"Suit yourself. I'll leave the door open." Sean headed toward his house, unlocked the door and stepped inside.

I walked up to the front, stopped and looked up. I hadn't seen that many stars in a while. At least, not that I could recall. The last time I'd been anywhere remote enough to enjoy that kind of view, my life had been in danger. Hard to enjoy nature when that happens.

Aside from the crickets, it was quiet out. I enjoyed it for a couple minutes before turning and opening the door.

A car passed behind me. I looked over my shoulder, but saw no head-lights or taillights. I took a few steps away from the house. Trees lined the opposite side of the road on either side of Sean's house. A car's headlights should light them up like Christmas trees. I saw nothing, yet, I still heard the car engine. It idled now. I started toward the street.

"What're you doing, Jack?"

I stopped and turned. "How close are those neighbors?"

Sean shrugged. "I don't know, maybe quarter-mile or so. Why?"

"Any of them work at night?"

"What's this about?"

"A car just went by, but I swear it didn't have any headlights on."

"Guy next house over is a doctor. Maybe he got called to the hospital and is returning home now. Come on in. You're gonna draw all the mosquitoes out of hiding."

I didn't move.

"You're not thinking of walking down there, are you?" he said.

I was.

"Jack, get in here."

The engine had cut off. I heard a door slam shut, though I couldn't tell if it was a car door or someone's front door.

"It's just my neighbor," Sean said.

I took five steps back, scanned the area the entire time.

"You really should get on some meds for that paranoia," Sean said. "You're a wreck."

"I'd be dead if I wasn't."

We went inside. I made sure he locked the door. He led me upstairs to my room. I'm sure it was nice, but I didn't bother turning on the light to take it in. I found the bed, fell onto it and went to sleep immediately.

11

THE TERCEL TICKED AND CLICKED FOR SEVERAL MINUTES AFTER Leon pulled onto the dirt road a couple blocks after the house the Mercedes had parked in front of. The stupid Toyota was going to get him killed. Or at least spotted.

Which meant he'd have to kill.

Not that he was opposed to that. He wanted to get home to North Carolina, not spend the night in the middle of Florida. He hated everything about the state, starting with the mosquitoes. They surrounded him now, and they would for the rest of his time here. It always worked that way.

He slammed his car door shut, hoping to mimic the sound of someone going inside. The noise echoed against the dead night. The crickets around shut up. The cicadas didn't. Leon stepped toward the road. The crickets resumed their shrill singing. Leon stepped a little heavier with their noise, masking some of the sound he made.

The wind carried whispers of voices, but they were too far away to decipher. He hoped they stayed that way. It was dark, and the territory was unfamiliar. He was a spotlight beam away from being taken out for being a predator in a sleepy, backwoods Florida town. They'd probably bury him in the woods and sink his car in a lake and no one would be the wiser for it.

He crept toward the final strand of trees, then headed toward the main road. Leon stopped across from the house where the Mercedes was parked. He shielded himself from view and watched.

The porch light shut off, then the landscaping lights. The windows of the home darkened.

Leon didn't move. He wanted to get a better look at the Mercedes to figure out what he was doing there. However, he assumed a house like this would have security inside and out.

So he remained and waited and nothing happened. After an hour, he headed back to the Tercel and placed a call.

"Yeah?" Vera said.

"I'm in Florida. He's inside a house."

"OK. Stay on him tomorrow. Report back with his every move."

The line went dead. Leon tossed his phone on the other seat.

"Yeah, every move," he said. "Gonna get me killed."

12

I WOKE UP JUST AFTER SEVEN IN THE MORNING. SUNLIGHT TRICKLED IN through a crack where the curtains met as it rose above the trees across the street. I rolled over, got out of bed and looked out the window. I didn't see Sean's Mercedes in the driveway. Must've been an in-office day for him.

I exited the room and retraced my steps to the stairs. The upgraded carpet felt like walking on a foam mattress. The air smelled of dark roast. My mouth watered. Every step I took brought me closer to the coffee. The scent led me into a kitchen lined with stainless steel appliances, cherry wood cabinets, and granite counter tops.

Only the best for my big bro.

"Hello, Jack." Debby leaned against the counter, lips pursed, arms crossed, left leg over her right. She held a mug in one hand, and a bottle of cream in the other. "Care for some?"

I smiled, nodded and said, "Black is fine, Deb."

She stepped forward and placed the mug on the island. Her stare never left my eyes. I reached for the cup. We continued to stare at each other for an awkward moment. We hadn't seen or spoken to each other since Mom's funeral. I knew the day would come, but I always avoided thinking about it.

"Jack, I—"

I threw up my hands, palms facing her. "Let me go first. I said something awful six years ago, and I've wished I could take it back almost every day since. I know Sean and I have had our issues, but that never had anything to do with you. You stuck up for him, and I lashed out at you for it. I've thought about this over and over, Deb. In that moment, I think I was pissed more about the fact that it was you who said it, not the words you said. We were friends way before there was something between you and Sean. You did what was right. I was in the wrong."

She shook her head as she reached out for my hand. "I knew it would piss you off. That's why I said it, Jack. I would have been surprised if you had reacted any other way. Now, I was shocked that Sean acted the way he did."

"I'm not. He's my brother. We're wired the same. You just never saw that side of him."

"But I saw plenty of it from you."

Little feet pounded on the floor behind me.

"Hi Mommy. Hi Daddy."

I turned around. The little girl froze.

"Kelly," Debby said. "This is your Uncle Jack. He's your Daddy's brother. You remember the pictures, right?"

She nodded. Her eyes were wide and her stare never left me. I knelt down in front of her with my arm stretched out. She tepidly reached for my hand. The tension left her face. She let go, raced around the island and asked for a bowl of cereal.

Deb fixed the girl's breakfast. The little girl hummed a song I wasn't familiar with. Probably the jingle to some kid's show. Her mother handed her the bowl on a tray and sent Kelly into the living room to watch TV while she ate.

Deb put the milk in the fridge and the cereal in the pantry. She returned to the island, looked at me and sighed.

"Were you and Jess still close?" I said.

She nodded. "We didn't talk as much as in the old days, but we spoke frequently."

"So those things Sean said, about her husband, he got some of that info from you. He pieced it together with what he had witnessed personally?"

"Yeah, and please don't mention that to her parents, or anyone else. I mean, maybe some of them already suspect it. But if they don't, I don't want to go around hurting feelings any more than they already are. Know what I mean?"

I pulled a stool out from under the island's ledge and took a seat. Steam rose from my coffee mug. I took a searing sip.

"You think she killed herself?" I said.

"That's what the police say, right?"

I knew enough to never trust an opinion until I had all the facts. "Did she ever say anything that made you think that she was in need of help or counseling?"

Deb shook her head. "She had her moments, Jack, but who doesn't? We all get depressed at times. Look at me, I live in this big, gorgeous house, but there are times I wish I did more than I do. That upsets me a bit. So, I don't know about any signs. She seemed normal. Frustrated at times. Her marriage was coming to an end and I think she knew that and I think she was ready to let Glenn know that she planned on leaving."

"Did she?"

"Leave?"

"Tell him."

Deb shrugged. "If she did, she didn't let me know."

I figured she might not have had time to. Glenn could have flipped out on her.

"Maybe she told him the night she died." I didn't need to see the tears welling in Deb's eyes to understand the impact of the words. "Don't dwell on that, Deb."

She bit her bottom lip, then said, "I've already gone there, Jack. Part of me can't see him doing it, but another part..."

I rose and walked around the island and placed my hands on her shoulder.

"I just want to hear her voice again," Deb said, crying.

I pulled her into an embrace and stroked her hair. Her tears soaked the sleeve of my shirt. I wished there was more I could do for her. For all of us. The only thing that could have helped was bringing Jessie back, and that couldn't happen.

"Looks like you two are getting along again," Sean said.

I hadn't heard him come in. I released my right arm and stepped to the side. Deb rested her head on my shoulder.

Sean's expression changed when he saw the tears on his wife's face. "What'd you say to her?"

I shook my head.

"It's not him," Deb said. "We were talking about Jess."

Sean moved in and took over for me.

"I'll leave you two alone." I grabbed my coffee and wandered around until I found the living room.

Kelly smiled as I approached. It reminded me of Mia. Their mouths were shaped the same. The dimple was the same. They got it from my mother. Kelly patted the empty seat on the couch next to her and waved me forward. Bold for a nine year old.

I sat next to her. For twenty minutes we talked about school and sports. She'd played soccer since the age of three and loved to watch football. She didn't have a favorite team. She just enjoyed the time with her dad. He didn't bury his face in his laptop or his phone when football was on the television. I tried to get her to talk about boys. Fortunately, she didn't.

"Why haven't you been here before, Uncle Jack?"

I sat back and thought about how to answer the question. What could I tell her? My life is too important? Too dangerous? Me and your dad and mom have issues? I glanced over at her. Why hadn't I come to see my niece? Last time was when she was barely a toddler. None of the excuses made sense, and they wouldn't cut it with her.

"Because I'm a fool," I said. "Just like that crazy duck-cow-fish thing on the TV."

She laughed. I wrapped my arm around her and leaned back. Her little head rested against my side.

Sean stepped into the room. "We should get going, Jack."

"How's Deb?"

"She's good." He waved me forward.

"Where are we going?"

"You'll see."

13

LEON HAD SCRAMBLED BACK TO HIS CAR WHEN THE MERCEDES took off earlier that morning. By the time he pulled out, the sedan rounded a corner. Leon made it to the main road and the Mercedes was gone.

He figured it'd be back sooner or later, so he exited the neighborhood and parked on the shoulder of Suncoast Blvd, about a hundred yards from Jack's only way out.

After about an hour, the Mercedes had returned. Now he saw it again. Leon brought his binoculars up and saw two men in the front seat. They were the same guys from the night before. The Mercedes pulled out and traveled away from him.

Leon shifted into gear and merged onto Suncoast. He kept a fair bit of distance between himself and the two men. His only job now was to keep an eye on Jack.

14

THOUGH I HADN'T BEEN HOME IN SIX YEARS, EVERYTHING LOOKED
the same. Trees, houses, fields, stores. I watched the familiar terrain pass by
at fifty miles per hour.

"Not much has changed around here," I said.

"Wait till we get to town," Sean said.

"Different?"

"A bit." He shook his head. "Actually, not much."

"Isn't that the same?"

"Semantics."

"Whatever." I rolled down my window. The morning air was cool, but
humid. It didn't matter what time of day or night it was down here.
Humidity was a way of life.

"Any chance we can do some fishing?" Sean said.

I shrugged. We used to go all the time as kids. There were many nights
dad told us to go catch our dinner. If we came home empty handed, we didn't
eat. We both grew up to be expert anglers. At some point, it lost its luster for
me. Too slow.

"Afraid I'll show you up?" Sean said.

"I know you will." I saw the river to my right. "Is that what we're doing?"

"No."

"Then where are we going?"

"To see Dad."

I said nothing.

We entered town doing twenty-five. I rolled my window all the way down and rested my elbow on the sill. I figured maybe I'd see someone I knew and could shout at them. Instead, I saw old guys sitting in rocking chairs outside Jay's Hardware and General Store. Two old ladies stepped out of the town diner. A group of kids loitered in front of the movie theater.

Nothing had changed. The faces got older was all.

"Where is this place you shelved Dad in?" I said. "I don't remember a rest home in town."

"On the other side," Sean said. "Figured you'd like to see the sights first."

Sean turned right in front of a sheriff's patrol car. I didn't recognize the woman behind the wheel. She had dark hair, pulled back tight. Sunglasses covered her eyes. She might have been attractive. Wasn't a long enough glimpse for me to tell.

I thought about asking Sean if he knew her. I didn't.

We exited town to the south and drove another ten minutes. The area used to be nothing but trees. Now the road was lined with shops and office buildings. Progress, some would call it. If it was this crowded all the way up here, it must've been a butchered mess clear down to Tampa.

Sean turned into the half-filled parking lot of a place called Johnson's Senior Care.

"This is it," he said, cutting the engine.

We got out at the same time. The Mercedes beeped twice at us. We walked toward the front door, hands in pockets, stares aimed at the ground. I imagined we looked like mirror images on the security feed.

Automatic sliding doors parted for us. I waited for Sean to go through. He walked up to the counter. A woman there greeted him by name.

"And this must be your brother?" A fascinated look spread across her face.

"Yes ma'am," I said. "Jack."

"Nice to meet you, Mr. Noble."

I nodded, and said, "Likewise."

She looked down at her desk and retrieved a sign-in book.

"Boy, your daddy likes to talk about you. Of course, I think he's referring to Sean half the time, and himself the other half." She laughed, deep and bellowing.

Sean looked back at me and shrugged. He gestured with his head toward the hall and walked in that direction.

"Nice meeting you," I said to the woman.

I caught up to Sean. We stopped in front of room 117. A dry erase board hung from the door. It said "Noble" on top. Someone had drawn a face with a frown underneath his name.

"What's that mean? He's sad?"

Sean shook his head. "Bad day, that's all. Could be any number of things. Don't worry. I've seen them all." He took a deep breath and held his fist in front of the door. "Anyway, you ready for this?"

"What's there to get ready for? It's Dad."

"All right, here we go then." Sean knocked, then pushed the door open. He stepped through and greeted the old man.

I walked in after. Shock hit me as I laid eyes on him for the first time in six years. He'd aged at least twenty, and he was old to begin with. Dad had waited until his early forties to start his family. Mom had been ten years younger. Up until the dementia set in, you couldn't tell the age difference. That changed drastically.

He looked at me and froze. His bushy eyebrows furrowed, almost covering his eyes. He extended a bony finger and aimed it at me.

"Is that my Jackie?"

I stepped forward. "Hey, Pop."

"Home from the Marines already?"

I shrugged.

"How on earth do you get away with that shaggy hairdo?" He shook his head. "In my day we'd have tied you down and shaved your head bald. Hell, I might try to do that right now."

He planted his hands against the arms of his chair and tried to push himself up. He didn't budge. Cursed up a storm, though.

"I've been on leave for a few weeks. They'd never let me walk around base looking like this."

He nodded, looked away. "You boys gonna stay around for a while? Your mother should be around soon. I know she'd like to see you, Jack."

I looked at Sean. He gave me a terse smile. Always something different. I could see it in his eyes.

"I'm not sure, Pop," I said.

"Actually, we've got to get going in a few minutes, Dad. There's been an unfortunate accident."

"Oh, no," Dad said.

"Yeah," Sean said. "Jessie passed away."

Dad shook his head. He brought his hand up to his mouth and bit on a knuckle. "I'm sorry, Jack. I know you two had plans to get married."

"I'm broken up about it, Pop."

He held out his hand. I took it. He squeezed as tight as he could. I barely felt it. He glanced up at me. Those blue eyes I remember were covered in milky cataracts. I wondered how he could tell it was me that had come in. I understood how he thought I was fifteen years younger.

"You're a good kid, Jack. Always have been. But you gotta work on those issues you have, anger and whatnot, before they take over and ruin your life. You don't want to end up alone, without a soul in the world to love you."

I bent over and kissed him on the cheek. His white stubble stabbed at my lips.

"Love you, Pop."

"You too, son." He smiled, turned to Sean. "And you too, kid."

Sean patted Dad on the shoulder and turned to me. "Let's get going."

We walked through the hall to the reception area. The nurse smiled at us as we passed. Sunlight poured in through a glass dome in the ceiling. We went through the automatic double doors and out into the parking lot. It was like walking out of a freezer and into a sauna.

A beat up Tercel nearly hit us when the driver leaned over and started looking for something on the floor.

"Don't do anything," Sean said.

I held out my hands. "I'm good."

After we were seated in Sean's car, he said, "Want to get a drink?"

I couldn't say yes fast enough.

15

LEON FOLLOWED THE PARKING LOT AROUND THE BACK OF THE facility. He stopped on the far side and waited there until Jack and the other man had left in the Mercedes. Once they were gone, he pulled into a parking spot by the front door.

He glanced at himself in the rear-view mirror. He looked like crap. A day without a shower and eight hundred miles of driving would do that to a guy. He grabbed a wet nap and cleaned off his hands and face. A pine tree air freshener hung from the mirror. He grabbed it and rubbed it on his shirt.

He scanned the parking lot to ensure that the men had not returned. It looked safe. He got out and walked up to the entrance. The doors slid open and he stepped inside.

The woman behind the reception desk rose and said, "Help you, sir?"

"Yes," Leon said. "My name is Roger Carter and I hear you guys run the best senior care facility north of Tampa. My Dad's been living with me the past five years, but it's grown to be a bit more than I can handle, what with my wife passing recently." He forced his eyes to water. Something he'd been able to do since high school. "I wonder, do you have any literature on hand, and maybe a nurse I can speak with?"

"Of course." She smiled and sat down and opened the drawer to her left.

Leon glanced down at the sign-in sheet on the counter.

"Rats," the woman said. "I'll need to go in back to grab that. I'll look for the nurse while I'm back there. Just a sec, OK?"

Leon said, "Sure, take your time, ma'am." He crossed his legs, dropped an elbow on the counter top and leaned to the side. After she disappeared, he pulled the registry closer. The last line with an entry had Noble written in both the visitor and resident columns. On the other side of the sheet was a messy bunch of scribble. No matter what way he looked at it, it didn't read 'Jack.' Leon looked up. That was the signature line. Between the signature and resident, Leon saw the number 117. He glanced at the column header. Room number. He pulled a pad from his pocket and used the pen on the desk and wrote down "Noble" and "Room 117."

The woman emerged from the hallway. She waved a few pamphlets in the air. "I've got it. And I found Nurse Jenny, too. She can answer any questions you have."

Leon lifted his hand in the air. He held his cell phone. "I just got called into the office. I better get going. But thanks for the literature."

"Maybe you can bring your father up one day this week to take a look around."

"I'll keep that in mind." He took the pamphlets and left the facility. He drove about a mile down the road and pulled into a shopping center. There, he placed a call to Vera.

"OK, so here's what I got. Jack and the guy, I'm figuring it's his brother. They left the house and cut through town. Ended up at a retirement home. I got a look at the guest register thing. Noble signed in to pay a visit to Noble."

"So a mother or father?"

"Yeah, that's what I figure."

"What did you tell the people inside?"

"That I was checking the place out for my dad."

"OK," she said. "I may have you follow up there. Whichever Noble is a resident may come in handy for us later."

"Hey, you get me an old black man down here, and I'm good as gold."

"You lost them, though, right?"

"Jack and the guy?"

She exhaled loudly into the phone. "Yes."

"Yeah, but at least I know where they'll end up. They headed back the way they came, too."

"Good. You feeling good on your own or would a teammate be helpful?"

Leon considered this. Two people could be better than one, but he hated working with a partner. They got in the way and always became a liability.

"Solo for now, but keep someone on standby."

"OK. Call me this afternoon." She hung up.

Leon rolled down his window. The smell of fast food filled the small car. He glanced around, spotted a Burger King and went in for a bite to eat.

16

I FOLLOWED SEAN PAST THE DENTED WOODEN DOOR INTO THE DIMLY
lit bar. The place had changed names a dozen times since I was kid. *Lou's,
Cal's, Crystal River Pub*, and several more that my mind couldn't conjure
the names. It always looked the same, though. Right down to the pool tables
in the game room. When we were kids, Dad brought us in here to shoot
while he pounded a few rounds with his buddies.

Bonding. Good times.

Sean and I took two empty stools at the far end of the bar. I had a wall
behind me, and the door in front of me. The mirror that stretched the length
of the bar let me keep tabs on the tables without looking in their direction.
Sean said nothing. Neither did I.

The bartender glanced our way. He nodded, put down the cups he was
drying and walked over. I recognized the guy. He, like the pool tables, had
been a staple in the pub for thirty years. And like the felt on those tables, he
looked weathered and worn.

"Well I'll be... If it ain't the Noble boys. What the hell are you two doing
in here? I don't see your daddy around. Don't tell me you two kids are old
enough to drink now?"

It took a minute for his name to come to me. "How are you, Eric?"

He shrugged. "Seriously now, something happened to your old man?"

Sean shook his head. "Nah, an old friend died, though."

Eric nodded. "Heard 'bout Jessie."

He glanced at me. There was a sadness to the way he looked. His eyes seemed to droop. His lips parted a crack. He wanted to say something. I looked away before he could.

"Anyway, what'll you guys have?" Eric said.

"Beer," Sean said.

"Beer," I said.

"Coming right up." Eric walked off.

Glasses clanked, feet scuffled and the jukebox kicked on. An old Stones song piped through the speakers.

Eric returned with two chilled bottles, caps off. Water drops ran down the labels.

I reached for my wallet.

He set them down in front of us. "Don't worry about it."

I looked at Sean. He shrugged. We'd make it up on the tip. Eric probably counted on that.

The Rays game was on TV. The music drowned out the commentators. Didn't matter. I watched without interest. Long gone were the days of enjoying sports. Maybe I'd get back into them after retirement.

If I ever managed to quit the business before it did me in.

Sean leaned over and nudged me with his shoulder.

"What?" I said.

"Look who's coming our way."

I looked ahead and saw two older women saddle up to the bar. I hoped that wasn't who he meant. He nudged me and lifted his finger off the bar top and pointed toward the floor. I shifted my gaze to the right, saw two guys I knew from my younger days. We had gone to school together from kindergarten on. During those thirteen years, we never got along. Half the fights I got in as a kid were with those guys. They hated me. I hated them. I wasn't surprised to find those feelings still existed.

They looked the same, only grown up and sixty or seventy pounds heavier. One of the guys was Glenn's brother. Glenn was Jessie's husband.

"This must be twofer day," one of them said.

"Yeah, two jackwagons for the price of one," the other said.

Sean dropped one leg to the ground. His shoulder grazed my back as he turned. I heard his other shoe hit the hardwood floor.

I glanced back, shook my head. "I got this."

Sean didn't move.

I slid off my stool. "If it ain't Mutt and Jeff."

"It's Matt and Jed, dumbass," Jed said.

Sean laughed. I smiled.

"What's so funny?" Matt was Glenn's little brother. They looked nothing alike.

"Look," I said. "I know there's this long standing thing between you guys and me, but you gotta let it go. That was almost twenty years ago. You're living in the past. I've moved on. You should move on. I mean, take your waistlines for example. They've moved on, and out."

"You're fixing to get your face pounded in, Noble," Matt said.

Words like that were either followed by a punch or more tough talk.

He continued. "And then when we're through with you, we'll take out your sissy brother."

I let my arms hang loose. "Then shut up and do it."

"What?" Matt said.

"You aren't going to do anything about it. You're all talk. At least twenty years ago you had the sack to throw a punch. All those years of sitting on your couch watching talk shows has sapped you of your testosterone. You go around bullying people like you used to. Only now you can't do anything but talk tough."

Matt narrowed his eyes. The pace of his breath quickened. His arms shook and his fingers twitched.

Jed grabbed his shoulders, and shook him, and said, "Knock him out."

That was all it took for Matt to wind up like he was throwing the first pitch out. His entire sequence was poorly executed. He tossed a lumbering right hook at me.

I leaned back and avoided the sloppy punch. With my right hand, I gained control of his right arm. I spun him around, grabbed the back of his head with my left and drove his broad forehead into the other guy's nose. Jed went down in a heap. I drove my heel into Matt's right knee. He buckled sideways. As he went down, I slammed his face into the edge of the bar and let go.

Sean pulled me back from the two bodies on the floor. Both men bled and rocked in place and moaned.

"Dammit, Jack," Eric said from the other side of the bar. "Didn't I have to ban you from this place for an incident like this before?"

I shrugged. "That time was my fault. This guy's to blame this time. He took a swing at me."

"And you did nothing to provoke it, did you?"

I held my hands up, sure that Eric wouldn't do anything.

A woman stepped out from the game room. She had on a sheriff's uniform. Dark sunglasses sat atop her head. Her hair was pulled back into a tight ponytail. I recognized her from earlier when Sean and I drove through town.

She looked at me, shook her head and continued toward the bar.

Sean grabbed my shoulder. "Just ease back a sec, Jack."

She said, "What happened, Eric?"

Eric said, "Those two knuckleheads were so drunk they fell off their barstools."

"Is that right?" she said. "There's only two barstools at this end. Can't fit anymore." She reached both arms out wide in front of the endcap, then turned toward us. She kept her arms out and extended her index fingers. "And you two must've acted the part of good Samaritans and come over to help. Am I right?"

Eric nodded. Then he looked at Sean and me, pointed to the other side of the room, and said, "Thanks for your help, now you two go back to your table. The Sheriff can handle this. I'll get you a fresh round of drinks."

Sean tugged at my shirt. I stared at the deputy as we walked away. She winked at me as I passed her. We found an empty booth near the back corner and sat down. I kept glancing at the woman.

"You'll never change, will you, Jack?" Sean said.

I hiked my shoulders an inch in the air. "In my world you have no choice but to act. If you don't, you're dead. You can't avoid trouble like that. Besides, what was I supposed to do? Let him hit me? Screw that."

"You didn't have to take out Jed and then slam Matt's head into the bar."

"Yes, I did. Otherwise it'd still be going on. Or they'd show up at your house later demanding we settle the score, or whatever crap lingo guys like that use."

"They might still show up."

He had a point. If those two were anything like they used to be, any scenario was possible.

"If they do," I said, "I promise they'll beg for a beating like I just gave them."

Sean leaned back a few inches. He stared at me without speaking. I don't know if he'd ever seen me make a threat like that. He had always had his suspicions about what I did. I never told him. I simply avoided the question. Perhaps that last statement convinced him that my standard, "Government work" response was a cover up.

I calmed down a notch. "Adrenaline, Sean. That's all."

"Whatever," he said, pointing toward the bar. "We got a visitor incoming."

The woman's thick-soled boots rapped against the floor. She walked slowly, confidently. She stopped in front of the table. I didn't look up.

"Hello, Sean," she said.

Sean nodded and said nothing.

"And hello, Jack," she said.

I looked at Sean. He stared blankly over my head. I looked up at the woman. "Do I know you?"

"You don't remember me?" She feigned being hurt.

"No, I don't. And Eric said the Sheriff would come take care of this. Where is he? I don't see Sheriff Woodard over there."

"I'm Sheriff Woodard, Jack."

I turned in my seat and looked up at her again. "Sheriff Woodard had one kid. A girl. I used to babysit his daughter. You are not her. She was rail thin, bucktooth and covered in freckles."

The woman smiled. Her teeth were perfect. Her body was too. "Some of the freckles are still there. Just too dim in here to tell."

"April?" I said.

"Hi, Jack."

"You're the sheriff now? What happened to your dad?"

"Heart attack."

"I'm sorry."

"He did it to himself. Doctor warned him that his fifth would be his last. And it was."

"Wow, I'm really sorry."

"Don't be, he's OK now, taking it easy."

Sean slid out of the booth. "Why don't you sit, April? Catch up with Jack for a few. I'll get some drinks."

"Water for me," she said as she took his seat, smiling. "You look good, Jack."

"I try," I said, still a bit stunned that the awkward little girl I knew twenty years ago sat across me as a fully developed woman. "You look... great."

"Time can do that."

I thought about the last time I'd seen April. She was still a kid, and I hadn't left for the Marines yet. I remembered taking her to the movies a week or so before I left for recruit training at Parris Island. I was eighteen, she was eight.

I heard Matt or Jed say something. Sean's voice rose a notch. I looked across the bar. Sean stood at one end. Jed and Matt stood by the front door. They both looked at me and pointed.

"This ain't over Noble," Jed said.

April stood, put her hand on the butt of her pistol and walked toward them. Her steps were no longer slow and cautious. She said, "Yes it is. Now you two get out of here before I haul your drunken asses in."

The men glared at her, then me, then Sean, and then left.

April returned to the table. She exhaled loudly and shook her head.

"Sorry about that," I said.

She shrugged. "Those guys are my biggest headache. I pray every night they give me one reason to lock them up for good."

"What about Matt's brother, Glenn?" I said.

April looked toward the bar, acted like she didn't hear me.

"April?"

"I know where you're going with this, Jack."

"Are you in charge of the investigation of Jessie's death?"

She nodded. The look she gave me told me to stop. I didn't.

"What do you think?"

"I can't say."

"I'm gone in a day or two. You can tell me."

"No, Jack, I can't. I'm not prepared for this. We don't have the staff for this. My dad would have handled an investigation like this alone. He's not in the department anymore, so it's all up to me."

"Did you reach out to him for help?"

"No, I can't do that to him. It could do him in. I'm supposed to have a detective from the city on his way, but so far, nothing."

Something about the way she spoke led me to believe that she didn't think the case was as cut and dry as a suicide. She removed a straw from its wrapper and cast it aside. Starting at one end, she ripped the wrapper down the middle. She glanced at me. I remembered that look. She was scared.

"There's more, isn't there?" I said. "You think she was murdered."

She said nothing.

"OK, I get it. Look, if you need someone to talk to about this, I'm all ears. I have some experience investigating."

"Something like this?"

"Close enough."

She nodded, slapped the table with her palms and got up. "I should get out of here." She took a step away, stopped, turned and held out her card. "Call me tonight and we'll discuss the case."

I reached for her card. It was printed on heavy paper, thick and coarse. She didn't let go.

"That's my cell. I can be reached anytime, for any reason. If those guys come around bothering ya'll, let me know."

I nodded. She let go. Her footsteps reverberated through the floor until she reached the door. She exited without looking back.

I couldn't escape the feeling that when I called her to discuss the investigation, things were going to change. And not in a good way.

I slid into the booth. Sean returned, set a beer in front of me and then slid in on the opposite side of the table.

"Where'd she go?" he said.

"Left."

"You all right?"

"Yeah. Memory lane and all that."

He left me to my thoughts. I let the music and the beer drown them out. Fifteen minutes later we got up. Each of us dropped a twenty on the table. We cut across the bar and stepped out into the humid early afternoon air.

"I don't understand how you live like this," I said.

Sean laughed. "Come on, you did it for almost twenty..."

I waited for him to continue. He didn't.

"What's wrong?"

"Look at that."

I glanced up from the sidewalk. Someone had vandalized his car. Across the windshield, they'd written, "Die Nobles."

We approached his Mercedes cautiously. I stopped a couple feet from the window, leaned over and put my hands on my knees.

"That ain't paint, Sean."

"What?" He stood next to me. "What is it then?"

"Blood."

17

"GOD, THAT'S DISGUSTING."

THE WATER from the hose mixed with the caked blood on the wind-shield. The fluids combined into a runny, red river that ran down the glass, took a detour to the side, and fell to the ground where it puddled. After the windshield was clean, he aimed the stream toward the bloody puddle and forced it toward the drain.

"At least it's not ours," I said.

"It could have been," he said. "Is this how you act all the time?"

Apparently cleaning blood off his car set off Sean's rage, and his big brother instinct.

"No," I said. "Just most of the time."

He shook his head and continued pushing the pool of faint red water away from his car.

I walked toward the road. It was just after twelve o'clock now. The lunch rush had begun. Everyone flocked to one of the four places to eat within town limits. That's how many there used to be, at least. Maybe there were more now. If I really wanted to know, I'd ask Sean. Turns out, I didn't.

I spotted the same beat up Tercel from the retirement home parked across the street in the Burger King parking lot. It faced me. There was no front tag. I shrugged it off as a coincidence. After all, if I'd have been paying better attention, I probably would have recognized half the cars in the facility's lot.

I turned around and walked toward the bay where Sean now dried his car with the cheap towels he had purchased out of a coin-operated machine. He worked the blue cloths back and forth across the window, then the hood, and finally the bumper.

He'd worked up quite a sweat. As a result, he took off his shirt. Fortunately, he wore a white tank for an undershirt.

I approached him, stopping in front of the Mercedes. "About done?"

He nodded, said nothing.

"What do you want to do now?"

He looked up. "Want to take Kelly out fishing?"

"Sure, why not."

The drive back to his house took fifteen minutes. We didn't say a word during that time.

We found Kelly on the couch playing a video game. She jumped at the idea of spending part of the day on the water. Sean went to find his wife. Kelly spent the next five minutes telling me about all the manatees that inhabited the water nearby. I figured she thought I grew up somewhere else. I knew all the facts she presented. I let her talk anyway. She filled me in on everything she knew about the creatures. Turned out to be a lot. I picked up a few new things.

After a bit of convincing, Deb decided to go along, though she made it a point to tell me that she wasn't much of an angler these days. We piled into her Suburban. Their boat was docked a few miles away and it was a quick trip over. After we parked, I grabbed a cooler out of the back. It was loaded with sodas and beer and sandwiches. Everything we needed for a day on the water.

Deb and Kelly sat in back while Sean started the thirty-foot vessel. I took a seat next to him. He pulled away, navigating slowly toward the river.

The two p.m. sun beat down on us from every angle. There was no escaping it. Deb tossed me a tube of SPF 70 and told me to lather it on.

I did.

It didn't matter. The sun still got me.

Sean found a nice cove for us to fish for a bit. He caught more than I did. I managed to tie Kelly with two bass.

We moved on from the spot and stopped a hundred yards from a manatee hole.

Sean jumped overboard. Kelly followed.

Deb said, "Going?"

I said, "Sure."

We jumped over together and swam out to meet the other two.

The water was a good fifteen feet deep and clear enough you could see the bottom. I saw manatees the size of Buicks gliding beneath us. Their scars were visible through the crystal water. Years of boats flying by too quickly, nicking and scarring the gentle beasts had taken its toll. Dad had been heavily involved in enacting regulations to cut down on the unnecessary deaths from careless boaters.

I hadn't thought about that in years. I found it hard to believe I hadn't cared either.

We moved closer to shore. A few manatees followed us over. They swam by slowly, allowing us plenty of opportunities to reach out and touch them. Whenever a hand touched their skin, they slowed down. I imagined they enjoyed it.

Kelly smiled and laughed and splashed and played. Deb looked happy for the first time since I saw her that morning. Sean seemed relaxed.

I'd forgotten how intoxicating a day on the water back home could be. The stress rolled off faster than humidity-induced sweat.

After an hour we made our way back to the boat and headed toward the dock. The sun hung lower in the sky now, out over the gulf.

"It'll be a great sunset," Deb said. "Too bad it's not till eight-thirty or nine."

I found my cell and checked the time. It was six p.m. Time had flown.

We reached the dock and three of us got off. Sean tidied up and joined us five minutes later. We all piled into the Suburban. The ride home was quick.

Time slowed when we pulled into the driveway, though.

18

THERE WERE THREE PATROL CARS. ONE IN THE DRIVEWAY, AND two on the street. April stood in front of the house. She ran toward us, stopped, and waved Sean forward. The tires chirped as he whipped onto the driveway. April directed him to pull to the side.

The front door of the house was open. The window to the left had been smashed.

"What's going on?" Deb said. She'd opened her door and was half out of the Suburban before Sean had put it in park.

Sean hopped out and raced to her side. Both of them swarmed April. They both pelted her with questions. The woman couldn't complete a sentence before they asked five more.

"Stay in here for a few, OK, kiddo?" I said to Kelly.

She forced a smile and nodded. She couldn't hide the concern in her eyes, though.

I hopped out and walked toward April. She'd already directed Sean and Deb to the front door where one of her deputies handled the couple.

"I thought you wanted me to give you a call first?" I said.

She pursed her lips and shook her head. "One of the neighbors was out walking and heard glass breaking. She ran home, got her husband. They both came back over in time to see a guy running away from the house."

"They get a good look at him?"

"Only from the back."

"And?"

"Hat, jacket, jeans. Perfect gear for a steamy Florida summer day, huh?"

I said nothing.

"They yelled at him, but he didn't stop. That's what they tell me. It wasn't until they got back home that they called us."

"What's missing?"

April took a deep breath and exhaled. "Nothing that I can tell. We'll need your brother and his wife to confirm, of course. The guy tore through the mail, left it scattered about. In the bedrooms, he dug out the luggage. Smashed out the side mirror of your brother's Mercedes." She pointed at Sean's car.

I hadn't noticed the damage. I wondered if Sean had. He seemed more concerned about the house.

She arched an eyebrow. "All kinds of things start happening when Jack Noble comes home, huh?"

"Anywhere I go, it seems."

In the light I made out a few freckles on her cheeks and her nose. Her eyes were the same crystal blue they had been when she was a child. Her teeth were perfect now. Her body had filled out in the right places. She was soft where she needed to be, and tight and toned everywhere else.

"I need to get them to a hotel for the night," she said. "You want to hang around here and I'll meet you in an hour or so?" She paused a beat. "We can go through the house together, and then review Jessie's file."

"Works for me."

I hung back while she instructed Sean and his family to gather a few belongings and meet her in front of the house. Ten minutes later, my brother and his family emerged. They looked scared, frustrated, angry. I could relate to the emotion of anger.

Sean walked by me, nodded. He didn't question what I was doing, or why

I wasn't going with them. Perhaps he figured I would arrive in a different car, show up later, something like that. Eventually, he'd figure it out once his emotions settled down.

They backed out of the driveway and took the road toward Suncoast. The car disappeared from sight.

I headed inside. One of the deputies was a guy I played football with. I couldn't remember his name. He didn't have the same issue.

"Hey, Jack," he said. "I heard you were in town."

"Hey, man," I said. It always worked. "Came down for Jessie's funeral."

He nodded. "That's a tough one, huh? Were you two still close?"

"Hadn't talked in over ten years. With some people, that doesn't matter."

"I suppose not." He turned away, stopped and looked back at me. "Just be careful what you touch. Boss might want to dust later."

I ignored his advice and picked up the phone and hit redial. If whoever did this was stupid, they might've used the phone. An answering service for Sean's firm picked up. I placed the phone on the cradle and went to the kitchen.

Nothing appeared to be disturbed in the room. Pots and pans hung from a rack over the stove. All the small appliances were in the same place as they'd left them. I opened the fridge, nothing appeared out of place in there either. I pulled open the freezer and stood in front of it for a minute.

Something about the kitchen wouldn't let me go. I spent a minute staring at the sink. Nothing jumped out at me. Whatever caused the feeling, I couldn't place it.

I jogged up the stairs and checked out my room. The bed was unmade. The sheets had been tossed in the corner. The closet door was open. Inside, anything that had been on a shelf or hanger was now strewn about on the floor.

But nothing seemed to be missing.

I left the room and went into Sean and Deb's. It was even more of a mess. Dresser drawers sat on the floor, upturned. Clothes were everywhere. I opened her jewelry box. It was filled with necklaces, earrings and rings.

Diamonds, gold, gems. None of it touched. Sean had a couple thousand in cash in his nightstand.

Why go to so much trouble and not take anything?

The only answer I could come up with was that they weren't looking to take *anything*. Only one thing.

What had Sean gotten himself into?

When I looked at it honestly, Sean and I knew little about each other. We spoke once a year at best. He could have been into any number of activities, legal or not, and I wouldn't have a clue. I knew a few people who might be able to tell me. But I didn't want anyone to know I was in Florida, much less the United States.

I left their room and took a glance at Kelly's. Nothing had been disturbed there. At least whoever broke in had some sense of moral code.

In all I'd killed about twenty five minutes checking out the house. I went out front, sat down on the porch. The sun ducked behind the house, shading the lawn and driveway. It had cooled off a bit, but there was no breeze and the humidity was still a killer.

Another fifteen minutes passed before April pulled up in her patrol car. She got out. I stood and walked toward her. We met halfway.

"They doing OK?" I said.

"As good as you could expect, I suppose," she said.

I nodded, said nothing.

"You check it out?"

"Yeah."

"Thoughts?"

"Someone was looking for something, but only that one thing."

She nodded. "Question is, did they find it?"

"Hard to tell."

"Is it?"

We stared at each other for a minute.

"Listen, Jack, I'm not trying to point fingers here or anything, but I've heard rumors."

"Rumors?"

"About you."

"What about me?"

"The things you do."

"Which are?"

She sighed and turned away. "Come on, follow me."

We walked inside. She dismissed the two men in there. I still didn't catch the name of the guy I played football with.

He said, "See ya around, Jack."

"You, too," I said without making eye contact. I continued toward the living room. Sean had a wide, deep worn leather couch. I fell back into it.

April closed the door and joined me. She took a seat in a more contemporary chair across from me.

We stared at each other. Neither of us spoke. It became uncomfortable. Was she waiting for me to spill my guts about my life?

I was about to get up and go into the kitchen when she broke the silence.

"Did you ever work for the CIA, Jack?"

I shrugged and said nothing.

"Don't brush me off."

"There's a lot of things I've done that I can't talk about, April. Just how it works. I never worked *for* the CIA, although I may or may not have been loaned out to them a time or two." I paused a beat. "Or three."

She seemed to accept the answer for what it was. An admission of guilt without admitting I was guilty.

"And what about a secret government agency?"

"I am not at liberty to discuss the existence or non-existence of any secret government agencies." I threw in a smile to derail her a bit.

"Have you worked as an assassin?"

"Why put labels on things like that?"

"What kind of answer is that?"

I rose. "Look, April, you're wasting time. Whoever did this, didn't do it because of me. No one knows I'm here right now. I flew in from England on a private jet. Landed at an Air Force base. No customs, passports, computer scans, or anything like that."

She sighed and fell back in her seat. "OK, then, so who did this?"

"What do you know about my brother?"

"Sean? He's well known, well liked. His law firm is taking off. Does a lot in the community."

She didn't read into my question the way I thought she would. I wondered if she really had her heart into the job, or if she'd taken it to get her dad to quit.

"Let me restate that," I said. "Have you ever heard anything about Sean—"

"No, Jack. Don't go there. He's clean, trust me."

"How would you know?"

She got up and walked past me, toward the kitchen.

I rose and followed. "You didn't answer me."

"I know because I questioned him already."

April had absolved herself. Perhaps she was cut out for her line of work.

We each took a seat at the kitchen island. The gut feeling that I'd missed something in there returned. I glanced around the room, looking for something. I didn't find it. My fingers bounced nervously against the granite counter top.

"What is it?" she said.

"What?"

She placed her hand on mine. My fingers settled down.

"You're a wreck," she said.

"Something about this room," I said. "Can't shake the feeling that I'm missing something. I've learned to trust that feeling. It's always right."

"Always?" She lifted a curious eyebrow.

"There's a dud here and there."

She squeezed my hand and then slid off her stool. For a day out policing, she smelled nice. She walked behind me, circled around the island and headed toward the fridge. Her head and her eyes never stopped moving. I doubted she'd find anything. Then again, it couldn't hurt to have her look.

"Wonder why they didn't disturb anything in here?" she said.

"Me either. They trashed everything else. What's so special about the kitchen? It's like they knew whatever they were looking for wouldn't be in here."

She let the door to the freezer fall shut. It created a puff of wind that blew her hair off her shoulders for a second. She turned toward me. Her nose and cheeks were red from the cold air. She smiled, but I looked past that.

I saw what I'd been looking for.

19

"STEP ASIDE," I SAID.

HER smile faded. She narrowed her eyes and said, "What?"

"Just do it," I said.

April took one step to the right and turned halfway. "What is it?"

I hopped off the stool. We stood shoulder to shoulder in front of the fridge. There were dozens of magnets on the door. It hadn't struck me as odd earlier, even though, as far as I knew, they couldn't stick to stainless. In the middle of the door were a bunch of magnetic poetry, words and phrases. Most were spread out into jumbled meaningless messages. Others said corny things like, "All my love belongs to you."

I pointed at the phrase in the center of it all. There was a gap of at least two inches on all sides separating the group of words from the rest of the magnets. It looked deliberate.

April read it out loud. "Back off get out."

"And look at it closely. See how that white is smudged? Kind of darker than the others?"

"Kind of red?"

We stood with our arms pressed tight to one another. She looked over at me. I felt her breath on my face.

"Is that blood?" she said.

"You got something to test with?" I said.

She shrugged. "We're a small department, Jack. We don't have anything fancy."

I placed my hand on my face and rubbed down to my chin. Someone had to be able to help. It was an hour's drive to Tampa. One of her deputies could get there in thirty to forty.

"Grab a camera and an evidence bag," I said. "We can have one of your guys run it to the city."

"OK."

"You've got some contacts down there, right?"

She nodded as she pulled out her cell phone and called back one of the deputies. She walked away from me and filled him in on the details.

I continued to stare at the message. I had a good idea who had left it, and why. What I didn't understand was why they didn't just track me down and deal with me? Why'd they have to bring Sean and his family into this? These guys knew me twenty years ago. They had no idea who they were messing with now. I could make their lives a living hell.

And I would.

I needed a car, and I had to get rid of April so that I could put an end to this.

I made my way to the living room. April stood in the foyer. The front door opened. She greeted her deputy, and together they walked into the kitchen. I followed behind. I didn't know this man. He took several pictures of the refrigerator, donned a pair of blue latex gloves, and placed the poetry magnets into an evidence bag.

April said, "Have them test it for blood first, DNA second."

The guy nodded, and said, "Yes Ma'am," and left.

April followed him to the front door. I waited in the living room. After her deputy left she joined me.

"I guess we wait," she said.

"You should go home," I said.

"I can't leave you here."

"Why not?"

She waved her hand around. "What if they come back?"

"I'm a big boy. I can handle it. Go home, April."

She took a few steps back. Whether she did it purposefully or unconsciously, she blocked my path to the front door.

"Why are you acting like this, Jack?"

"Like what?"

"Like you're going to do something."

"Probably best you don't ask a question like that."

She hesitated before answering. I could see her struggling with the choice. Leave or try to detain me. She threw a curve ball at me.

"I'm going with you," she said.

"Where?"

"You know where. Those two jerks from the bar."

I hadn't considered this option. It made sense. She could keep me from doing something stupid, or she could cover up anything stupid that I did.

"You know where they live?" I said.

She lifted her eyebrows an inch, nodded. "Been there several times."

I followed her outside. The sun had set. It was dark and muggy. Crickets and cicadas competed for our attention. A water bug the width of a golf ball skated across the driveway. Halfway to her patrol car, I began to sweat. I started to long for London.

She started the engine and blasted the AC before she closed her door. I stole a glance in her direction. She took a few deep breaths. Her hands white knuckled the steering wheel. She whispered something. I had no idea what she said.

"You sure you want to do this?" I said.

"Yes," she said.

"You can just drop me off and give me directions. No one will know. I sure won't tell."

"I'm not leaving you there alone. You nearly killed them in the bar and that took a couple seconds. I'd probably roll up to their house in the middle of the night and find their heads on stakes."

Ironic, considering where I'd been only a few days ago.

"Besides, these guys are armed to the teeth. They won't do anything if I'm there."

She backed out of the driveway, threw the transmission into drive and gunned the engine. We flew around the bend in the road. I saw a turtle off to the side. She slammed on the brakes at the stop sign. Burned rubber seeped in through the vents. I rolled my window down once we began moving in an effort to dissipate the odor.

"How far is this place?" I said.

"Other side of town."

I wanted to ask her about Jessie. Despite being in town for a day, I knew nothing other than she was dead and they suspected it had been suicide. Our earlier conversation led me to believe that April doubted this. I tried to bring it up a couple times, but couldn't find the angle.

April gave me one.

"She lived in that neighborhood."

I followed her gaze toward the community of brick ranch houses. The roofs were all low pitched. The yards all had palm trees and lots of flowers and manicured lawns.

"Kids?" I said.

"Two," she said. "Boy and a girl."

"Drive by it," I said.

She hit the brakes and made a hard left into the neighborhood. Kids playing soccer in the street took to the sidewalks. April slowed down and pointed at a brick house painted light yellow or off-white. Too dark out to tell for sure. The car rolled to a stop a few feet past the driveway.

Yellow police tape covered the front porch and the door.

"How'd she die? I mean, I know it's being looked at as suicide, but how?"

"Gunshot."

"Did it look self-inflicted in your opinion?"

"Jack, I'm an amateur when it comes to this stuff. I've never investigated a suicide, much less a murder. I've been promised a detective from the city, but they haven't showed up yet."

I reached out and placed my hand on her forearm. "It's OK. I'm not grilling you here, just asking a couple questions."

She took a deep breath. Her gaze left the front of the house. She stared at me.

"It doesn't look right to me," she said. "The position of her body, her hand on the gun, the blood on the wall... none of it seems right."

"Have you sent the pictures to Tampa's homicide department?"

She shook her head. "They're all at the morgue. Anyway, I've spent some time online, researching. So far, the feeling in my gut seems right. I guess the detective will let me know if I'm wrong."

"Can we go in?"

"Key is in the glove box."

I reached for the latch. It didn't open.

She pulled her keys from the ignition, fished around for a second, then handed it to me with a small key pointing up. I inserted it into the lock and opened the glove box.

"Grab the flashlight, too," she said.

I grabbed the key to Jessie's house and the large stainless steel flashlight. "Got gloves?"

"In the trunk."

We both got out. The wind had picked up. It blew in from the gulf. Fresh air. Salt air. It felt good and made the humidity a little more bearable.

I met April at the trunk. She popped it, grabbed a box of gloves.

She turned to me, and said, "You need a gun?"

"I'm good." I didn't care how she took that. I was armed. If she knew, she did nothing to stop me.

We walked up the driveway and across the paved walkway to the porch. She ducked under the yellow tape. I followed close behind. She cut the tape on the door. It fell in two even length strands along the frame.

"We'll replace it before we go," she said.

I heard voices behind us. Looking back, I saw a couple sitting on their porch. Orange embers at the end of a cigarette glowed in the dark. I was surprised I hadn't picked up on the smell.

The door clicked open. April looked back at me. "Ready?"

I shrugged. "Guess so."

I clicked on my light and stepped into the dark house. Nothing could have prepared me for what I encountered.

20

LEON BARBER IDLED ON SUNCOAST'S DIRT AND GRAVEL SHOULDER. He had a view of the police car and the front of the house. The cruiser had pulled up next to the curb and lurched to a stop. Jack and the woman had remained inside for a minute before getting out. They met at the back of the car. She had reached inside the trunk. Leon couldn't tell for what. Jack reached behind his back, tugged at something.

His piece, Leon presumed.

They walked up the driveway. He lost visual contact with them when they ducked under the darkened porch.

Leon counted back from fifty, slowly. When he reached zero he checked his mirrors then cut across the two-lane road. Gravel pelted the Tercel's undercarriage. The rear end of the compact car fishtailed. He let off the gas and regained control on the blacktop. By the time he passed the first house in the neighborhood, he drove a steady twenty miles per hour. He slowed down and coasted past the police cruiser. Turning his head toward the house, he searched for Jack. Didn't see him, though. Police tape covered the porch. The door to the house was closed. Either they'd gone inside, or walked around back.

He slowed down a bit more. The Tercel crawled forward. Two strands of yellow police tape hung from the door frame, about four feet up on either side.

They'd gone inside.

Leon continued another couple hundred feet down the road, made a three point turn and parked about a hundred feet from the house. He studied the tangle of asphalt, grass and siding in front of him. The sky grew darker by the second. The final glimmer of red light over the gulf faded.

He pulled out his cell phone and called Vera.

"He's at some house with a cop," Leon said.

"OK." It didn't sound like the information surprised her.

"Want me to get closer?"

"No," she said. "Stay put."

Leon hung up the phone and tossed it on the passenger seat. It skipped twice and came to a rest next to the door. He was tired of sitting around doing nothing. It's all he had done to this point. They had people for this. He wasn't one of them. His job had always been to come in, and strike fast and hard. Sitting in parking lots waiting for the go-ahead was for the desk jockeys. And since he'd been around the whole time, it might not even be his go ahead.

He couldn't stand being played. Vera was jerking him around. She might be able to keep him from taking Jack out, but she couldn't keep him cooped up in a car for a week. He slapped his steering wheel.

"To hell with this."

He leaned across the passenger seat, opened the glove box and pulled out his Glock 17. He'd decided to see what Jack Noble was up to, and how the man would react when faced with Mr. Nine-millimeter.

Leon reached for his door handle and shoved his shoulder into the window. He stopped short of placing his foot on the ground.

If he acted out of line, it would come back to haunt him. Maybe not today, or tomorrow. But one night, he knew, he'd wake up with a sharp blade pressed to his throat. There'd be no meeting beforehand. He'd get no trial or committee hearing.

He'd disappear.

Simple as that.

But first, they'd have to find out.

21

ROTTING FLESH AND DAY OLD BLOOD HIT ME LIKE A SACK OF BRICKS. I stood inside, next to the front door. April closed it and the odor enveloped us. She gasped a few times. Her hand hit my shoulder, presumably to steady herself.

My flashlight beam hit the opposite wall. Blood coated it. The crimson pattern started about six feet in the air, blossomed, then traveled down in a thick, wide line. The flow of blood continued on the carpet, forming an area that covered three feet out and to the side. Two spent shells lay on the floor. They were within two feet of each other. Someone had placed evidence cards next to them.

The bullet casings stood out.

Why two?

April must've read my mind. She patted my arm with one hand and shined her light at a spot on the wall with the other.

"First bullet missed and went through the wall right there. Nervous, I suppose. I know I would be."

I walked forward, stopped in front of the mess. I looked down, trying to find an alternate path.

"There's booties in the bottom of the box of gloves," she said.

I slipped a pair on. The hole in the wall intrigued me the most. I inched closer, then took a step back. I used the flashlight to zoom in on another section. The cone of light spread as I leaned back. The comparison between the small section against the entire wall proved interesting.

"What're you doing?" April said.

"It's hard to be positive, but doesn't this section here," I circled the area with my flashlight, "look different than the surrounding area?"

She moved in, turned her body sideways and stood close to me. She took short, quick breaths. She wasn't used to this kind of carnage, and, even though she'd seen it once, it still made her anxious.

"Yeah," she said. "It looks faded. Muted, maybe."

"Like some of the paint came off, right?"

"Could be."

"You guys checked all the linens, the washer, so forth."

"Yeah, best we could, at least."

I lowered into a squatting position. The light followed me down. April combined hers with it. The faded pattern matched the blood stain on the wall a couple feet away. A bloom up top, and a streak heading to the floor. This one was thinner. I turned my flashlight toward the floor. The carpet looked fine. Unsoiled. It matched the rest of the room, except for where Jessie's body had lain.

I inched the flashlight up, panned left and right.

"Look at that," I said.

"What?" she said.

I pointed at the small drop of red on the millimeters wide baseboard ledge.

"Is that blood?" she said.

"That'd be my guess."

April looked up at me. Her eyes were wide, her lips parted. We were close enough that I felt her breath hit me in spurts.

I said, "The faded wall, that could be dismissed, despite the bullet hole. One of the kids could have gone crazy with markers there one day, or spit their juice there. But that single drop of blood there tells us something."

"She didn't kill herself."

"Nope."

"Someone missed the first time."

"They hit." I pointed to my ear. "But not in the right spot."

"She started to run that way." April shined her light to the left. "That explains it."

"What?"

"Why the angle seemed odd. It makes sense now. See, that's what bothered me. Everything about the way she would have had to hold the gun to get that angle of entry, the blood, it was off because she didn't do it."

"Did you find two wounds?"

"Just the entrance and exit."

"April." I paused a beat and rose. "That wasn't an exit wound. That was the second shot. It either grazed her or went through and through. Either way it hit the wall, and so did her blood. It wasn't as much as the other shot, but it was enough that someone cleaned it. They failed to wipe away one little drop."

"You're kidding me," she said.

"Agreed," I said.

"What now?"

"Where's the body?"

"Clearwater. At the morgue."

"OK. We seal this place up now. You need to get someone out here to guard it. Then we head down south."

We turned and walked to the door. The warm air that rushed in was a welcome relief.

"What about those two idiots from earlier?" she said.

"We pay them a visit after," I said.

April went back inside and collected samples while we waited for one of her deputies to show up. I expected her to botch it after her claims of limited training. Whether she'd picked up her skills online, or from TV, she acted like a pro. Best I could tell, at least.

I leaned against a pole supporting the porch and watched her work. I had glimpses of playing video games with her when she was a kid. As a girl, she'd been awkward in every way, even with a game controller in her hand. It was still hard to believe this was the same person. Relatively speaking.

I must've had a strange expression plastered across my face, because she glanced up and gave me a cross look.

"What?" she said.

"What?" I said.

"You're looking at me all funny."

"Sorry, just remembering when you were a goofy looking kid."

"Ah, yeah." She rose from her crouching position and walked toward me. "Well, I remember when you were a good looking young man. Guess we both changed."

I smiled. So did she. Then she apologized.

"I shouldn't act like that here. Your friend died in that room. You'd think as a cop I'd be able to cope better."

"People adapt to horrible situations by acting like this, April. I saw a man in Iraq get both his legs blown off. He cracked jokes with the medics until he passed out."

She looked frustrated, like she knew what she needed to do, but couldn't. Her dad had held the job for thirty years or so. He was the law in Crystal River. With that, came a level of respect from the community. I doubted April received the same level of consideration from half the old timers in town. And what was Crystal River but a bunch of retirees now? What there was of the younger generation was probably the same as anywhere else. They didn't care.

"It'll come with time," I said.

She smiled, nodded and went back to work. I decided to step away for a few minutes so she could complete the task without feeling like I was watching over her shoulder.

I walked to the end of the porch, scanned the street. The people across the road were still outside on their porch. They'd extinguished their cigarettes. I heard them talking, but couldn't decipher what they said.

Elsewhere, the kids had all gone inside. It was hard to play soccer with the sun down. The streetlights that lined the road were dim and spaced far apart.

I stuck my head past the railing and looked up. Clouds had rolled in from the north. The breeze had died down. The air felt thick again. I heard a rumble of thunder in the distance. We might beat the storm on our way down to Clearwater, but we were sure to hit it on the way back.

A car pulled into the neighborhood. I saw the light rack on the roof as it passed under a street lamp. The headlights lit up the street. I followed the flood of white and saw the same beat up Tercel I had seen across from the car wash and in the parking lot of Dad's senior care facility.

I walked to the porch entrance and ducked under the police tape.

The cruiser parked behind April's vehicle. The guy got out.

"Jack," he said. "Where's April?"

I still couldn't remember the guy's name. Perhaps Sean had a yearbook lying around somewhere in his house.

"Inside," I said as I hiked my thumb over my shoulder. We passed each other on the driveway.

"Hey Craig," April said.

Craig, that was it. But was that his first name or his last? I questioned whether I really remembered the guy.

They spoke on the porch for a few moments. I turned right at the end of the driveway and headed toward the Tercel. It was parked in a dark area, making it impossible to tell if anyone was inside it.

About halfway between Jessie's house and the Toyota, April called for me.

"Jack, what are you doing?"

Any cover I had had been blown. I turned around and walked toward her, casting the occasional glance over my shoulder. She waited for me beside her car, next to the passenger door.

I stopped two feet from her. "That's the third time I've seen that Tercel today."

She glanced over my shoulder. Her eyes were narrowed and her lips pursed.

"About a hundred feet back," I said. "Older model. Primer gray."

"Where'd you see it?"

"At my dad's retirement home, across from the car wash, and now here."

She shrugged. "Coincidence, that's all. He visited his mom or dad earlier, had a bite to eat, and he's home now. People do live and work around here, you know. They have lives, families, dietary needs."

"Fast food is far from a need."

"Whatever, come on."

I didn't accept her take on events as gospel, but they made sense. At least, they would to someone who didn't carry around the same level of paranoia as I did.

She held her cell phone up. "I've got an ME who is going to meet us at the morgue."

"ME?"

"Medical Examiner. Don't you watch TV or read?"

"No."

"Huh." She studied me for a moment. "Well, you should."

"I'll keep that in mind. Maybe add it to my resolutions next New Year's Eve."

She waved me off. "Get in the car, Jack. We've got a bit of a drive ahead of us."

22

"I'M TELLING YOU, THAT WAS close, Vera." Leon's heart pounded. He had to force air through his nose. He was lightheaded.

It felt good. He felt alive.

Jack Noble had stood ten feet away from where Leon hid. The hedges were thin, too. If the man had aimed the heavy-duty flashlight in Leon's direction, Jack would have spotted him. If he'd have sneezed, or been stung by a bee, Leon would be dead now.

"I told you to stay in the car," she said with no inflection in her voice.

"I'm tired of that."

"Take me through what happened so I can try and make some sense of why you stepped out of line?"

"They were inside the house for a while. Another cop showed up." Leon paused a beat. The cruiser pulled a tight U-turn, hopping a curb, and raced toward the end of the street. "Hey, Vera, they just left. Pulled out in a hurry. You want me to follow them?"

The line was silent for a minute except for Vera's steady breathing.

"Is the cop still there?" she asked.

"Yeah, he is, but Jack ain't. Should I go?"

"No. I can trace a cop car. They don't have many in that town. I know where you're at, so it won't be hard."

He heard her tapping on her keyboard. He tried to imagine what Vera's office looked like. He'd never been in there. Never been close. Hell, he hadn't ever met her. He only knew the voice, that stiff, monotone voice. Did she sound like that all the time? When she had sex, was it like screwing a robot?

"Leon, why don't you go inside and talk to the cop? Find out what he's doing there."

Leon glanced at the police tape surrounding the porch. "How am I gonna pull that one off?"

"Tell him you're the detective from the city."

"What? What detective?"

She sighed. "Don't question me. You have to accept that I know more about what is going on than you do. When the time is right, I'll fill you in. Until then, you'll be told what you need to know and you will keep doing what I say to do when I tell you to do it. Understand?" She paused a beat. "I don't need to tell you what will happen to you if you don't. After all, you're usually my go to guy to get rid of a rotten apple."

"Bad apple or rotten tomato."

"What?"

"Nothing." Leon hesitated. Though he'd never asked, he always assumed that there were more like him. Someone had to assassinate the assassin. "Yeah, I know, V. Whatever you need, I'll do."

"OK, then. Call me back when you're *done* with the guy."

"Yeah, sure."

He hung up, opened the door, turned in his seat and placed both feet on the ground. He didn't have his good shoes on. He hadn't counted on this job lasting this long. Now he regretted it. And his feet hated him for it. As he walked toward the house, he slipped his cell in one pocket and a blackjack in the other. It weighed down his pants, causing the Glock to slip a little in his waistband.

A holster would have been a good idea, too, he thought.

Leon walked down the sidewalk at a steady clip. He stopped in front of the house. The windows were dark. The door propped open. Leon crossed the street. He stepped lightly up the driveway, across the walkway, and ducked under the yellow tape and stopped on the porch. The cop stood in the front room, facing away.

Leon whistled at the guy.

The deputy spun around and reached for his pistol.

Leon already had his drawn. "Hey, ho, man, take it easy."

"Who…who are you?" the deputy asked.

Leon smiled a little. The other guy had no business being in the house. He wasn't a cop. The guy was a glorified secretary.

Leon said, "I'm Detective Jones from Tampa. Was asked to come down here and check this crime scene out. I saw your car out there, but I wanted to make sure you weren't a perp."

Perp? Where had that come from? Too many movies.

"I'm a deputy in the Crystal River Sheriff's department. I was told by my boss to wait here and protect the scene."

Leon wondered from what. He smiled, nodded, and said, "Looks like you're doing a stellar job, my man."

The deputy's flashlight hit the floor and lit up a decent space around it. Leon caught sight of the blood on the wall.

"Man, what happened here?" he said.

"Suicide," the guy said.

Leon chuckled. "Ain't no suicide, man. Who the hell shoots themselves while they're standing up so that the blood sprays on the wall like that? People tend to develop nervous leg syndrome when a gun is pointed at them." He caught the deputy's attention. "Meaning their legs don't want to work anymore. Knees get all rubbery and give out. They fall to the ground, crying and whimpering and begging for their life and whatnot." He still held his gun. He aimed it toward the ceiling and wagged it around, let it come to rest on his temple. "Now, I seen a few men put a gun to their own head. They sat down for it, though. I figure, maybe someone could stand, but they ain't gonna go up to the wall and hold one side of their head against it."

"What?" the deputy said as if every word had passed around him. "Who the hell are you?"

"Like I said, I'm Detective Johns from Tampa."

"You said Jones a minute ago?"

Leon smiled. "Did I?"

The deputy took a step back. "Let me see your ID."

"Don't move." Leon aimed his Glock at the man.

The guy lifted his hands in the air.

"Turn around," Leon said.

The man did.

Leon walked up to him. He grabbed the man's handcuffs, yanked his arms back, and placed the cuffs on the deputy's wrists.

"It's nothing personal," Leon said right before he knocked the deputy out with his gun.

The man fell to the floor in a heap. Leon dragged him into the kitchen. A trail of blood followed them. Leon saw it, cursed. He grabbed some peroxide and a towel and cleaned it up. Then he dropped the towel on the guys face and the peroxide on his stomach. The man had no reaction.

Out cold.

Leon pulled out his cell phone and called Vera.

"Well?" she said.

"He's down. This place is a mess. Blood all over the wall, the carpet, the deputy's face." He held back a laugh.

"I want you to tamper with it."

"How?"

"Get creative."

"Don't you think they already have what they need from it?"

"Let me worry about that, Leon."

"What about the cop?"

"Did he see you?"

"Yeah."

She sighed. "Take him someplace."

Leon glanced at the man on the floor. He didn't need to hear anything else. "OK."

After Vera ended the call, Leon looked around for something to use to destroy the crime scene. He knew enough about forensics to keep from getting caught. There was little he could do to get rid of all the blood at this stage. Besides, the crime scene was old enough that they would have gathered all the evidence they needed. But Vera gave him an order, so it was best to carry it out.

He found the laundry room at the end of a hall off the kitchen. On a shelf he saw a bottle of bleach and a bottle of ammonia. He grabbed both, and carried them to the kitchen. The deputy moaned and rolled over. Leon kicked him in the head three times. The guy stopped moving.

Leon opened the back door. He saw a hose coiled up on the ground. It had a spray nozzle attached to the end. He turned the faucet on and dragged the hose through the kitchen and into the living room.

He squeezed the nozzle's trigger and aimed the powerful stream at the wall and the floor. Dried blood began to liquefy and slide down the wall. After a minute of dousing the area, he emptied the bottles of bleach and ammonia on the wall and the floor. The mixture of the two burned his throat and nostrils. He ran through the room and the kitchen and burst through the back door. He filled his lungs with thick fresh air.

He knew that was a bad combo, but he hadn't expected that reaction.

Leon waited a few minutes. He wanted to hang outside longer, but knew time was critical. He followed the green hose through the house and scooped it up by the spray nozzle. Then he aimed the jet of water at the wall and the floor.

"That'll have to do," he said.

He carried the hose into the kitchen. The guy had scooted to the wall. Leon sprayed him down. The deputy screamed as the high-powered jet of water hit his open wounds. Leon laughed at the guy as he tossed the hose outside.

He walked back to the deputy and squatted down in front of him. The man looked away.

"That's what I thought," Leon said.

The deputy said nothing.

Leon pulled him to his feet and pushed him into the garage. The deputy tripped. Somehow he managed to turn so that his side hit the concrete floor first.

"Wait here," he said. "You so much as move, I'm going to kill you."

Leon exited the house, picking up the deputy's pistol along the way, jogged down the street and got into the Tercel. He raced toward the house, backed into the driveway and butted the rear bumper up to the garage door.

He waited behind the wheel for few minutes, watching his surroundings.

Inside the garage, Leon belted the sheriff again, almost knocking the man unconscious. He lifted the garage door just enough to shove the deputy into the trunk of the Tercel. Leon watched as the man rolled his head back and forth, trying to talk. Blood covered spittle flew a few inches into the air and crashed back down on his face.

"Save it," Leon said, closing the trunk lid.

He got behind the wheel and pulled out of the driveway. The guy banged against the frame and the backseat. Leon turned up the music and drowned the noise out.

23

THE MORGUE LOOMED AHEAD LIKE A GATEWAY TO HELL. THE dark hid the bulk of the building. Landscape lights set at ten-foot intervals were aimed upward, highlighting long thin stretches of the building's concrete facade.

April pulled into the parking lot and double-parked near the door. She left the car running for a minute. For the first time, it felt like the air conditioning had cooled me off.

She said, "You sure you're ready for this, Jack?"

I said, "I've seen plenty of bodies, April. Some were my fault, others weren't. Some were friends. Some of those friends died because of me. I can handle this. It's the only way we'll figure out what happened."

We exited the vehicle and met in front. We walked silently to the morgue's entrance. Inside, April signed us in. The older guy on the other side of the counter wore a white coat, blue jeans and a t-shirt. He had messy hair and was unshaven. We'd woken him up, and he looked pissed about it. He looked at me, then at her. I presumed he wanted to say something. He didn't.

"That's him," April whispered.

He led us down a narrow hall that deposited us into a chilled room. The walls to my left and right were fifteen feet high and lined with chambers. There were three rows on each side, with fifteen frozen caskets to a row.

When the hell would there be ninety bodies needing a place in the morgue in Clearwater?

The guy looked at his chart. "Let's see, Jessie Staley." He traced his finger down the page. "Ah, there we go." He led us to the other end of the room. He turned a handle and pulled Jessie's chamber open.

Her dark hair was matted against the pale skin of her face. Her eyes were closed. Blood caked her eyebrows. Her lips were parted slightly. The top one was split in the middle. One of her teeth had been knocked out and another broken.

The ME moved her head to the right. He pointed at the obvious bullet wound above and slightly forward of her ear. "Entrance." He turned Jessie's head a little more. His fingers walked around her skull and came to a stop a few inches behind the first wound. "Entrance. And, you can't see it, but exit just an inch behind. That bullet grazed along her skull and popped back out."

"That explains the hole in the wall," I said.

"And the blood on the baseboard," she said.

"You notice anything else?" I said to the ME.

"Obvious trauma to her mouth."

"How did she fall?" I said.

The ME shuffled through her file and pulled out a photograph. Jessie lay on her side right. Her right arm stretched out along the floor. Her left fell across her chest. One leg was straight, and the other pulled forward. The back of her head rested on the floor. The last thing she saw lay somewhere between the man who shot her and the ceiling.

"That rules out the fall knocking her teeth out," I said.

The ME reached out and opened Jessie's mouth. "I found the full and partial teeth inside. I'm waiting on results."

"What would that tell us?" April said.

"If a weapon other than someone's fist did it."

"You'll be able to tell?" she said.

He shrugged. "That's why I sent it off."

We stood without speaking for a moment. I stared at Jessie. April stared at me. The ME tapped his foot and cracked his knuckles.

I looked over Jessie's body. Her face and head took the brunt of the attack. She had a fresh scar on her arm. I noticed nothing else.

"Anything else?" he asked after a minute.

"Jack?" April said.

I looked up. I had plenty of questions. Not for him, though. I wanted to be able to ask Jessie what happened. How did it happen? What led to it happening? I wanted to tell her I was sorry for how things ended, and the trouble I dragged her into a decade ago.

"Jack?" April said.

"Yeah, sorry. Let's go." I nodded at the ME. He turned away.

I heard Jessie's body being slid back into the frozen tomb that precluded her eternal stay underground.

We sat inside the car. I grabbed the back of my head and exhaled. It didn't feel real. Even after seeing her corpse, I couldn't believe that Jessie was dead.

"You OK?" April placed her hand on my shoulder.

I shifted in my seat so I faced her. "Tough to take in, you know?"

"Remember what happened to my mom?"

I thought about it for a minute. There had been an accident a year before I left for the Marines. April's mother and father had been out on the water. He went below deck to grab a couple beers. When he came up, she was gone. That was the story, at least. It never sat well with me. But the man telling it was the only witness and he was also the town's sheriff. How could you doubt him? An independent investigator came in at her father's request. The Mayor picked the man out. The guy found no evidence of foul play, said it was an accident. She had been drinking, fallen overboard, and the tide carried her body away.

"I remember," I said.

"Still keep hoping she'll just show up one day. Come walking up along the river and find her way to my house." April looked away. "Or at least that her body will wash up. I suppose I should let that go considering it's been twenty years."

Neither of us spoke for five minutes. She started the car, but we didn't leave. The air that came out of the vents smelled like stubbed out cigarettes at first. The smell faded, leaving behind an ice-cold breeze that hit the middle of my face.

"You know what I think?" I said.

"What?" she said.

"I think those guys know more than they were letting on. I think that little message was more than them trying to get under my skin."

"You think they were involved?"

"Them, and Glenn. Hell, Matt's his brother. Think about the scene. That could have been a two-man job. Definitely not suicide. I think one of them held her while the other went to shoot. She moved. The bullet hit but didn't kill. One guy punched her. She stopped. The other shot and killed her."

"Plausible."

"Probable."

"So what should we do?"

"I think you should go over and question them."

"What about you?"

I stared out the front window at the blackness beyond the parking lot. "I'm going with you."

She shifted into drive and crossed the parking lot, turning right and taking us toward town. She bypassed Main Street. We prowled along the outer edges of the historic center. Streetlights lined one side of the street, not the other. She turned into an older neighborhood. Thirty years ago, my grandparents lived there. Now it looked nothing like it did then. The houses were worn down. The lawns were messy, full of weeds, or just brown. Some of the homes we passed looked abandoned, or inhabited by squatters. I saw the house my grandfather and his brother had built themselves. Someone had painted it purple.

"What the hell happened here?" I said.

"The economy," she said. "Most folks bugged out some time ago. Went to Jacksonville, Gainesville, Tampa and Orlando. However few jobs those cities have, it was better odds than here."

The economic state of the country wasn't something I dwelled on. Since becoming an adult, I worked either for the government or as a contractor. There were plenty of jobs available in my line of work. And they paid well.

"There it is." She pointed ahead.

The house looked like the rest in the neighborhood. The gutter hung off the roof on one side. Siding was missing in a few places. The lawn had grass two feet high mixed in with bare spots.

April blocked the driveway with her cruiser. She left the engine running.

"Take this." She tossed a key toward me. "That's a spare. If you need to run, you do so."

"I'm not going anywhere without you."

There were no blinds or curtains covering the wide front window. The TV lit up the far wall. Images flashed on the screen. I couldn't tell what they were watching. Two of the men occupied opposite ends of a couch. Glenn sat in a recliner against the left wall.

A dog barked as we walked up the driveway.

Matt rose off the couch and walked toward the window. His frame blocked my view of the television. He cupped his hands to his face and leaned into the glass. He shouted something. The other two men rose. Glenn went to the back of the house. Jed went to the front door. Matt met him there. The door swung open and both men stepped out. Jed held a baseball bat.

"You might want to rethink that," I said.

"Wasn't the warning at the house enough for you, Noble?" Matt said.

"Put the bat away, Jed," April said.

"You brought the cops, Jack?" Matt said. "Can't fight fair and square?"

"Fair and square got both of you knocked out in five seconds. She's here for your safety."

Matt took a few steps forward and spit in my direction. It missed me and hit about ten long blades of grass on its way to the ground.

"Where'd Glenn go off to?" I said.

"Don't know what you're talking about," Jed said.

"Saw him through the window. He went to the back of the house. It'd be best for you all if he came outside."

"Piss off," Matt said.

"I can get a warrant," April said.

I almost questioned her.

Matt did. "For what? We ain't done nothing. If anything, I want to press charges against Jack for assaulting me. So, there, take him away Ms. Sheriff."

Both men laughed.

I looked at April. "I'm growing tired of this."

Matt took a few more steps toward me. "So what are you gonna do about it?"

I said nothing.

"As far as I'm concerned," he said, "you're trespassing on my property. Get the hell off it before I kick your ass."

April said, "You rent this house."

"Don't matter," Matt said. "I know that much."

He stood inches from me. A wave of tequila and corn chips and his body odor blew past me. I might as well have been standing in a dumpster.

"Get going, Jack."

I didn't move.

"Jack, we can get another car out here. Craig's close. I'll call him. We'll watch the house. These drunks aren't going anywhere."

I said nothing, kept my eyes on the man in front of me.

Matt moved quicker than he had at the bar. It caught me by surprise. He drove his big hands forward, into my chest. I lost my balance for a second. He followed it up with a head butt. I managed to move to the left, but not far enough. He caught the side of my forehead. The maneuver didn't have the intended effect of splitting my face open. It left both us reeling a bit though.

I shook my head and regained my balance. He threw a right hook at me. It was wide and sloppy. I ducked it and delivered a blow to his midsection. The air left his lungs like a balloon deflating. He bent over. I grabbed the back of his head as I drove my knee into his face. He fell down, gagged on his blood.

Jed came running toward me swinging the baseball bat.

I didn't have enough time to reach the M40 tucked in my waistband and avoid his next swing, so I waited. He waved the bat back and forth like a kid stepping up to the plate for the first time. There was no cohesion. His next attempt would be wild and in my direction. I prepared to avoid it and gain control of the bat.

"Freeze!" April yelled.

Jed stopped in place. He glanced at me, then her.

"Take your shot, man," I said.

He thought about it. I could see him inching forward. He stopped just out of arm's reach. That gave him plenty of room to work the bat. Unfortunately for him, he didn't count on me kicking him, so it came as a surprise when I slammed my foot into his crotch. He dropped the bat and fell to his knees. I kicked him in the face and then pushed him over. He landed on top of his friend.

"That's the second time you two ended up in a pile today. There's a lesson in there somewhere."

April and I left the two guys on the ground and walked to the front door.

"Glenn," I said. "Come out here. We need to talk to you about what happened to Jessie. We know it wasn't an accident."

There was no response. The door was open. I couldn't see or hear any movement.

"What do you think?" April said.

"We can wait him out."

A roaring sound filled the still night air.

24

I TURNED AND RAN TO THE DRIVEWAY. THE MOTORCYCLE CREATED A breeze that crashed into me as Glenn drove by. I grabbed the bat off the ground, cocked my arm back. By that point, he'd traveled too far beyond my reach. I couldn't do anything but watch the red taillight shrink into the dark.

"Dammit." April rushed past me. "We can't let him get away."

One of the guys on the ground laughed. The other moaned.

"Let's go," she said, already halfway to the car.

"Don't think about leaving town," I said to Matt and Jed as I walked by. Jed got to one knee and flicked me off. I altered my course and kicked him in the face. He collapsed again.

April stood behind her open door, shaking her head. "Why?"

I dropped the bat on the driveway and shrugged. "Why not?"

She put the cruiser in reverse and gunned it. My head whipped forward then back as the rear tires hopped the curb behind us. Two quick thumps. April didn't seem to care. She kept her foot on the gas and shifted into drive. Tires spun in the grass, dug into the earth. We lurched forward. The rear axle dropped six inches. The tires squealed until they got their grip set on the asphalt.

Didn't matter how fast April drove. We'd lost Glenn. He had a head start on a motorcycle. He could have cut through someone's yard and pulled into a shed by now. Or ditched the bike and taken off on foot. Woods surrounded the neighborhood on three sides. There were more across Suncoast, although the tributaries and gulf lay beyond. April slammed on the brakes, opened her door and stepped out. I joined her by the cruiser's trunk. We were near the entrance to the neighborhood, facing the way we had come.

"I'm getting Craig over here. He can bring those two drunks in." She pulled out her cell and held it to her ear. Seconds passed. She made a twirling motion with her hand, then said, "Craig, get over to 2424 Magnolia. There's two guys passed out on their front lawn. I want them locked up."

"He on his way?"

"Voicemail." She hung up. "What do we do now?"

Porch lights flicked on. People wandered through their front doors, down their driveways, and gathered along the side of the street. Hard to tell what would happen in a neighborhood like this. Their stares and gestures made it obvious they weren't fans of the local law enforcement. How far would they go, though?

I kept my eye on the growing crowd, and said, "His wife's funeral is tomorrow morning. No way he doesn't show. Have a couple of your deputies waiting there and arrest him afterward."

April followed my stare. She glanced at me, then turned back toward them. "Arrest him for what?"

"I don't know. You're the cop. Force him to go in for questioning. Catch him jaywalking for all I care. Get him to the police station and let me work on him."

She looked at me again and leaned back, her brows furrowed and her arms crossed. I remembered her giving me the same look when she was five or six after I told her she couldn't stay up to watch TV. Only this time the hurt was real.

"I'm sorry," I said. "My temper got the better of me, and he got away."

"What's done is done," she said with a sigh. "Why hasn't Craig called back?"

"Maybe he fell asleep."

"Maybe we should go over and check up on him."

I shrugged, jutted my chin toward the crowd fifty feet away. "I think we should go somewhere before that group of people decides to do something stupid."

She nodded. "Maybe we should go get a drink."

"I can handle that."

We turned and walked to our respective sides of the vehicle. I kept my head on a swivel and my stare focused on the crowd. They did nothing. We both slipped inside the car.

She drove through town, past the only bar I knew of within five miles. She didn't slow down. I said nothing. She'd spent her entire life here. She knew the places to go. Something new could have opened up, and I wouldn't have had a clue. Maybe she was taking me to a new restaurant where I could get a steak and a beer.

That would be heaven.

Downtown Crystal River was deserted. The roads were lit up with new orange street lamps. The only sound was the purr of the engine and the near jet-like sound of the air conditioning blowing through the vents. It was the coolest I'd felt since arriving in Florida.

We left Main Street and the lights behind, headed north. I knew there was nothing that way, at least not on Suncoast.

"Where are we going?" I said.

"You'll see," she said.

Five minutes later she turned right. The darkened street offered no clues. She hugged the road's curves. Second nature. She'd driven them hundreds, if not thousands, of times. Finally, she pulled onto a gravel driveway, cut her headlights and parked the car in an open garage. With a twist of her wrist, the engine and the vents went silent.

We sat in silence for a minute. The ticking of the cooling car sounded like shotgun blasts.

"Want to come in?" she said.

"Do I have a choice?" I said.

"You can walk back to your brother's house."

I thought about it. The mental map I pulled up told me it'd be a three or four mile walk. It was dark and hot and muggy, and that didn't appeal to me. Also, I couldn't recall seeing a beer in my brother's fridge.

I wasn't sure if hers had any, but I'd risk it.

"All right," I said. "Lead the way."

The exterior of her house looked old enough that the shingles might have been made of asphalt. The yard was well maintained. The grass was short. Hedges were trimmed. There were plenty of flowers, all in bloom. Red, yellow, orange, purple. She didn't care about cohesion. She must've liked the vibrancy of them all.

Her keys jangled as she pulled them from her pocket. They reflected the streetlight in front of her house. She stuck one in the doorknob. The lock clicked. She pushed the door open and flicked on a light. A pool of white washed over the front step. A tabby cat greeted her with a long meow. It rubbed against her leg, gave her a long stare, and then walked away.

"Perfect pet," she said. "Says 'hi' when I come home and then takes care of himself. Haven't even been able to find a man who can do that."

"Say hi, or take care of himself?"

She smiled. "Either."

I said nothing.

"It's a joke, Jack. Just trying to lighten the mood. It's been a rough day for both of us."

"Day? Try decade."

She walked away from me. Her arms crossed in front of her. Her hands went to the opposite sides. She grabbed her shirt and pulled up a few inches. It slipped out from her utility belt clad waistband. The bottom of the shirt rose up a few inches. Her skin was tanned. A colorful tattoo adorned her right side. She let go of the shirt with her left hand. The hem fell to her hip. She used the same hand to unclasp her utility belt. It hissed through the belt loops of her pants. She held it out to the side. It looked like a dangling water moccasin. She let it fall to the floor.

"I'll be right back," she said, looking back at me. "Make yourself at home."

The foyer had one picture on the wall of the Eiffel Tower, and no furniture. I glanced down the dark hallway. Looked like it led to the bedrooms. To the right, I saw the dining room. An old oak table with four chairs sat under a dark light fixture. I walked forward, into the living room. She had a full size couch and a love seat. Both were upholstered with the same faded denim fabric.

I walked past the furniture to the back door. White vertical blinds covered it. I pulled them back. It was pitch black beyond the thick glass. I reached my hand to the side and found a switch. A light cut on, dim at first, then bright once it warmed up.

Her backyard wasn't much. Fifteen feet deep and as wide as the house, all enclosed with a six-foot privacy fence. There were no trees or shrubs or flowers back there. Didn't even see a grill. I figured April spent little time in her backyard. The front yard appeared to be her tranquil place.

"What are you doing?"

I turned and saw April standing there with two bottles of Miller Lite. She'd changed into gym shorts and a pink tank top. She'd pulled her hair back. Her arms and chest and legs were as tan as her side.

"I thought you said you had beer?"

She extended her arm toward me. "You a snob now?"

I hiked my shoulders in the air and held my hands out to the side. "Spent some time in Europe. They've converted me. A bit, at least."

April walked toward me and stuck the bottle in my hand. "You're in Florida now, bud. Act like it."

I brought the bottle to my lips and took a pull off it. It was cold and refreshing and once I got past the aftertaste, it was pretty good.

She crossed the room, stopping to place her beer on a coaster on top of the wooden coffee table. The longer I looked at the table, the more I realized it had been made from pallet boards.

She caught me admiring it. "You like it?"

"Yeah. You make it yourself?"

"Yup."

"Neat."

She laughed. "Yeah, *neat*. When'd you start talking like a Cleaver?"

"Sorry, long day."

"So, have a seat."

I did. Her couch was more comfortable than Sean's expensive leather sofa. I moaned as I leaned back. My body sunk into the cushions. I wondered if I'd be able to get back up.

"You all right, old man?"

I didn't respond.

She knelt down in front of her entertainment center. Her buttocks rested on her heels. Her tank top inched up. I saw part of the tattoo again. I wondered what it looked like in its entirety. I heard a loading tray open, then close. A bossa nova beat commenced a few seconds later. A guitar and tenor sax combined to create a tune I hadn't heard in years. Perhaps I had, but not in this way.

April rose, spun halfway, and approached with a smile on her face. "You remember?"

I took a second. A man sung in Portuguese. A smoky sax accompanied him. "Girl from...?"

She nodded, slowly.

"Some beach in Rio de Janeiro, Brazil?"

She shook her head, quickly. "Really, Jack? That's the best you can do?"

"Ipanema, right?"

April rolled her eyes. "About time. Now, do you remember?"

I shook my head. She looked disappointed. I said, "Give me a clue."

She took a deep breath, sat down on the coffee table in front of me, placed her forearms on her knees and leaned forward.

"The summer before you left, you watched me almost every day because my mom was gone, and my dad worked that crazy shift and didn't get home until nine or so. You weren't here alone all the time, but the last couple hours was always just us. I used to—"

"Put this song on and make me dance with you."

April smiled. She reached out and grabbed my hands. She rose, tried to pull me up with her.

"No," I said.

"Yes," she said.

"Not a chance."

"You don't want to disappoint me, do you?"

"I really don't care."

She pushed the coffee table back with her legs. She took a step back, pulled on my arms harder. Eventually, I relented. She laughed at first as I fumbled through the steps. Then she moved in closer. The day had taken its toll on both of us. Her scent was natural, appealing, even mixed with the beer.

Her body pressed against mine. Her lips went to my neck. For a moment, I thought I'd tell her to stop. I didn't. She kissed my neck, my jaw, my cheek, and my lips.

She wasn't stopping. Neither was I. My hand went to the hem of her tank top. I lifted the right side. I pulled my head back to see more of the tattoo. She blocked me with her arms. A smile crossed her lips and she lifted an eyebrow.

"Not yet."

"When?"

She shrugged.

Then both our phones rang.

We both exhaled, loudly.

"I have to take that," she said, stepping back.

"I should too," I said, reaching into my pocket for my phone. I answered without checking the number, figured it was Sean.

"Jack?"

"Sasha?"

From the other side of the room, April said, "What? What do you mean he's not there?"

"What's that?" Sasha said.

"Nothing. My brother's wife. What's going on? Why are you calling? It's well after midnight there."

She started to answer. I cut her off.

"Hold on a sec."

April's voice faded to a murmur in the background. I wanted privacy, though, so I went to the back door. It was locked in three places. I managed to get them all unlatched and stepped into the backyard. A dozen mosquitoes greeted me. They dive bombed me, two or three at a time. I swatted them away.

"OK, Sasha. What's up?"

"She got a death threat."

25

DEATH THREAT.

THE PHRASE ECHOED through my head. A scene played out in my mind where Erin had gone to Sasha, desperate and pleading after being unable to find me. Someone had put the pieces together. They couldn't get to me, so they threatened her and Mia.

I don't know if it was the humidity or fear, but I broke out into a cold sweat. I swallowed back the lump in my throat.

"Who?"

"Marcia Stanton."

My pulse dropped below one hundred. "Credible?"

"Best I can tell it is."

"What was said?"

"The gist of it, 'you're dead.'"

I moved to the corner of the small backyard and leaned against the fence. This afforded me a view into April's house. Our beer bottles stood next to each other on the coffee table. I took a moment to compose my thoughts.

This wasn't the first time that Marcia Stanton had her life threatened. I was outside that cafe a few days ago because we knew about the threat before she did. I had to find out if that was the case this time.

"Did we intercept any intel about this like the last attempt?"

"Not a word. And we've been listening hard enough to hear a mouse fart."

"Christ." I glanced up at the sky. Clouds raced past. "You need to get a team assembled and put around her now."

"That's what I suggested, too."

"OK. Sounds like you have this under control, and I wouldn't expect any less. So, why are you on the phone with me?"

"She wants you, Jack. She said she needs you here and with her until this threat is eliminated."

"I'm unavailable."

I heard her take a quick breath, as if she was going to respond. She paused for a moment. "The funeral's tomorrow, correct?"

"Yeah."

"So you can come back after that, right?"

"It's not that easy, Sasha." Something caught my attention inside. I took a step to my right. April entered the room. "There's things here that I need to see through."

"Like what?"

"It's best that you don't know."

"I can find out," she said. "You know that."

"You don't know where I am."

"Crystal River, Florida."

I said nothing. Location breeched. I'd be checking over my shoulder every minute now.

"Come on, you didn't think all your records were destroyed, did you?"

The clouds overhead slowed down. Like in a traffic jam, they piled into one another. Soon the cloud would grow out of control and have nowhere to go but down.

"Give me a day, Sasha. After that, you can send someone to pick me up and I'll come back. Keep Marcia underground tomorrow. If she insists on going out, get the best men you can find. If any of the Prime Minister's guys are off, surround her with them."

The back door flew open and April stepped out. She struggled to breathe.

April said, "Jack, we need to go."

"Hold on," I said to her.

"Brother's wife?" Sasha said.

"Something like that," I said.

"You're not going to tell me who she is?" Sasha said.

"She's the sheriff. We're working on something."

"Sure you are. You got a thing for women in uniform, don't you?"

"I'll talk to you tomorrow." I hung up and stuffed the phone in my pocket.

April motioned frantically. "Let's go."

I followed her through the house, attempting to get her to tell me what was wrong. I feared for Sean and his family's safety. My chest and gut tightened, like someone had nailed me in the solar plexus with a two-by-four.

I grabbed onto her bare shoulder at the front door and spun her around. I said, "What is it?"

She said, "Craig's not at the house."

"Jessie's?"

She nodded, ducked her shoulder and slipped out of my grasp.

"OK, and...?" I said.

"His car is there. The crime scene is ruined. Someone poured bleach and ammonia and hosed it all down. There's fresh blood, too. I think it's Craig's." Her bottom lip quivered. She bit it. Her eyes had grown wet. Tears slipped down her cheeks.

"Listen to me, April. Go change. You don't need your uniform, but throw on some jeans and grab your pistol. We're going to head over there, quickly, but calmly. We'll figure out what's going on. But let's wait until we see this with our own eyes before we start making assumptions. OK?"

"OK." She wiped her eyes with the back of her hand.

She disappeared down the dark hall. When she returned, she had on faded blue jeans. They had holes in the knees. We left the house and walked to the car, side-by-side. Our hands brushed against each other. Thunder rumbled. It sounded far away. No flash accompanied it.

We got in the car. She drove. On the way, she asked, "Who called you?"

"Lady I'm working with."

"Everything OK?"

"Typical problems at the office," I said. "Looks like I'll have to return after tomorrow."

"Oh." Her lips went to one side of her face and she glanced at me. "Will you come back?"

I shrugged. "There's no way I can give an honest answer to that question. I could tell you yes, but I'd be lying. I could say no, and show up a week from tomorrow."

"I can't believe I waited almost twenty years to see you again and it had to be like this."

I said nothing. What could I say? I'd forgotten about her after a week of getting my butt kicked in recruit training. She'd grown up with a distorted memory of me, and built me up from that. I could tell her everything about me, everything I had done, and she'd dismiss it because in some part of her brain, she thought of me as some kind of hero.

"I'm not who you think I am," I said.

"What?" she said.

"This image you have of me, it's not who I am. April, I'm not a good man."

"Don't say that."

"It's true. Trust me. The best thing you can do is forget all about me."

She shook her head. "There's too much going on right now, Jack. Can we talk about this before you go?"

I sighed, looked out the window. Beyond the road I saw nothing but black. The gulf lay a couple hundred yards away. Crystal blue water as far as you could swim. I wanted to be out there more than I wanted to be in the car.

"Jack?"

"Sure."

We reached Jessie's neighborhood. Red and blue lights bounced across the sky. Craig's cruiser was parked on the street, in front of the house, right where I'd last seen it. Another one of April's deputies had pulled into the driveway and left his strobes running.

She slammed on the brakes and threw the car into park before coming to a complete stop. The car lurched forward and jerked back. She threw open her door and jumped out. I followed. We ran to the front of the house where her deputy waited.

"What's going on, Skagen?" she said.

The man stepped forward. "He's gone. No answer. Nothing. There's a mess inside. Fresh blood in the kitchen, living room, and the garage."

I scanned the area while the man spoke. Across the street I saw the faint glow of a cigarette behind the front window.

"Jack," April said. "Coming in with me?"

"You go ahead. I want to check something out."

She and Skagen walked inside. I crossed the street and cut across the neighbor's lawn to their front door. I didn't bother with knocking. I reached for the handle, found it unlocked, and pushed it open.

The guy dropped his cigarette and hurried backward to the wall.

"What are you doing?" he said.

"What'd you see?" I said.

"Huh?"

Every time I'd been there, the guy had been watching, whether from the porch, or inside. He saw what happened to Craig.

"That's a nasty habit you got there," I said.

"So," he said.

"It'll kill you."

He said nothing.

I walked toward him, stepped on the cigarette and put it out. The man's breathing grew wheezy. I reached behind my back and pulled out the M40.

"When I say kill you, I don't mean in the sense of heart disease and lung cancer. I mean it'll get you noticed by the wrong person at the wrong time."

"Don't shoot me, man."

His dark eyes focused on the M40's barrel. He sucked in breath and blew it out in under a second. I caught the odor of whiskey. The guy was frail, his hair was gray and thin. He hadn't shaved in a week or two. Long lonely hairs poked out from his open shirt.

"Where's the other person?"

"What? Who?"

"Don't screw with me, man. I saw someone on the porch with you earlier."

"She...she's in bed."

"If you're lying, she's dead."

"I'm not lying," he said.

"Tell me what you saw."

"Get that gun out of my face." He whispered the words.

I took a step back and lowered my weapon.

The guy took a few deep breaths. He patted his chest a few times. "OK, after you and the woman left earlier, this black guy, he came walking over from down the street that way." The man extended his arm and pointed over my shoulder. "The other cop, well, he talked to him, then turned his back on him."

"What do you mean by that?"

"It was as if he recognized him, or accepted him as belonging there. The cop turned and waved the guy forward."

"OK."

"They was inside for a while." He pursed his lips and blew out quickly. It sounded like faint machine gun fire. "I started to get bored. Figured I might come in and watch some television. Gotta be a game on, at least. Right?"

"Of course."

"Then I seen that black dude come running out of the house, down the street again. He pulled back up a couple seconds later in a beat up little car."

"What kind of car?"

The guy shrugged.

"Maybe like an old Toyota?" I said.

"Could've been," he said.

"You get the color of it?"

The guy shook his head and tapped his nose. "Maybe gray."

"OK."

"Anyway," he said. "He gets out, pops the trunk, opens the garage, and then puts the cop in the trunk."

I waited a beat. "Did you call the police?"

The guy shook his head. "No, sir. I didn't know who else might have been out there. I've been called a snitch before. Been beaten 'cause of it, man."

"What's your name?"

The guy said nothing.

"We can get it through other means."

He looked toward the window. "Your girlfriend's out there."

"Your name," I said.

"Fults," he said. "Herman Fults, with an *ess*, not a *zee*."

"Don't make any plans to leave town, Herman."

He nodded. "That all?"

"No, I've got one more question."

"Can I get a drink first?" He turned and walked toward the kitchen without waiting for my response. "Come on, man."

I followed him. He grabbed a bottle of Wild Turkey, tossed the cap and started drinking.

"Have a seat," he said.

I sat across from him. My seat felt unsteady, and the table wobbled.

"You want to know what happened to Ms. Jess, don't you?"

I nodded. "Did you see?"

Under the kitchen light, he looked like a different man. Not in a good way, either. The man in the living room was old and frail. This looked like that guy's deceased father. Deep lines were etched into his face. What hair he had looked brittle. His skin was gray, and his eyes were glazed over and milky.

"She was home with her husband. The kids was out. I was watching the game. Heard a loud engine pull up, so I got up and went to the window, cracked it and had a smoke. Two big guys got out and went right inside the house."

"Had you seen them before?"

"Tubby and Tubby Jr.? Oh, sure. They were over a lot. Ms. Jess told me she hated them. One was her husband's brother."

I said nothing.

"So, anyway, nothing seemed out of the ordinary. I went back to my game. Fell asleep. My front door was open, just the screen there. Windows, too. Nice breeze that night blew directly into my house. And then, two explosions woke me up."

I straightened up.

"What time did that happen?"

He looked up. "Maybe around one or two."

"How long between the explosions?"

"Not long. Couple of seconds."

"What happened next?"

"Well, I ran to the window. Nearly did myself in, that time. Couldn't breathe for a minute."

"Did you see anything?"

"Not a thing, man. The car was gone." He took a minute, sighed a couple times. "I went over there. The front door was unlocked. I pushed it open and saw her." His eyes watered over. He tried to speak again, but couldn't.

"OK, Mr. Fults. I got it. I'm going to have someone come by tomorrow and get a statement from you."

"Can I do it after the funeral?"

"I'll talk to the sheriff."

We sat there for a few minutes. Neither of us looked at the other. I rose, excused myself, went through the front door and jogged across the street. April stood in front of her cruiser.

"Jesus, Jack. It's a mess in there. This doesn't look good." She kept her composure.

"Yeah, well, you gotta hear the story the old man across the street just gave me."

"He's a drunk," Skagan said.

"And he also sits on that porch or behind the front window and watches everything that goes on out here. Normally, that's not much. But these past few days, a ton."

"What's that mean?" April said.

I recounted the story Fults had told me. Everything from the African-American guy gaining access to the house, Craig being dumped in a trunk, and what happened the night Jessie died.

April pushed past me, headed toward Fults's house.

"What are you doing?" I said.

"I'm going to find out why he didn't let us know this before. Why didn't he call in when Craig was being beaten and abducted?"

She spun around and drew her sidearm. Skagen and I both went after her. I got there first and grabbed her with both arms. She tried to pull away. I didn't let go. She relented and turned toward me.

"Tell me what I could have done differently, Jack?"

"This isn't your fault," I said. "It's mine. That car, the one I saw three times today, that guy was following me. He's the one that did this. We need to find him." I paused a beat. "I need to find him, and figure out what the hell he's doing here."

"Why would he take out Craig?"

"Maybe Craig saw something he shouldn't have."

I couldn't say anything more than that. I knew that anyone following me would be ruthless and coldblooded. And, presumably, Craig had been in the way at the wrong time.

26

LEON DROVE THROUGH THE CENTER OF TOWN. HE DIDN'T SPEED. He didn't glance around. There were a few people out. They didn't seem to pay any attention to him.

He left the old historic area. The speed limit increased to thirty-five, then forty-five miles per hour. He kept his speed steady. As long as the road ahead of him was barren, the high-beams were on.

He came across what looked like an abandoned road. The turn off was visible, but beyond that, the asphalt was cracked and overrun with grass and weeds that had forced their way through. Nature had reclaimed what was once hers.

He turned onto the road. The headlights washed over the area. The road led into a stretch of woods a couple hundred feet away. Unsure what laid in wait at the end, he cut his lights and crept forward.

Tall pines rose up on either side of him. The road came to an end. He stopped, rolled down his window and waited with the engine off. The car ticked and clicked for a few minutes before going silent. A breeze blew past him. Insects sung and hummed. An owl screeched a time or two.

Satisfied the road was nothing more than a relic, he got out and walked to the rear of the Tercel.

The man inside the trunk banged against the lid. The little car shook and swayed.

Leon stood at the rear for a minute. He had to get rid of the guy, and letting him live was not an option. He popped the trunk. In the darkness, he could only make out the shape of the deputy. The man squirmed. Leon pulled out his pistol, aimed toward the man's head and pulled the trigger twice. The man's flailing legs and wriggling torso went still.

Leon inhaled the smell of nitroglycerin and sawdust, turned, and spit. That was the smell of death.

He had to get the body out. He walked around the side of the car to check if he had anything between the front and back seats that he could use to bury the guy. He didn't need a shovel, just something to move a little earth around. The less visible the man was, the better.

He opened the door and stuck his head inside. He found nothing but a few fast food wrappers. Disappointed, he exited the car. As he turned to the back, he spotted a light a hundred feet or so away, in the woods.

Leaves rustled. Branches popped. Someone approached.

Leon had been around the block enough times to know that no sane person would head toward gunfire unless they were armed as well.

And standing next to the car, he was a sitting duck.

He crouched behind the rear wheel. The approach continued. He shuffled toward the rear of the car, and tried to get a look into the woods. The headlights were on, but the cone of light didn't extend toward the light in the distance. Whoever approached had come from that direction.

Leon was bathed in red light behind the car. He couldn't stay there. He moved back to his spot behind the rear wheel. Trees surrounded him on three sides. Running back to the highway wasn't safe. Neither was running toward the oncoming person.

Leon took a breath, closed his eyes, and composed himself. Then he took a sprinter's stance and darted into the woods.

27

APRIL GRABBED SKAGEN BY THE ELBOW AND PULLED HIM TO THE side. She told him to keep the house locked, and not to let in anyone but her. He went inside. The front door shut. She paced the length of the porch for a minute or two. She came to a stop, wrapped her hands around the back of her head.

"You can't blame yourself for this," I said.

She'd been staring at the house across the street. It seemed to take a few seconds for my words to settle in.

"Who should I blame then?" she said.

"Craig, for one," I said.

"That guy could barely figure out a revolving door, Jack. I should have never put him in this position. Give him a radar gun and tell him to pull someone over when they did ten over the speed limit, he did fine. But something like this? It was too big. He was probably thrown off by the scene inside and relieved that someone showed up. He'd have bought any story."

"You think something about the guy seemed familiar or trustworthy?"

She shrugged. "Only Craig knows that. Hopefully we'll be able to ask him when we find him."

She joined me on the walkway. We headed toward her cruiser. I offered to drive her home. She protested at first, but gave in after a few minutes. When we reached her house, I cut the engine. We remained seated with the windows up and the ignition off. Our breathing was rhythmic, in time with one another, and the only sound in the car.

"I'm not going to be much for company now," she said.

"Understood," I said. "I need to be out there, anyway. You have a car I can borrow?"

She gestured to nothing. "Take my patrol car."

"You sure?"

"You're not going far, are you?"

"Maybe to the other side of town."

"Just stay away from those guys. Let us handle that, OK? I've already got the on-call on his way over."

"I've got other concerns, April. Someone is here because of me. Your man is missing because of me. I've got to get this figured out quickly."

She said nothing.

Neither did I.

Another minute passed. The windows fogged up from the bottom. The streetlight cast a faint pool of light through the back window. It lit up the right side of her face as she turned to face me.

"What is it?" I said.

"I really hope you're going to come back."

"I'll be back in the morning."

She smiled, leaned over and kissed my cheek. "That's not what I meant."

I knew that, but I didn't say so.

She reached out and grabbed the door handle and cracked it open an inch. The crickets sang. The cicadas screamed. She hesitated.

"What is it?" I said.

"Nothing."

She walked to her front door and went inside. A minute later half her torso emerged from the dim opening. She held out her hand and stuck her thumb in the air. Then she was gone. The door closed. The lights cut off.

I didn't feel safe leaving her there alone, not with someone skilled enough to kidnap a cop on the loose. So I drove to the end of the street with my lights off, made a U-turn and remained there for fifteen minutes.

The street remained quiet, empty, still. Houses looked dead and deserted. The trees had a rhythm of their own. They swayed with the breeze at random intervals. A heavy gust blew through. It sounded like the ocean. Waves breaking.

I started the cruiser and shifted from park to drive. I slowed as I passed April's house. The windows were still dark. The front door still closed. April, I presumed, was in bed. Alone.

I'd only managed to get a hundred feet away when a call came over the radio. Someone had found Craig's body in the back of a mid-nineties Toyota Tercel. He'd been shot at point blank range, twice, in the head.

I whipped the wheel around and raced to April's house.

She had the front door open before my foot hit the pavement.

"Have you heard?" I called out.

"Yes," she said.

"Get in," I said.

"Let me drive. I know where we're going."

I met her at the front of the car. She reached out and squeezed my hands. She looked steeled, determined.

It took her twenty minutes to reach the location. She turned onto an old, abandoned road that dead-ended in the woods.

"What was back here?" I said.

She shrugged. "I've never been back there before."

Her headlights washed over the unkempt field. The cruiser straightened out. The beams of light settled straight ahead. I saw the Tercel parked at the end of the road. Skagen had arrived before us. He'd pulled up next to the car. I wondered if he'd locked up before leaving Jessie's house.

April gunned the engine and hit the brakes a second before it would have been too late. She left the engine running and hopped out. I cracked my door open to the sound of thunder. Lightning splayed across the sky over the gulf.

Skagen met April at the back of the Tercel. He shined his light inside the trunk. April stared down into the makeshift tomb for a moment. She didn't gasp or cry out or reach for something to steady herself. I stood behind her, squeezed her shoulder. She took a deep breath and turned and shook her head. Her eyes watered over.

Skagen said, "An old man lives in a cabin behind us. He heard the shots. Caught a glimpse of the man that did it, but it was dark. Said by the time he got over here, the man was gone."

"How long ago was that?" I said.

"Half hour, maybe more," Skagan said.

"He wouldn't get far through the woods," April said. "Maybe a mile."

"If he went through the woods he'd find a place to hide," I said. "But if he took to the road and ran, he could be four miles away, if he's in decent shape."

April walked past me, beyond the cone of light cast by her headlights. She stopped a few feet past the cruiser. She faced the highway.

I walked toward her.

She said, "There's dozens of streets four miles in either direction. Some dead end, others will lead you back to I-75 if you follow them long enough and make the correct turns." She turned around, shaking her head. "Christ, we don't even know what this guy looks like."

"Fults saw him," I said. "Told me the guy was African-American."

"Fults is delusional, Jack," she said. "The other day he told me that aliens came down and took Jessie away. We can't put out anything based on what he told us."

"Sounds like we're..." I was going to say 'screwed,' but didn't.

She walked past me, and called for Skagen. "Finish up with the witness and head back to town. Check every street there, then start back this way. I want you to go up and down every road. Got it?" She paused long enough for him to nod. "We're going to head south."

I joined her in the patrol car. She flicked on the high-beams as she spun around and drove toward the highway. I scanned the area to the right. She took the left. The grass was high, probably up to the middle of my thigh. If anyone had been through it, or hid in it, I couldn't tell. A K-9 unit would have been helpful in this situation.

"Can you get a dog out here?" I said.

"Not now. Maybe in the morning. I told dispatch to notify all the adjoining towns and highway patrol. I'm sure they were all happy to get a notice to be on the lookout for an armed man, possibly African-American, definitely a cop killer."

The first of several fat raindrops hit her windshield. I saw a flash of lightning stretch from the heavens to the gulf. A crack of thunder followed. Then the sky opened up and pelted the area with rain.

"Guess the dog's out of the question now," she said.

I shrugged. I didn't know enough about how they worked to agree or disagree. "Call in the morning and find out anyway."

We drove eight miles down the highway, going about half the speed limit. The rain let up after a mile or so. She slowed down at every intersection. It took three times as long as it should have to make the drive. We saw nothing.

She stopped in the median and called Skagen. He hadn't seen anything, either. She aimed the cruiser toward town. We drove down every side street we passed until we reached the murder scene. Houses rose out of the earth like skeletons. Silent dark cars waited for their owners. Trees swayed with the gusts coming in off the gulf. But there was no sign of the man. He'd vanished into the night.

April pulled onto the dirt shoulder. Blackness surrounded us. The coroner had come and gone. At the end of the abandoned road the Tercel sat empty, wrapped in police tape. We couldn't see it, but we knew it was there.

"It's almost four, Jack. The funeral is at ten."

I nodded, said nothing.

"I have a spare bedroom." She looked away. "You can stay in there."

"No, take me back to Sean's."

She hesitated, made eye contact with me. "You sure?"

"It's for the better. Trust me."

And so she took her foot off the brake and the cruiser rolled forward. We arrived at Sean's house after twenty silent minutes.

I opened the door and stepped out. She said nothing. I ducked my head inside and leaned forward. She stared at me, her eyes wide. They looked black in the dark.

"I…"

She shook her head.

"Yeah." I rose and shut the door.

28

IT DIDN'T TAKE LONG FOR Leon to find a car. He had cut through the woods for a few hundred yards after someone came out guns blazing. Cops would be on the way, but he knew he had time, so he crossed the field to the road and made his way south.

The cloud-covered sky made it pitch black out. Optimal conditions for him. He stayed close enough to the road to keep from sinking in the wet field. One car passed. Leon ducked and lay down in the grass to his right while they passed.

The first street he came across looked promising. The houses older. They were spaced far apart from one another. As far as he could see, all the windows were dark.

He skipped the first two and hit the third. There he found an F-150 prime for the taking.

Dumb luck, some might think.

Country folk, Leon thought. Always gullible enough to leave their keys in their vehicles.

And this was a double down as far as luck was concerned. Not only were the keys in the ignition, the truck was a five-speed.

Silent escape into the dark night.

Leon didn't leave right away. He stayed back fifty feet. He took cover under a tarp strung between three trees when the rains came. For a time, he watched the house, the street, and the highway. Fifteen minutes of nothing was his plan. As long as the house stayed dark, the street motionless, and the highway deserted for that amount of time, he'd take the truck and go.

It took a couple hours, but everything fell in place.

Leon left his hiding spot. The ground crunched under his feet. Pine straw, dried out after a hot summer. Not even the thunderstorm could do enough to soak it.

The truck door creaked as he opened it. Leon paused, glanced back at the house. The lights didn't cut on. The curtains didn't move.

He reached in, released the emergency brake, put his right hand on the steering wheel, his left on the door frame, and started pushing. His thighs burned as his feet dug into the ground. The truck started rolling. He cut the wheel near the end of the driveway. The turn wasn't perfect, but he didn't end up in the ditch either.

With the truck rolling at a couple miles per hour along the asphalt, Leon hopped inside, pulled the door to the point where it was closed, but not fully latched, and turned the key in the ignition. The big V-8 engine roared to life. He turned on the highway and drove ten miles in ten minutes.

When he reached the highway 19 and 98 junction, he veered to the left and stayed on 98, which placed him on a path to I-75.

He pulled out his cell and called Vera. It took a couple minutes to fill her in on how things went down.

"Where are you now?" she said.

"About twenty minutes from 75, but this truck is hot. I imagine I got maybe two or three hours before it's reported missing."

He heard her tapping on her keyboard. "OK, in that time you could easily be in Fort Lauderdale. I've got someone between there and Miami who can take you in. They'll be able to hide the truck until we can dispose of it."

"What about Jack?"

"Don't worry about him. I've got things in place that are going to take care of Noble."

"OK. So where exactly am I headed?"

"Get on 75 and go south. It cuts across the state from west to east an hour or so away from you. Call me when you get close to Fort Lauderdale."

He was about to hang up when she said something else.

"Leon, what's the license plate number."

He pulled over, got out and went to the back of the truck. He used his cell phone like a flashlight and called out the sequence of letters and numbers to her.

"Thank you," she said. "I'll keep monitoring for that. If it is reported sooner than we expected, you'll have to ditch it and hide until I get someone to you."

"All right, you make sure you..." It was pointless. She'd hung up.

He set the phone down in the console and pulled back onto the road.

29

I MANAGED TO KEEP MY EYES SHUT FOR TWO HOURS. WHETHER I actually slept during that time is up for debate. I tossed, turned and punched the cushions a few times. I was still on London time, which meant it felt like eleven in the morning when I rolled off the couch.

In reality, it was only six a.m.

I called the facility to check on Dad's status. The woman that answered told me that Sean had him transported to the hotel last night.

One less thing to worry about.

I figured that the guy who killed Craig wouldn't hang around, but couldn't bank on it. The man was there for me. Someone could argue otherwise, but the fact that the guy showed up in three separate places at the same time as me left little doubt in my mind. One of those places had been Dad's facility. Presumably, he had my father's room number. I hoped that's where it ended.

I called my brother.

"How'd last night go?" I said.

"OK," he said. "Kinda crowded in here, but other than that, we're good. I slept with Dad. Deb and Kelly slept in the other bed. Dad's got a pretty loose digestive system. Anything interesting on your end?"

"Too much."

"What happened?"

"I'll tell you later. You planning on going to the funeral today?"

"Yeah."

"OK. I'll pick you up in Deb's Suburban. Cool?"

"Sounds good, baby brother."

I hung up and headed for the kitchen. The tile felt cool on my bare feet. I found the coffee, popped the lid off the container and stuck my nose in the opening. Good start. Hot coffee would be better, though. I knew from before that it took ten minutes to brew. I opted to pour a cup once there was enough in the pot. The strongest possible cup of the morning. I needed it.

My cell phone buzzed and skated across the island. I set my mug down and scooped the phone up. The country and city code combination indicated the call came from London. I didn't recognize the rest of the number.

"Yeah," I said.

"Jack, this is Marcia."

"Hello, Ms. Stanton."

"You can call me Marcia."

"OK."

She said nothing. Was she waiting for me to say her first name?

"What can I do for you, Marcia?"

"I need to know when you are going to be back."

"I don't think you need to know that at all."

"I'm putting off important campaign duties at the request of your boss. I think I deserve to know when you'll be here to take over my security."

"Listen to me, Marcia. I never agreed to anything like that. We've offered you an alternative solution more than once. I can't help it if you keep turning us down. I've said multiple times now that I am not the one to handle your personal security. That's not what I do. I've never been in charge of such a thing. You're at greater risk if I'm out there with you."

"If it weren't for you I wouldn't have survived in that cafe."

I said nothing. The only response that came to mind was that I wouldn't have let her go to the cafe. That would only solidify her position.

"Jack, if you ever tell anyone I said this, I'll deny it. But I'm scared for my life. Every time I step outside, I brace for a bullet to tear my head off. I study every face that passes. I don't even trust my closest associates anymore. This has been going on so long, I don't feel safe anymore."

Her words influenced me. I had to remind myself that she put herself in her current position.

"You knew the risks when you started taking down corrupt officials. Did you think their associates would roll over and die?"

She forced a laugh. "You think this is over a few bad cops and politicians?"

I said nothing. I heard a door open in the background, close to Marcia. A woman said something. Marcia replied, but she must've had her hand over the mouthpiece.

"Jack, I have to go. Please don't tell Sasha I called."

"OK."

"And please consider this. OK? I'll call you later."

The line disconnected. I dialed Sasha's number.

"Are you ready?" she said.

"Not quite," I said. "Funeral's in a few hours. I have some things to take care of afterward. Maybe tonight. Probably tomorrow."

"Everything OK there?"

"It's a mess down here, Sasha. But that's everywhere I go it seems."

She had no response.

"I just got a call from Marcia Stanton."

There was a long pause. Sasha spoke slowly. "Why? What did she want?"

"Me to hurry up and get home."

"I told her to let me handle you."

"I need you to level with me. What is it that you aren't telling me about Marcia?"

"I'm not following."

"Sasha, this woman has at least three groups targeting her. And that's what you're aware of. From what she told me, she's not scared of anyone we know about. I mentioned corrupt politicians and cops, and she laughed. She's not afraid of them getting to her. There's a reason she wants me close by, but she won't tell me what it is. There's something else at work here. I've got a ton on my mind, and it's making it difficult to piece this together. Can you dig a little deeper for me and find out who the hell else she pissed off?"

Sasha sighed. "We've been through it a couple times already, Jack." She paused a beat. "There's nothing under the surface."

"I get the feeling you're withholding something. Before I go holding hands on a walk through the park with her, I want to know who the hell has me in their sights."

I hung up without waiting for Sasha's response. My phone lit up ten seconds later. I left it buzzing on the counter and walked out with my coffee. The floor transitioned from cool tile to plush carpet. I cut through the living room, past the couch I had slept on, and went out back.

A wooden deck stretched twenty feet into the yard. It was at least forty feet wide. I dragged a seat to the far edge. The sun crested over the house and hit the back of my head. It was still cool out, and the humidity hadn't started its steep climb. The rains the night before had left the ground wet. Water drops clung to blades of grass and sparkled in the morning light.

I finished my coffee and remained outside for another fifteen minutes. I felt like a sitting duck out there, surrounded by woods on three sides. Maybe it wasn't safe. I didn't care. In fact, I closed my eyes for five minutes and dumped everything cluttering my head.

Finally, I left the serenity of the porch and the sun and the sparkling grass and went back inside. My phone beeped from the kitchen. I left it there and went upstairs. I needed a suit to wear to the funeral.

Sean's room looked the same as it did the night before. Clothes and linens covered the floor. I stepped around them and went into Sean's closet. I found a dark blue suit, white button up shirt, and a conservative blue tie hanging in his closet. I didn't need to try them on first. They'd fit. The shoes would be a different story. Sean's feet had always been a size and a half smaller than mine. I would have no choice but to curl my toes, or wear the beat up pair I owned.

I chose comfort.

I showered, shaved and got dressed. Unsure whether or not I'd return to the house, I grabbed a pair of khaki shorts and a pull-over shirt off the floor. They smelled clean. I headed downstairs and back to the kitchen. My phone continued to beep. I ignored it. I needed a boost. A second cup of coffee did the trick. After I drained the mug, I was ready to face the day.

30

LEON'S CELL PHONE BUZZED INSIDE THE CENTER CONSOLE. HE grabbed it and double-checked the incoming number. *Blocked.* Considering only one person blocked their number when calling, and that same person was the only one with this number, he answered.

"You're hot," Vera said.

Leon cursed under his breath as he glanced at the green sign on his right. It said he had twenty miles until he reached I-95. "I'm close to Fort Lauderdale. Twenty miles or so now."

"Get off the road. I'll have someone meet you."

She hung up. Leon pulled into a shopping center. He drove around back and left the truck behind the Payless. He found a rag in the glove box and used it to wipe down the dash, seat, steering wheel, shifter, and the door handles.

He glanced in the direction he had come from. The back lot was deserted. He turned and walked in the opposite direction.

He tried calling Vera, but there was no answer.

The strip mall stretched on for a half-mile before he found a covered walkway between two sections of a building. It led from the back lot to the front. The walkway was one big puddle. His shoes and socks became soaked. He saw a sporting goods store three doors down. It was early, though, and they might not be open. He jogged along the sidewalk. The sign said he had to wait thirty minutes.

He found a bench nearby. It was in full view of the sun. Leon sat down. He pulled off his shoes and stripped his socks off.

Half an hour later, Leon went into the store, barefoot. He found a pair of Teva's that were fifty percent off. They were a size too big, but the adjustable straps meant they fit well enough. He made his way to the checkout line. The girl behind the register looked like she'd spent as much time sleeping last night as Leon had. Although, he figured she'd had more fun than he'd had.

He handed her a fifty. She gave him five back. Leon exited the store with a new pair of sandals on his feet.

Outside, he called Vera again. This time he got through. She let him know that she already had his location and a man was on the way to pick him up. He'd be there in fifteen minutes, no later.

Traffic in the strip mall's parking lot picked up. Every car that drove by increased Leon's adrenaline level. A cop car came flying down the highway. Leon's heart nearly stopped. But no one paid any attention to him. Lulled into a state of relaxation, he stretched his arms along the back of the bench. Head leaned back. Eyes closed. The sun beat down on him and warmed his face.

A car pulled up and stopped. The passenger window rolled down. Leon looked at the man in the driver's seat. He had shoulder length brown hair and a full beard.

"Vera sent me," the guy said. "Get in."

Leon hopped up. He looked left and right, taking in the scene along the walkway. The few people out there paid no attention to him. He walked to the car and pulled the door open. His hand went to his pistol.

"You won't need that in here," the guy said.

Leon pulled his hand away. He didn't know this guy. His faith in Vera was the only thing he had to go on.

"All right, man," he said as he slid into the seat. "No problem. You got a name?"

"Sure do." The guy grabbed the shifter, slammed it into first and peeled away without saying another word.

31

I PULLED INTO THE HOTEL PARKING LOT AND FOUND A SPOT CLOSE TO Sean's room. His door was open. I couldn't see inside. My heart skipped a beat. Every possible worst case scenario ran through my mind. They all ended with Sean, Deb, Kelly and Dad dead.

I swung the Suburban's door open, hopped down and ran to Sean's room.

Kelly stepped through the doorway, her back to me. My footsteps echoed through the covered walkway. She looked over her shoulder, and said, "He's here."

I stopped, pulled in a deep breath and held it.

"Hey, Uncle Jack," she said.

"Hey, kiddo," I said as I exhaled. "Your mom and dad inside?"

She nodded. "Grandpa, too."

I tousled her hair as I passed her on my way toward the door. It took a second for my eyes to adjust to the dimly lit room. Sean stood in the hallway, on the other side of the closet and bathroom door.

He said, "You look good in my suit."

Deb stepped out of the bathroom, said, "He looks better than you do, Sean."

"I always have."

"He takes after his mother," Dad said. "Sean's ugly like me."

Everyone smiled. No one laughed. The gravity of the day pressed down on us all. I wondered if we'd escape it.

We left the room and piled in the Suburban. Deb drove, Dad sat up front with her. Sean and I sat next to each other in the middle row Captain's chairs. Kelly sat on the bench seat behind us.

I decided to drop the bomb on them.

"I've got something to tell you," I said, reaching for my wallet.

"What is it?" Sean said.

I pulled out a picture of Mia and handed it to him. I watched his expression as he studied the blue-eyed girl with a slight gap between her two top front teeth. She had pale freckles on her nose. Her hair was pulled back. Blond strands hung down on the sides and across her forehead.

"She looks like mom," Sean said. "What? When?"

"About eight years ago, I guess."

"Where is she?"

"London."

He looked at me, looked up, back at me. "Erin?"

I nodded.

"How come you never said anything?"

"I only found out recently. We're still getting to know one another. Erin and I are on friendly terms, but there's nothing between us, so I see the kid every other weekend and take her to dinner during the week if I can."

"So that's where you're living now? London?"

I nodded. "For now."

"I have a cousin?" Kelly said.

"Sure do," I said. "Her name's Mia. She's a little younger than you, but not by much. Maybe you'll get to meet her soon. Christmas, perhaps."

"You're gonna come back for Christmas?" Sean said. "Two visits in one year?"

"I was thinking you guys could come out to visit."

"What are you doing out there?"

I looked away.

"Right, right," he said. "Can't say."

I looked up at the rear-view mirror. Deb glanced back. She smiled.

"Glad to see you've grown up, Jack."

Dad said nothing. I figured he was off in another world at the moment. I hoped things worked out so that I could introduce him to his granddaughter.

A couple minutes later we reached the small church. It was on the western edge of town and sat on a hill. The cemetery was set off to the side. You could see the gulf from both spots.

A line of people stretched from the front door to the street. We exited the Suburban, made our way to the line. Someone passing by said that the service would be standing room only. I offered to stay back with Kelly so Deb and Sean could go in. I had a past with Jessie. Deb had talked to her weekly, if not daily. She deserved to be in there, and Sean needed to be at her side, supporting her.

People stepped aside and let her go through. Generous, considering.

I stood amazed at the throng of people who showed up to offer their respects to Jessie. Was it the result of living in a small town? Or was it the impact that Jess had on their lives? A little of both, I supposed.

Kelly and I walked around the back of the church. We spotted three cranes. They flew off as we approached. When we reached the front of the church again, three sheriff's department cruisers pulled in. Skagen got out of one. A guy I didn't recognize out of another. April was already walking toward me.

She hadn't pulled her hair back yet. The wind kicked it off her shoulders, and the sunlight shone through from behind, turning brown into gold.

"Get any sleep?" she said.

I shook my head. "You?"

"A bit." She looked down and smiled at Kelly. "I see I've got competition for your attention."

Kelly giggled. "I'll be finished with him soon. You can have him then."

It was a light moment set against a heavy backdrop.

Behind me, Jessie's lifeless body lay in a casket in the middle of the church. The blood on her body had been washed off. Her wounds had been concealed. Someone would have put her in a pretty dress, did her hair, and covered her face with makeup. All this in the attempt to make it appear as though she were only sleeping peacefully.

Everyone does at the end.

So Kelly, April and I waited off to the side, near the church entrance, for thirty minutes. We hardly spoke. When we did, it was small talk. Neither of us wanted to say anything important with Kelly around.

Skagen and the other guy were positioned near the parking lot exit. I didn't need April to tell me why. Glenn and those two drunks weren't getting out.

Most of the line had made it inside. Two dozen people were left on the front steps. The doors had been propped open. The congregation sung in unison, louder than they had all morning.

"That's the final hymn," April said. "They'll be coming out soon."

The crowd out front stepped down off the steps. The doors were no longer blocked by flesh, unleashing the sound of a couple hundred feet shuffling along the old, weathered hardwood floor of the church. Six men I didn't recognize held Jessie's casket, three to a side. Her parents followed behind. A couple kids were with them. I recognized them from the family photos in her house. Glenn followed behind. Matt and Jed were at his side. No reason for them to be so close unless Glenn had expected company.

Matt saw me. He reached out and slapped Jed in the gut. They both walked toward me.

I ignored them for the moment and kept my focus on Glenn. He touched Jessie's dad on the shoulder, said something, and broke free from the line. Matt and Jed stopped about twenty feet away and waited for him.

"Kelly," I said. "Go find your parents."

She ran toward the church, avoiding the oncoming men.

"What the hell are you doing here, Noble?" Glenn said. "I oughta lay you out right here, man."

I said nothing.

April stepped forward. "Just keep it down, Glenn." She waved a finger at the other two. "And you two keep back."

"Get lost, little girl." Matt headed right for her. "You ain't fit to be a cop. I don't recognize your authority."

April reached for her belt, pulled out a black jack. One flick of her wrist was all it took to drive the club into Matt's stomach and knock him to the ground. His hollow gasps for air were overruled by a collective gasp from the crowd.

I looked past Glenn and Jed. My dad stared at me. He nodded once, clenched his fist and held it out in front of him.

I stepped in between April and the men. They'd killed Jessie. I knew they'd have no issues attacking April.

The crowd shifted like an amoeba. Sean stepped away from the group and headed toward me. He bulldozed his way between Glenn and Jed. The latter tumbled to the side and stuck one hand in the dirt to keep from face planting.

"Just in case you guys think about doing something stupid," Sean said.

Glenn held his hands out in front of him. Reason escaped his mouth. "Jack, this is my wife's funeral. Why are you doing this?"

"You know why, Glenn. We know what you did."

"What's that supposed to mean?" he said.

"I've got a witness that puts you and your fat goons at the house the night Jessie died. He heard two shots. They woke him up. When he got to the window, you'd already taken off."

Glenn shook his head. "Nah, man. We were gone two hours before they figured it happened."

I stepped forward. "Yeah, where were you then? You got someone who can back it up besides these idiots?"

Glenn said nothing. Jed looked at him, lifted an eyebrow and shrugged. Glenn shook his head. Matt was still on the ground, on all fours. He'd got his wind back, but his face was still dark red.

"That's what I thought," I said. "You got nothing, because the only thing you were doing was putting distance between yourself and the murder scene."

A murmur rose from the crowd.

"I didn't kill her, Jack." Glenn threw up his hands and turned around.

"Just tell him," Jed said.

Glenn took a deep breath. He turned around. His left hand was on his hip. The right covered his eyes. When he spoke, it was slightly louder than a whistle.

"We were at my girlfriend's house, OK? She had a couple of her cousins there, up from Tampa, for these two numb nuts. She's got..." He dropped his head back and shook it. "Christ, how do I say this? She's got video, man. It's all timestamped, too. But the contents of it can't get out."

I held up a hand. I didn't need to hear anymore to know where that was going.

"It doesn't matter what you want," April said. "If you want to be cleared in this investigation, we'll need to see it. And wherever it goes from there isn't up to me."

"You're a piece of trash, Glenn," I said. "She gave you two kids, and this is how you repay her? And how convenient you're out of the house and on tape during that time? Even if you weren't there, I'm betting we can make a case you arranged it."

"Me?" Glenn took a step forward. He was about my height, but he had a good forty pounds on me. While his friends were fat, Glenn wasn't. It would be an even match if it came to blows. "Listen up. I know she's been talking to you the past couple of years, Jack. I walked in on her plenty of times and she dropped the phone, or shuffled some papers, or closed whatever it was she was looking at on the computer. No matter how many times I caught her and asked what she was doing, she never told me. Always had some excuse. But I saw past that, man. I saw the lies on her face. She went away with the kids not too long ago. I tore the house upside down. Found all kinds of documents with your name on them. Places and times to meet. That explained some of her business trips for that garbage makeup she sold. You two coordinated it all behind my back."

"What's he talking about, Jack?" April said.

"I don't have a clue," I said. "Glenn, the last time I talked to Jessie was spring of 2002. I saw her for a minute at my mother's funeral, and that was from twenty feet away. She smiled, I waved, then she patted her stomach and grabbed your arm and walked away."

Glenn's cheeks turned red. "Man, don't lie to me. I'm serious, Jack."

At the same time I was trying to diffuse the situation with Glenn, I was also trying to make sense of the fact that he supposedly found papers with my name on them in Jessie's possession.

"Kos," he said.

"What?"

He spat on the ground in between us. "About six months ago, Jessie told me she was in the running for a trip to Greece. Never said much about it later, only occasionally. Keep it fresh in my head, I guess. But I found a paper that had your name and Kos on it, written in all caps. K. O. S. That's the code for their airport there. It's near some resort. Didn't take much to put that one together. You were going to meet and spend a week together there."

"I spent some time in Greece not too long ago, but nowhere near Kos. And you're wrong, the airport code is KGS."

He said nothing.

"Glenn, I need you to put aside what you think happened. Now reach past the beer and the fast food and dig into your memory for me. Did it say KGS, or KOS?"

"What does it matter?" He held his arms up. "I caught you."

"You stupid hick. Where's this paper now?"

"At the house. I made a copy of that one. The lawyer I spoke to said I should do that, since some of the stuff went missing."

"What do you mean missing?"

He didn't respond.

"I need to see that paper."

Glenn shook his head.

April said, "I can get a warrant."

Glenn said, "Up yours, Noble. You ain't getting inside my house again."

"Let it go, man," I said. "Your wife wasn't murdered."

"Then who's that in the casket."

"Listen to me, Glenn. She wasn't murdered. She was executed."

32

"YOU REALLY MADE A MESS up there in Crystal River," the guy said.

Leon counted the mailboxes as they passed. He spotted one with an owl painted on it. He smiled. He had the same one at home. When his son got home from school this afternoon, he would open it up and get the mail. Leon appreciated that. Saved him the trip outside.

"I did what she told me to do," Leon said. "In fact, I cleaned up a mess. No one's gonna get anything from that murder scene now."

"But you killed a cop," the guy said.

"What else was I supposed to do?" He shifted in his seat and faced the man. "What would you have done?"

The guy glanced over, smiled. "I would have killed the cop."

Leon pointed at himself and then the guy. "See, you and me, we're the same. I'm surprised I never met you before. You do hits, too? Thought I met most everyone."

The guy nodded. "I'm the same as you. There are a few more of us. We're never supposed to be in the same place at the same time. Something really went wrong if we are."

"What's your name, man?"

The guy said nothing. He slowed the car down and turned onto a driveway. It curved behind tall hedges and led to a white garage door. The man pulled the keys from the ignition and got out.

Leon glanced around. The house was nice, big. The yard looked spacious and unnaturally green. This guy had it better than he did. Did that mean he was better? Or had he been around longer?

Leon hopped out and headed for the front door.

"Not that way," the guy said. "Follow me."

Leon followed the man around the side of the house.

"Still can't get over that mess you made up there," the guy said.

"Ah, come on. One cop. When things go bad, we gotta do what we gotta do. Right?"

"Yeah, I agree, but you put yourself in a position where you might have been spotted by your mark."

"Who, Jack? Man, that's what I wanted to say to Vera. She had me out there as a spotter. I ain't cut out for that. You know what I'm saying. You'd be pissed if you'd been asked to do what I had to. Right?"

The guy nodded, and said, "Through the garage."

"That ain't never happened to you before?"

"It has."

"The cop or having to spot for yourself?"

"Both, maybe."

"Why won't you tell me your name?"

"I never tell anyone my name."

Leon looked back at him. "But you said we're equals. Doesn't that count for something?"

"I guess it doesn't really matter if you know it. My name is Alessandro."

Leon nodded, smiled, opened the door and stepped into the garage.

"Although," Alessandro said, "if you hadn't been spotted, I wouldn't have told you."

The ground crinkled underneath Leon's feet. He looked down. He stood on a blue tarp. The door closed. The garage went dark. His arm lurched into motion, but couldn't get to his gun fast enough. He heard a tinny sound.

It was the last thing he ever heard.

ALESSANDRO STEPPED over the dead man and folded the end of the tarp across the corpse. He didn't need to check vitals beforehand. The hole in the back of the Leon's head was enough confirmation. He wrapped the man in the tarp, then strung together heavy-duty zip ties to secure the bundle.

His panting was the only sound in the empty garage. He pulled out his phone and placed a call.

"It's done, V."

"Thank you. Leave the body in the garage and the car in the driveway. There's a blue Impala out back. The keys are in the glove box. The code for the door is nine-four-four-eight-two. I want you to drive to Tampa. Call me when you get there."

Alessandro hung up. He pulled out a cigarette and lit it. He took two deep drags while looking down at the tarp surrounding his victim. Had he ever come this close to his employer terminating him? Sure, he'd had a couple snafus in his time. Who didn't? The only thing he could figure was that this Jack guy had to be more dangerous than Leon, and maybe even more dangerous than himself.

And more important than any of his previous targets.

One thing was for sure. Alessandro couldn't make the same mistake Leon had.

33

PEOPLE POINTED. THEY GASPED. THEY CURSED AT US. EVEN TRIED to block our path as we led Glenn toward April's cruiser.

"Back off," Glenn called out. Matt and Jed stepped in and helped keep the rowdier attendees at bay.

It was odd, to say the least, working together with them after a lifetime of dislike and disrespect.

April switched on her lights and we raced through town toward Glenn's house. On the way he described the documents he had seen. He explained that on the surface they seemed like nothing more than itineraries and meeting notes. But he never liked the names that appeared. Especially mine. His suspicions developed a few years ago after the first time he saw a correspondence to me. Of course, only Jack showed up. When I pressed him, he couldn't produce a last name.

He assumed.

"If my name appeared, what else did the documents say?" I said.

He shrugged and glanced away. "I really can't remember. Maybe it had a city name or something."

"You remember which city?"

"Nah. What does it matter anyway?"

"Sometimes a word isn't just a word, Glenn. Sometimes it means something else."

He made a noise, but said nothing.

"Anybody ever call and hang up, say they had the wrong number? Did you ever see anyone suspicious outside your house? Ever answer the door and the person said they had the wrong house after asking for a random person?"

Glenn looked at me. He leaned back in his seat and crossed his arms. His eyes narrowed. He wagged his right index finger.

"You know, I remember seeing a black sedan out there recently. Never seemed like anyone was in it. I figured one of the neighbors had family in town or something. But it showed up kinda regular, like a few times a week for a while there. The phone calls thing, yeah, I mean, we'd get a lot of calls asking for some random name. Who doesn't? I always supposed someone had wrote our number on a few bathroom stalls."

Glenn smiled for a second. I didn't.

What the hell had Jessie gotten herself into?

April barely touched the brake as she made the turn into the neighborhood. I had to hold onto the handle on the ceiling keep from sliding out of my seat and into hers. She stopped in front of the house.

I stepped out into a cloud of smoke. The burned rubber stunk like a paper factory. I ran up the driveway. I heard Glenn's heavy footsteps not far behind my own. April's joined his a second or two later. I ripped the police tape off the two columns on either side of the porch entrance. Glenn pushed past me. He pulled out a key and stuck it in the door.

The smell knocked all three of us back. We coughed and gagged before adjusting.

"What the hell is that?" Glenn said.

"Bleach and ammonia," I said.

He pulled his undershirt up and over his nose. "That'll kill you, won't it?"

I nodded. "Let's go."

He led me down the hall to a spare bedroom. It looked more like a closet with a window that provided a view to the front yard and the street. They had a computer set up next to the window. Whoever sat in the chair could swing to their left and look. Presumably, they set it there so they could watch the kids playing outside while Glenn or Jessie worked on the PC.

Or they were like the old man across the street and liked to stare through a couple glass panes all day long.

I made a note to run the black sedan by the old guy. Perhaps he'd noticed it during one of his stake outs. Reports of aliens aside, the guy pegged Craig's killer as far as I was concerned.

Glenn squeezed past me. He sat down. The chair groaned under his weight. Dust rose and trickled through the sunbeams that filtered through the cracks in the blinds. He placed his arms on armrests wrapped in neon green duct tape.

I scanned the contents of a floor-to-ceiling bookshelf. Mostly fiction, a combination of romance and mysteries. There were a few non-fiction books on disaster preparedness, Special Forces training, and wilderness survival. Next to the bookcase there were three framed paintings on the wall. One was of a mallard. Another of the gulf at sunset. The third was a family portrait done in charcoal.

"What the hell?" Glenn said.

I looked over my shoulder. Glenn had his arms raised. His mouth dropped open. He shook his head.

"What is it?" I said.

"There's nothing on this hard drive," he said.

"What?"

"Look."

I took a few steps and stopped behind him. I grabbed the back of the chair and leaned over. He might have cleaned up for the funeral, but he still stunk.

I focused on the computer. The operating system had started up, but it was as if it had been given a clean slate. The programs directory was empty. So were all the document folders. He pulled up the second hard drive. It was blank.

"When was the last time you used the PC?" I said.

"Couple days before Jessie was killed."

It was the first time I'd heard him use the word killed.

"You mentioned files," I said. "I assume paper files. Where are they?"

He spun in his chair. I moved out of the way. He pulled open a drawer in a wooden file cabinet behind me.

"The hell?" he said.

"What?" I said.

"It's all gone. Look. Nothing's in there."

My patience started to wear. I had a feeling that Glenn had purposefully led us astray so that the real killer could get away. I glanced toward the doorway. April stood in the hall. She lifted an eyebrow and made a gesture with her hand toward the front of the house. I shook my head.

"Glenn?" I said.

"Wait a minute." He straightened up. "I know." He got up and walked past me, past April, down the hall and into his room.

We followed.

He pulled clothes out of a drawer and tossed them onto the floor. Had he done the same at Sean's house? I pushed the thought aside. That didn't matter at the moment.

"Here." He held up a piece of paper. It had vertical and horizontal creases through the middle of the page. Didn't seem to affect anything though.

I walked over and snatched it from him. On the top I saw my first name. Below that were forty letters and numbers, evenly spaced, and in some kind of random order. None of it made sense. It had to be a code of some kind. There were two inches of space below the jumbled code. At the bottom, written in big letters I saw what Glenn had referred to earlier.

KOS

"What's it mean?" April said.

I looked up. They both stared at me. I cleared my throat.

"Kill on sight."

34

WE STOOD IN GLENN'S STUFFY BEDROOM IN A TRIANGLE FORMATION, elbow to elbow. I held the paper in my hand. Flat, so everyone could see.

"Jack," April said. "Who would want to kill you on sight?"

I said nothing.

"What the hell are you into, man?" Glenn's cheeks turned red. I could see him piecing together an imaginary puzzle. "What did you get my Jessie into?"

I squared up to the man in case he tried something. "Glenn, I told you the truth earlier. I haven't had any contact with Jessie since '02. Whatever this is about, she got herself into it."

"So, what is it?" April said.

"To figure that out, we need to break this code."

"Can you do that?"

"No," I said. "But I know people who can."

"Why'd they kill Jessie if you're the KOS guy?" Glenn said.

"Good question. Just because my name is on that page doesn't mean I was the target. You don't know when she wrote all of this down. The code could have been from months ago. KOS added a week ago. My name three days ago. Just the fact they are on opposite ends of the page adds doubt."

The three of us remained silent for a minute. The circular hum of the fan filled the void. Cold air hit my forehead. I looked up and saw a vent overhead.

April spoke first. "Glenn, is there anything else you can tell us?"

"There was more than this. I wish I'd have..." He backed up and sat down on the edge of his bed. It looked like he was about to have a breakdown.

I looked at April and shrugged. Picking up on the fact that I didn't intend to comfort the guy, she walked over to him and placed one hand on his shoulder.

"If you think of anything else, you call me," she said.

He said nothing. He didn't look at us. We left him in the room and made our way to the front door.

"You buy this?" April said.

I nodded, said nothing.

"You live in a world where something like this is possible?"

I nodded again. That was as much as she needed to know. Bad things happen to people when they get involved in my world. It was best I leave her out of it.

We walked toward her cruiser, which idled in the street. I saw Fults on his porch. He leaned against the front railing. He had a flask in one hand, a cigarette in the other.

"Let's go have a talk with the neighborhood watch," I said.

We crossed the street and cut across the man's unkempt lawn. He staggered back and found a mildewed white plastic chair to park himself in.

"Sheriff," he said.

She said, "Mr. Fults, we have a couple questions for you."

"Sure," he said.

"Did you see a black sedan out here recently?" I said. "Parked in the street a couple days at a time?"

"Oh, yeah, sure did. Thought it kind of strange. It'd be there for a few days, then disappear. Come back again for a few hours, leave. Sat out there for a week one time."

"How long had this been going on?" April said.

"Couple months, at least," he said.

"Ever see anyone get in or out of it?" I said.

He looked up toward the ceiling. "You know, can't say that I did. It was just...there."

"Thanks, Mr. Fults."

I stepped off the porch and headed across the street. April stayed behind, presumably to ask additional questions. I had no need to hear anything else.

Glenn stood next to April's cruiser. I stopped a few feet short of him. He said nothing.

I said, "Sorry about, Jessie, Glenn."

"Thank you." He paused, glanced up at the sky, rubbed his face, then looked me in the eye. "I'm always gonna believe this is your fault, Jack. Somehow, someway, you led her into this. Whether directly, or by her trying to find you. She must've stumbled upon something way over her head."

Unwittingly, Glenn had given me a direction to follow.

"Just make me one promise," he said.

"What's that?"

"I know you're into some special forces, mercenary crap. It's a running joke with some of us that went to school together, played football, you know."

I nodded, said nothing.

"You find this bastard who killed her, and you torture the hell out of him. Don't let him die right away. Take your time. Make him suffer. Cut him up part by part."

Though I had no plans to torture her killer, I felt obligated to Jessie to do something. Eleven years ago, I almost got her killed by showing up at her doorstep in the middle of the night. Something happened after that. I don't know what, though. She picked up a trail, or someone picked up hers. She fell into the trap that so many do. It's something that no one else in their life knows about. Ultimately, they have to do what they're told to keep those they love alive. In the end it leads to their own death.

Glenn walked back to his front door.

"You want a ride?" I called out.

April walked up behind me. "What?"

Glenn came back to the car. "Sure."

I looked back at April. "Least we can do."

We took our places in the car. Halfway between Glenn's house and the church, my cell phone rang. I pulled it out and checked the number.

Marcia.

"Pull over," I said.

April slammed on the brakes. The car fishtailed. She got it under control and veered onto the dirt and gravel shoulder.

I stepped out into a cloud of dust, answered the phone.

"You need to get out of there now, Jack," Marcia said.

"What?"

"You're in danger."

"We chased the danger off last night. He killed a cop, not me. I doubt he's—"

"Shut up and listen to me, Jack. You have no idea what's going on. The web is huge and you're flying right toward the middle of it. Before you know it, it's going to close around you."

I paused a beat. "If you know what's going on down here, then tell me."

She said nothing.

Neither did I. It was a game of chicken, and I wasn't about to swerve first.

After a minute, she spoke. "Call Sasha, tell her to get the flight ready. Also tell her that you've decided to work for me. She'll bring an extra car and you and I can leave without her."

"Why should I do this?"

"I have the answers you're looking for."

"Then why won't you tell me now."

"I can't, Jack. I need to see you first. Once I do, I can tell you what happened to Jessie."

The line went silent. I lifted my hand in the air and then flung it down. Somehow I managed to keep the phone in my grasp. I decided to call Sasha before my mind began processing Marcia's words.

"Jack?" she said.

"I'm ready," I said. "Where do I need to go?"

"I've got a jet waiting at a private airport north of Tampa. How soon can you get there?"

"Probably forty minutes."

"OK. They'll be ready. I'll message you the address."

"Sasha?"

"Yes?"

"I'm going to do it. I'm taking over security for Marcia. Bring her with you. Have an extra car waiting at the airport."

"You got it."

We hung up. I placed one more call before getting back in the car. April leaned across my seat and tapped on her watch. I held up one finger.

My brother answered on the second ring.

"Sean, listen to me. You need to get out of town. Far out of town. Take Deb, Kelly and Dad and go."

"What? Why?"

"Just do it."

"Where should we go?"

"Drive to Texas for all I care. Get out of town. Don't use your cell phone. Don't let anyone know where you've gone. Don't even tell them that you've left."

"I've got a practice to run, Jack."

"Dammit, Sean. Do it. Now."

He paused, said, "OK," and then hung up.

I got in the car. My skin was flushed. I didn't notice the air conditioning at first. "I need you to take me to Tampa."

"Why?" April said.

"I can't say."

She hit the gas, pulled away from the shoulder and drove to the church. We let Glenn out next to the parking lot entrance. The crowd gathered near the back of the graveyard, presumably waiting for him. I didn't see Sean or

his family or the Suburban. He'd taken off already. I hoped he heeded my
warning and stayed away from his house.

April turned on her lights and did ninety down the highway. She only
used her sirens in spots where traffic cluttered the road. The closer we got to
Tampa, the more often she needed to use them.

Sasha texted me the address along the way. I plugged it into the car's
GPS. It would only require a couple turns to reach our destination.

We were silent for the majority of the drive. April had questions for me.
I had questions in general. Neither of us voiced our concerns.

It took twenty-five minutes to reach the private airport. It was easy to
find the jet. Every other plane we saw was a single prop. April stopped the
cruiser a hundred feet away. I didn't move. We didn't speak. The cold air
pelted our faces.

Two minutes passed. April broke the silence. She shifted in her seat.
Said, "Will you ever come back?"

"Probably not."

She turned her head toward the windshield. "Can I come visit you?"

"That's not a good idea."

"Why?"

"My life is complicated. Take those things that you thought about me,
and multiply them by one hundred. It's not so much that I'm in danger most
of the time, rather than those around me are. I can watch out for myself. But
I have to live a detached life. Everyone close to me ends up in trouble. Sometimes dead. I can't do that anymore. I can't do that to you." I reached out and
placed my hand around the back of her head. "I've got this little girl back in
London, and I struggle with it every day. I want to see her more, but I know
I shouldn't see her at all. It's not her fault that things are this way, so I give in
because I don't want her to grow up believing that she did something to
drive me away."

April said nothing. Tear tracks ran the length of her cheeks.

"There's no record of her and I having any kind of connection. Our visits
are secret. I've got friends that help with that. I'm starting to wonder if that's
good enough, though. If I ever piss them off, who knows what will happen?

Look, I know this sounds like an excuse to you. This visit, it is what it is, but you shouldn't risk your life to explore it further. I won't risk your life, that's for sure."

She opened her mouth, closed it, and turned away. "Just go, Jack."

My hand slid down her neck, along her shoulder and settled on her arm. She pulled it away. I hesitated a moment, then tugged on the door handle and stepped out. Before walking away, I leaned inside.

"I'm sorry."

35

I SWUNG THE DOOR SHUT. April shifted into drive and hit the gas. She pulled away before I could think to tell her to stop. She exited onto the highway and drove off. I watched her go until I could no longer see her car.

I could have handled the situation better. All she wanted to hear was that I'd return. We might've kissed, hugged, said goodbye. It would have been me dealing with the reality of the situation. Instead, I put it off on her.

"Are you Jack?"

I turned around. The man standing a few yards away from me was bald, short and skinny. His legs looked like toothpicks sticking out from his shorts. He couldn't have weighed much over a buck forty, if that.

"Sir?" he said.

I nodded, said nothing.

"Baggage?"

"Just what I carry on the inside."

He gave me a funny look, shrugged and turned. "Let's go."

I followed him onto the jet. He had a hitch to his walk, as if one of his legs was artificial. I knew it wasn't. A bad hip injury at one time, I presumed.

The jet was smaller than the last, and not as nice inside. The seating was standard. Nothing custom about it.

"Sit anywhere you'd like," he said. "We'll be taking off in twenty minutes. You need anything?"

"A drink."

"Soda?"

"Alcohol."

"Nervous flyer?" He smiled and nodded.

"No, just thirsty and tired and not wanting to waste any mental energy on this flight."

His smile faded. "I'll be right back."

The far right seat in the last aisle had an open space in front of it. I sat there, and stretched my legs out in front of me. While not as comfortable or appealing as the couch on my last flight, the seat had plenty of cushion. I might not even need my drink to fall asleep.

Before the thought could settle in, the small man emerged from the narrow hall carrying a cup and five mini-bottles of rum. "This enough?"

I reached out and took them. "I know where to find you if I need more."

He stood there, and for a moment shuffled between his left and right foot. Was he nervous? Did he need to use the toilet?

I avoided his stare and focused on emptying two of the mini-bottles into the cold plastic cup. The ice cubes had holes that ran through the center. The brown fluid washed over and through them. I downed the first cup in two gulps. The spiced rum burned my throat. I didn't cough.

The guy backed up, turned and walked toward the front of the plane.

He had too much nervous energy. I didn't like it. I set the bottles on the seat next to me, stood, pulled the M40 from my waistband. I still wore Sean's suit. Everything happened so fast I didn't have time to change. The shorts and shirt I had brought were in his Suburban.

I had finished the fifth bottle by the time the plane taxied. My eyes were closed when we lifted off the runway. And I was asleep before the pilot leveled out.

36

ALESSANDRO PULLED INTO THE PARKING LOT OF A DELI NAMED Cool Cuts. He saw a small car parked near the front door. Inside, a woman stood on one side of the counter, and a teenage kid wearing an apron was on the other side.

He parked in the middle of the lot, facing the entrance, and then called Vera.

"Are you in Tampa?" she said.

"About twenty miles north," he said.

"Have you ever heard of a man named Noble?"

Alessandro thought for a minute. "Sounds familiar, but I have no recollection of ever having met him. What's his background?"

"Marines, loaned out to the CIA. After that he worked for a government agency you've probably never heard of. He left abruptly and went into business for himself. He had a partner for a while, but that's irrelevant. More recently, he did some work in London with British Intelligence."

Alessandro caught a flash in the rear-view mirror. He angled his head to get a better view. The front door had opened. The woman emerged carrying a white plastic bag. She stepped out from under the awning and shielded her eyes from the sun with her hand. She walked to her car, got in and pulled away from the parking spot. He looked over his shoulder. The kid in the store was out of sight.

He said, "So what's any of that got do with me?"

Vera cleared her throat. "You know not to ask questions like that."

"You had me take out one of your best guys today. Now I'm taking my second trip to Crystal River in less than a week. What the hell is going on here? If there was more, why'd I leave instead of finishing up?"

"He messed up." She paused. He said nothing. She added, "And you're the best I have. You left because the job was done. Then it wasn't. I didn't want to put you in the same place days after completing your task. I thought Leon could get the job done. Apparently, I was wrong."

He had been able to surmise everything she said on his own. There was more to this, and he wanted those details.

"Look, Vera, you know I'm a good soldier, and I don't make waves. But this time, I need to know what's going on."

She said nothing. If it weren't for her breathing, he'd have thought she'd put the phone down and walked away.

"Don't freeze me out."

"Listen to me. I can have done to you what you did to Leon. If this goes down successfully, then I'll consider bringing you in on what happened. But for now, you would be wise to do what you're told, when you're told, like the soldier I hired you to be."

"Sure thing." Alessandro ended the call. He squeezed the phone. He knew when he signed up that there was no way out. Even if he could track down Vera and kill her, there was someone behind her. He had no idea who. He had no idea who ultimately employed him, or who she reported to. The calls came from her. The money was deposited into any number of bank accounts, which changed regularly.

He had to do what he was told, like when he killed that unarmed woman, or he would end up like that poor sap, Leon.

37

THE JET ROLLED TO A STOP IN AN AREA LIT UP BY HUGE LIGHTS FIXED to the top of tall poles. I stood at the top of the metal staircase that had been wheeled up to the side of the plane. Sasha stood at the bottom. She had a smile on her face. It did little to hide the concerned look in her eyes. Behind her, almost identical Audis sat parked side by side. I assumed the black one had been brought for me. Through the semi-tinted front windshield, I made out the shape of Marcia in the passenger seat.

"How was your flight?" Sasha said.

"I slept. Guess that makes it good." My feet hit the pavement. I took two steps toward her. "Now tell me what's going on here."

She shrugged. "You saw how she is. She won't—"

"Not her," I said. "Nothing has come up about me? No one knew I went to the States?"

She turned and gestured for me to follow. Once we reached her car, she said, "All I can tell you is that we came across credible intelligence that indicated your life was in danger."

I decided against telling her Marcia had said the same thing. "What kind of evidence?"

"Someone was in town to kill you," she said.

"I already knew that. He got someone else. Best we can tell, he fled."

She said nothing.

"Where did this tip come from?"

"I can't say."

"It's my life on the line, Sasha. You need to tell me."

"I can't say, because I don't know, Jack. It was anonymous. But when I put my resources to work, they confirmed it."

My comfort level shifted to the negative. We were in a wide-open space. At least two people in London knew where I was. How many more knew?

"Why didn't you come right out and say it?" I said.

"Would you have wanted me to? Besides, we found out after they fled."

I didn't get the feeling that the women were sharing information. Marcia had stated that the man who fled was not the danger.

"Anything we can do to follow up on this?" I said.

"Like what?"

"You're the one that works in Intelligence, Sasha. You tell me."

She looked away. Her cheeks turned red.

I held up my hands. "I'm on edge."

"I understand, Jack. And I need you to realize that I'm doing everything I can to get to the bottom of this. In the meantime, you've got a new responsibility, one that you agreed to. So get in that car and do whatever Marcia Stanton tells you to do."

"Anything she says?"

"Within reason." The tension drained from her face. She smiled, reached out and touched my cheek. "Be careful. Check in with me in the morning before you guys leave."

"OK."

I took a step back. Sasha pulled her door open and slipped behind the wheel. I turned, rounded the front of the car she'd brought for me and got inside.

Marcia stared through the windshield, toward the jet. She didn't acknowledge me at first. I wondered what went through her mind. I started the car and followed Sasha's taillights. She'd lead me toward the city.

After a few minutes of silence, Marcia said, "I live about twenty minutes from here."

I nodded, said nothing.

"They provided this car. It's not mine. We'll talk more at my place."

The car could be bugged. Someone could be listening to our conversation. She was smart not to say anything important.

I drove on through light nighttime traffic. Traffic lights worked against us. We were stopped at half of them. We drove along Whitechapel. She told me to turn right onto Commercial Street. I kept going straight.

"What are you doing?" she said. "I live back there."

"You're under my care now," I said. "That means I'm taking you to a place where I know that I'm safe."

"Your apartment?"

I said nothing.

"You think that place is going to be safe? Sasha and her team probably have an army of bugs in there."

I still said nothing.

"Jack, don't be stupid."

I pulled into a deserted lot and stopped the car. I flung my door open and got out. Marcia hesitated, then did the same.

"We're not going anywhere they know about," I said. "Got it? Not your place, not mine. I've got a little house on the other side of the city. It's rented in a false name. I paid a year up front in cash."

She protested, but once it became clear that I wasn't turning around, she gave up. We took our seats and passed through the city. I picked up the M4 and drove to West Drayton. A few minutes later, I parked behind an apartment building.

"Let's go," I said.

Once outside, she said, "You know the car's being tracked."

"Yup, that's why we're getting in a different vehicle and *then* going to my place."

She caught up to me. "Are you always this paranoid?"

"The day I stop is the day I die." I pointed at a white sedan. "There it is."

I got back on the M4 and drove west another ten miles to the far end of Slough. The streetlights in the neighborhood were few and far between. My house had a wooded lot. It was almost impossible to see the front door from the street. I pulled into the driveway and parked in front of the garage.

Marcia followed me up to the front door. I had installed an electronic lock when I moved in. I blocked the pad and punched in the code. I swung the door open for the first time in two months. Stale air escaped and surrounded us. I entered first. She followed.

Marcia glanced around the barren great room. "Not much for looking at in here."

"I'm never here. It's a backup option. That's all."

"How long are you planning on keeping me here?"

"We'll start with tonight and see where it goes."

She looked like she wanted to argue with me. Instead she took a seat at the dining table.

I went into the kitchen. A small white fridge with a chrome handle stood next to the stove. I opened the door, grabbed two bottles of water. I placed a bottle in front of Marcia, and took a seat opposite her.

"You said my life was in danger," I said. "You said the web was closing in on me. Care to elaborate now?"

She brought the bottle to her mouth and tilted her head back. She swallowed, then licked her red lips. Her lipstick coated the rim of the bottle.

"I'm not who you think I am," she said.

"I could say the same," I said.

She smiled, looked down at her hands. Her fingernails were long. They matched her lipstick. She drummed them against the table in a slow, steady motion, starting with her pinky finger.

"You're Jack Noble. You were born in Crystal River, Florida. You grew up there. Your mother is deceased, your father is still living. You have one brother. His name is Sean. He has a wife, Deborah, and a daughter, Kelly. There are no aunts, uncles, cousins, or anything like that. You had a sister.

She was four years older than you, two years older than Sean. She died at the age of sixteen."

I looked away. No one knew about Molly, not even my closest friends. "She was murdered. I witnessed it. Did nothing when it happened. Paralyzed by fear. It was the last time something like that happened to me. I let the rest of the details deteriorate over time."

Marcia nodded, continued. "You entered the Marines at the age of eighteen, although it wasn't long before they realized you were special. A co-op with the CIA followed. You did things in the States that the CIA wasn't allowed to do. Then you went to Europe for a few months. Then the world changed in September, 2001. You and your partner Riley were sent to Iraq before most anyone else. Information gatherers, right?"

"More like henchmen who guarded front doors."

"The program you were in was dubbed a success by some, a failure by others. Some wanted to shut it down. Someone else didn't. That someone was high ranking and he got greedy. You confronted General Keller head on. The evidence you gathered did you no good, though. Nothing ever came of it. Keller stepped down in time. You moved on."

"How do you know all this?"

She took another drink from her bottle. A trickle slipped past the corner of her mouth and ran down her chin. She wiped her face with the back of her wrist.

"You pulled some strings and got out of the Marines. After what had happened, no one protested. They thought it would keep you quiet. And it did. You were scooped up by another organization. It was no accident that the SIS came calling, Jack. Only, they were pushed into action almost too late. In fact, if they hadn't managed to delay Jessie's flight, she would have reached you before Frank Skinner did. Then what would have happened?"

I slid my right hand off the table and wrapped it around my pistol.

She continued. "You did plenty in your time with the SIS. But, in the end, it wasn't for you. Your true calling came to fruition when you set out on your own. Right?"

I said nothing.

"The thing is, Jack, you still flirted with the pretty girls whenever they called. You took job after job. It didn't seem to matter who called. You'd do a job for one guy, and then turn around and kill him if someone else paid you enough money. You took the calls from the SIS, and other organizations. You did work for your friends in London. The French called on you from time to time."

I slid my hand from my pistol to my pocket and retrieved the paper from Jessie's house.

"I appreciate the history lesson, Marcia. But what does any of this have to do with right now?"

She pushed back in her chair, rose and turned. Her black pants hugged her curves. She walked across the room. Her footsteps echoed against the wall. She stopped, appeared to stare at the wall. Her hands were clasped behind her back. She tugged on her fingers one by one.

I leaned back and waited for her to continue.

"What did you learn in Florida, Jack?"

Was now the right time to present my evidence?

"I'm not sure what you mean, Marcia."

She turned around. Her lips were pursed. She swung her arms forward, grabbed her right wrist with her left hand, let them fall to her waist. She was a powerful woman on the inside and outside. She knew how to present it and appear intimidating without being threatening. I dwelled on what she had said earlier.

"I'm not who you think I am."

She said, "Did you find out anything about your friend?"

I said, "We've been talking a lot about me. Let's hear about you."

She shook her head. "In time. Just go along with this, please. It is relevant."

"She didn't kill herself. At first, I thought it was her husband and his brother and brother's friend. The evidence I uncovered suggests otherwise."

Marcia walked back to the table. She pulled out the seat next to me. She placed her hand on my forearm. "You can do better than that, Jack."

"Why should I?"

She said nothing. She looked serious, apprehensive, frightened even. Up close and under the lighting I saw the faint traces of crow's feet extending from the corners of her eyes. Shallow lines spread across her forehead. They did nothing to detract from her beauty. I refocused and answered her question.

"OK, here's how it went down. I suspected her husband and his brother. There had always been bad blood between us. It seemed natural. He had an alibi, apparently solid. He accused me of having a long distance affair with Jessie."

"Had you?"

"I last saw her over ten years ago, after the Keller affair. It sounded like you already knew that."

"OK, continue."

"Glenn, her husband, had evidence. He showed it to me. To him, it indicated secret rendezvous and things like that. To me, it was a hit list, and my name was on it."

She didn't seem surprised. "Was there anything else?"

"It was all gone. I assume whoever took her out, stole or destroyed everything. Hell, she might have been expecting them and had it all in a folder. Maybe she knew they were coming and destroyed it herself."

She placed one elbow on the table and propped it under her jaw. "Can you describe the evidence you saw?"

"I can do better than that."

I tossed the folded paper onto the table. She grabbed it and opened it up. Her eyes scanned left to right, focusing on the code.

"What do you make of that?" I said.

She said nothing.

"Any idea who has me on a kill on sight list?"

She still said nothing. Her lips moved as she went over the jumbled mess of letters and numbers on the page. She looked up at me.

I waited for her to say something.

She glanced down at the page again. Her lips moved some more. I couldn't make out the words she formed. She finished, and looked up at me again.

"Jack, have you ever heard of FATF?"

"Yeah, sure," I said automatically. "On second thought, no."

"FATF is a special task force within the OECD. Have you heard of them?"

"Yeah, it's an international organization that has something to do with economic policy, right?"

She nodded. "Close enough. The FATF task force deals with money laundering on a global scale. This is big due to terrorism, and there is a large focus on Africa right now. Those groups are the primary target."

"OK. What's that have to do with me?"

She glanced down at the paper. "Was this all there was?"

"We searched the office. The drawers were empty. Their PC had been wiped. Like I said, whoever was sent to take out Jessie did a nice job of cleaning the place, or she did it first."

She held up the paper. "This is all written in the same hand, but I'd venture to say it was at the very least days apart. You can see the ink is different. The code is in black, and your name is in dark blue."

"What's the code say?"

She rose and paced around the table. "It talks about the FATF and a target. It has nothing to do with you. At least, not as far as I can tell."

"Who's the target?"

"I can't tell that part, unfortunately. It doesn't match with the rest of the message."

"What?"

"Code within the code."

"Marcia, how were you able to tell what that paper says?"

She stopped, placed her hands on the table and leaned forward. "Before my foray into law, I worked in MI5, undercover."

"How come Sasha hasn't mentioned this to me?"

"She doesn't know. Our paths never crossed. I was never on the payroll under my name."

"You left about five years ago?"

She nodded.

"Why?"

"My cover was blown."

"How?"

"I was exposed during an investigation of Jessie Staley."

38

HEARING JESSIE'S NAME KNOCKED ME BACK. I BROUGHT BOTH
hands to the top of my head. For a moment, I forgot how to breathe.
Hearing her husband's accusations was one thing. Seeing the paper with my
name on it, another. A woman who claimed to be a secret agent for Britain's
counter-intelligence agency telling me that she investigated Jessie felt earth
shattering.

"What were you investigating her for?" I said.

"It was so long ago, Jack, I can't remember all the details."

"It was your last case. I'm sure you remember some of it."

She took a seat next to me again. "Your evidence against Keller was
destroyed all those years ago."

I nodded.

"Jessie did that."

I nodded again.

"Do you know why?"

"They threatened her parents."

"Yes. And what does a bully do when they know threats work?"

I looked away. "They keep making them."

"Correct."

"Who?" I said.

She shook her head. "It doesn't matter, Jack."

"Don't tell me it doesn't matter. They killed her, and judging by that paper, they want me dead, too."

"You're not the only one," she said. "I'm a loose end."

"When this happened, did they get your name, or your cover?"

"Cover, but it is obvious that someone recognized me."

I studied her for a moment. "So, these attacks that are happening, the reason you wanted me around, was because you aren't dealing with thugs. These are professional killers? Why are you out in the streets every day? Why are you running for public office? Why not run off and hide?"

"They can find me anywhere. Don't you get it? They'll get to me one way or another. I'm going to go out on my own terms."

I thought through what she had said. Part of me refused to believe it. It wasn't possible.

"Tell me what you know about Jessie's role in all of this," I said.

"I knew about Jessie's death before you did. I received an anonymous call. That's why I pressed for you to join me. I knew they were close."

"Tell me what you know about what she was involved in."

"She was used as a runner. When something had to be transported, she was called. I'm talking about very sensitive documents, Jack. They stopped using electronic communications because we caught too much of it."

"How would she transport them? They wouldn't risk giving her a folder, would they?"

"Often it's in the form of a chip. They'll implant it in the flesh."

I thought back to the morgue. She had a recent cut on her arm about an inch long.

Marcia pushed the sheet in front of me. "Other times they'd memorize it."

I studied her face. She was unwavering.

"I spoke to her several times during my investigation years ago. We encountered each other. She put on a tough front, but I could tell she was scared. She opened up to me. That's how I know about the threats to her family. They never let up. They threatened her kids, who were babies at the time."

"How'd you get busted?"

"I let my guard down."

I waited for her to continue. She didn't.

"All that stuff you know about me, is that from being in MI5?"

She nodded, said nothing.

"So you don't know anything recent?"

"No, not really."

I pushed my chair back and rose. She stared up at me. I walked past her, toward the front door.

"I'm going out for a bit. You can take the bed. I'll sleep on the couch."

I stepped outside. After a few days of oppressive humidity, I welcomed the cool night air. I walked down the driveway. The trees rose up into the sky and blocked the streetlight two houses down. I reached the curb and turned right.

My mind raced from one thought to the next. The revelation about the extent of Jessie's activities came as a partial shock. I saw it coming, even if I'd tried to avoid it. She gave up our evidence against Keller. They had her from that moment on.

Who, though? What did they have her do? How often? Where did I fit into this? If Marcia was right, and my name had been added to that paper after the fact, why had it come up?

I looked up at the clear sky. "I wish you could talk to me, Jess."

She couldn't, though. And for all I knew, the clues had been there and I'd missed them.

I continued along the street. A dog barked from behind a chain link fence. My thoughts turned to April for the first time since I'd left. I wondered if she knew anything about this. That was doubtful. Perhaps Deb did, though. She and Jessie had remained tight. Maybe something had slipped over a glass of wine. I pulled out my phone. It was eight o'clock in Florida. They'd still be up.

Sean answered.

"Are you guys OK?" I said.

"We're all good. We made it up to—"

"Don't tell me. It's best I don't know."

"What's going on, Jack?"

"Is Deb around?"

"Sure, but can you tell me first?"

"No." I paused. "Sorry, I just can't yet. I'm not sure."

"OK." He said something in the background, then Deb came on.

"Jack?"

"Deb, I need you to think back over the last five years. Did Jessie ever say anything to you that indicated she was in danger?"

"With her husband?"

"No, not him, just in general. Did it ever sound like she feared for her life?"

"Her life? No, not that I can think of."

"When she went away, what did she tell you?"

"She went out of town for sales conferences and on trips she had won. She took me once. We went to Jamaica."

"Did anything out of the ordinary happen there?"

"Pretty ordinary, Jack. We were well past our party days."

"OK. Tell Sean I'll call in the morning."

I turned and headed back to the house. The same dog barked when I passed his yard. I hoped that a moment of clarity would find me as easily as the dog. It didn't. I walked up to the front door more confused than when I had left.

I glanced to the side. The bedroom window was lit up. Marcia had found it. I figured she had lain down, so I quietly opened the door.

I heard the sound of her voice. It was muffled. I couldn't tell what she'd said, but it seemed as if she spoke with an American accent. I stood in the entryway for a moment. The call ended before I could hear anything else.

The bedroom door creaked open. Marcia stepped out. With nothing to change into, she had on the same clothes.

"I didn't know you were back," she said.

"Just got here," I said.

She walked past me.

"I swear I heard an American accent coming out of your room."

She looked back, smiled and nodded. "I was on the phone with my sister."

"Your sister?"

"She's worried about me."

"And she speaks like she's from the States?"

Marcia stopped and turned. "My father ran off to the U.S. when I was young. He remarried and had three more children. Anna, the oldest of the three, and I are close. That's who I was speaking with. She is very American. Even more than you."

I let it go at that. She got a glass of water from the kitchen, and went back to the room. I lay down on the couch. Despite my nap on the plane, I had no trouble falling asleep.

39

ALESSANDRO STRETCHED OUT ON THE BACK SEAT OF HIS CAR, asleep. His phone woke him. He opened his eyes. The moon hovered high overhead. It looked like a flashlight, a hundred yards away. If he traveled a few hundred yards to the west, he'd see it reflected off the calm gulf waters.

He let the phone ring four times before answering. He contemplated letting it go to voicemail. It wasn't as if Vera wouldn't call back until he answered. And she'd be pissed. And a pissed Vera was not ideal for Alessandro's well-being, so he answered her call.

"The husband knows too much," she said.

The statement caught him off guard. He'd been prepared to face another man. He expected she would call to relay pertinent information.

"About what?" he said. "He wasn't there."

"About something I don't want him knowing. You'll have to kill him. But, before you do, you'll need to find out what his brother knows."

"So you want me to start with his brother?"

"No, deal with the husband first. Prior to killing him, press him for information on his brother. If we can avoid killing that man, let's do so. The mess is spreading and I need you to contain it before the leak is out. We're on the verge of the wrong set of eyes falling upon Crystal River."

Alessandro glanced up, through the rear window. Thin clouds raced by the moon, hiding portions of it, but never the entire orb. He tried to think of a question to ask Vera that might lead to more information. He disliked being in the middle of something this convoluted without all the facts.

"OK," he said. "Anyone else?"

"Keep an eye on the sheriff. I don't know how much she knows. I'll send you the addresses, including the location of the sheriff's department."

Vera ended the call before he could say anything. After a minute, he climbed between the front seats and slid in behind the wheel. He had turned the key in the ignition when his phone buzzed. It was a message from Vera. She wanted him to return to the house first. He plugged the address into the Impala's navigation unit and pulled onto Suncoast.

The drive took five minutes. He didn't pass a single car on the way. He pulled into the familiar neighborhood. Judging by the darkened front windows along the street, everyone had already headed to bed. He glanced at the clock on the dash. It was just after eleven p.m.

He spotted the house, drove past it, parked two lots down.

Alessandro hopped the neighbor's fence and darted across their back-yard. He hit the next fence full speed and vaulted over it. He repeated the process once more, then raced to the back of Jessie's house.

It was dark inside. The air handlers were silent. It didn't look like anyone was home. He moved to the rear door. It was unlocked. He pushed it open and crept through the house with his sidearm drawn. He cleared the place, room by room, verifying they were all empty.

He called Vera to tell her. She sent him directions to Matt's house with instructions to neutralize the men only if threatened. He ignored the warning.

No one would know either way.

He bypassed town and arrived at the entrance of a neglected neighbor-hood twenty minutes later. The place looked run down. The houses were old and in various stages of disrepair. He imagined that half of them were empty or contained squatters.

He cut his headlights off and cruised down the street with his foot off the gas. The dilapidated condition of the neighborhood didn't bother him. The residents in a place like this weren't the kind that would talk to cops. It didn't matter if they witnessed something. They would never admit to it. Alessandro could appreciate that. He might even flip a hundred dollars to anyone he saw outside when he left.

Extra incentive.

He tapped his brake as he passed the house. The front window was lit up. He saw three heads turned toward a wide screen television. Two of the faces were out of view. The one he could see led him to believe the man was stoned. He presumed the others were, too. It was an assumption he'd have to ditch before entering the house. Best to assume they were capable of putting up a good fight.

He pulled to the curb, exited the vehicle, and cut across the lawn to the front door. Alessandro didn't bother knocking. He reached for the handle and turned it. Not one of the men moved as he stepped into the foyer. He singled out the man most likely to give him trouble. That man would be the first to die. The other two were heavy, stoned, and looked like they'd move slowly. From his position, he could kill all three before one got a hand on him.

"Which of you gentlemen is Glenn?"

The man against the far wall looked at him with a blank expression and said, "I am."

One of the other guys started to get up.

Alessandro aimed his pistol at the man. "No need to move. I'm only here to see Glenn."

The guy said, "Well, that's my brother."

"If you want him to live, you best get back in your seat."

The guy held out his hands and lowered himself onto the couch. The three of them breathed heavily and erratically. Their panic levels were high. If they all tried to make a move, it would be uncoordinated. It would play into Alessandro's hand.

The men didn't move. This was going to be too easy. He fought to keep a smile at bay.

Then he shot Glenn in the head.

The suppressor affixed to the end of his pistol drowned out most of the noise. It sounded like a pellet hitting a tin can. He spun, fired another shot before either of the two men reacted. It hit the guy to Alessandro's right in the head. He slumped over the arm of the couch.

The third man moved quickly. It surprised Alessandro. He fired before he aimed. The shot missed. The big guy lunged for him. Alessandro threaded one arm through the guy's arm as he sprawled backward. The man flung his free arm. It connected with Alessandro's hand, dislodged the pistol. He heard it hit the floor and skate across the room. He was unable to get a visual on its position.

The big guy threw another punch. It connected on Alessandro's side. One of his ribs cracked. He fought through the pain, wincing, and delivered an uppercut to the man's down turned face. The guy screamed, then gurgled. Without seeing the damage, Alessandro assumed he'd broken the man's nose.

So he hit him there again. And again.

The big guy dropped to his knees. Alessandro kicked him in the solar plexus. The man wavered, but didn't fall. Alessandro kicked him twice more. Once in the gut. Once in the throat. Finally, the man fell to the side.

Alessandro crossed the room, picked up his pistol and walked back toward the man. The big guy struggled to breathe. His face was dark red. Alessandro stepped forward. The man tried to move his arms, couldn't.

Alessandro spat on him, then pulled the trigger four times.

So much for information gathering.

40

I OPENED MY EYES, TILTED MY HEAD BACK AND GLANCED AT THE BACK door. No light penetrated the sheer curtain that covered the windows. I considered going back to sleep. I knew that would be a losing cause. I lifted my cell phone, checked the time.

Five a.m.

I lay there for a moment, stared at the ceiling, listened. The house was still, quiet. Marcia slept. Or had left. I could deal with either.

The events of the previous day flooded my mind. I had plenty to catch up on, so I kicked my legs over the edge of the sofa. They found the floor. My knees and ankles popped as I rose. I lifted my arms over my head. My shoulders and elbows had the same reaction as the lower half of my body. A cool draft ran through the room. It felt good against my bare arms, legs and chest.

I went into the kitchen. The tile floor felt twenty degrees cooler than the air surrounding me. I grabbed a protein drink out of the fridge. I lifted the lid to the garbage can to throw away the cap. The sheet of paper with my name and the code and the letters KOS sat atop a used paper plate and two empty bottles of water. I pulled the document out and carried it into the other room. My pants were folded on the floor. I grabbed them and stuffed the paper into one of the pockets.

I tried to assume that the document had been placed in the trash by accident. But a feeling gnawed at me. It left me doubting that conclusion. I'd figure out a way to casually bring it up to Marcia. Her reaction would tell me whether she did it on purpose.

The only shower in the house was located in the bedroom. I decided against disturbing Marcia. She could sleep for another hour or so. I went back into the kitchen. A twenty-year-old coffee maker sat on the counter top. It worked. The coffee it brewed was strong in strength, taste, and effect. That was all that mattered. If Marcia was anything like me, the smell of it would be enough to wake her up within the next ten minutes.

The coffee dripped through a filter made from recycled paper. Drop by drop the pot filled, and I felt sleepier. I let it finish brewing before pouring a cup, though. When it was finally ready, I bypassed the cream and sugar, and took my tall mug of black coffee out back.

Through the trees, I watched the sky turn from blue to red to orange and back to a new shade of blue. It looked new, crisp, fresh. The sun climbed higher over the next few minutes. Bright light found its way through clustered leaves. Birds piped up. The air warmed. The breeze remained cool.

I had my cell phone in my lap. I glanced down at it as it buzzed against my thigh. The call came from Florida. I dragged my finger across the screen and answered it.

"Glenn, Matt and Jed were murdered." April sounded winded. It was past midnight there. Presumably, she hadn't slept much. And the sleep she had managed might have been beer-induced.

"Are you at the scene?" I said.

"I'm leaving my house now."

I pictured her brushing the tabby cat to the side and slipping through the front door. I doubted she put on her uniform. Maybe she had on blue jeans and a tank top, her sheriff's shirt draped over her shoulder. There wasn't time to worry about being in the proper attire when on the way to a triple-homicide.

"What do you know?" I said.

"Nothing, yet. A neighbor called in to nine-one-one after she saw a man fleeing the scene. She was on her porch, across the street. Said she saw the guy enter the house. She thinks she saw him in the living room. They had their blinds open, like last time."

"OK."

"The guy executed them. She heard what she described as bolts dropped into a coffee tin. That's all I got right now. I'll find out more after I secure the scene."

A triple homicide was not something an amateur would likely pull off. A pro did this. And he might still be close.

"Don't go over there alone," I said. "Got it?"

The phone thumped and clanked. A pause followed. "Sorry," she said. "Dropped it putting on my shirt."

The tattoo flashed in my mind. I brushed it aside. "April, make sure you have at least one, preferably two deputies with you."

"I will." She paused a beat. "What do you make of this?"

I made plenty of it. Three men were executed after one of them revealed that he found a cache of government secrets. Even though he hadn't a clue what he looked at, I was sure that got him killed. April and I weren't the only ones he told. Now someone was cleaning up a mess. They started with Jessie. Then April's deputy Craig got in the way and paid for it. I was in the middle of it all. Without me there, who else would they go after?

April?

Sean and his family?

I said, "It's too soon for me to speculate, April. Call me when you get to the house. Make sure you message me pictures of the crime scene."

We hung up. I downed my coffee and went back inside. I had a change of clothes in the bedroom. The door remained closed. I still had on the pants and undershirt I borrowed from Sean the day before.

For five minutes I paced the room. My footsteps grew louder with each pass. The square trek did little to clear my mind. I had no great insights. Things grew more muddled.

Marcia still didn't wake.

I stepped out back, called Sasha. I filled her in on the new developments. She told me she'd dedicate as many resources as she could, when she could.

I went back inside. Marcia stood in the middle of the living room. She watched me enter.

"Is everything OK, Jack?"

"No."

"What happened?"

"Something bad."

"Care to elaborate?"

I shook my head, went in the kitchen.

She followed me. "Jack—"

"Why did you throw away that paper?"

"What paper?"

"The one I brought back from Florida."

"I didn't throw it away, Jack."

"I found it in the trash this morning."

She looked at the garbage can, then back at me. Her eyes were wide. She held her hands out. "I...I must have done it by accident when I tossed my plate and the empty water bottles away. Why would I get rid of that? We might need it to figure out what is going on."

Her eyes were unwavering. Her lips didn't tremble. She stuttered once, but that was it.

I said, "You told me on the phone that you knew who was targeting me."

She took a step back, folded her arms over her chest. She glanced toward the window over the sink. A tall hedge blocked most of the view.

I said, "If that were true, you would have said something by now. Right?" She had no reply.

"Why'd you tell me that when you clearly don't know?"

"All I know is that something is going on, Jack. I had to get you back here. I knew if I told you that, you'd reach the conclusion that while you were there, others weren't safe, and you'd come back." She leaned toward me. Pointed at herself. "It was a gamble, but I was right."

I reached into my pocket and grabbed the paper. I realized at that moment I'd left my pistol in the other room. It wasn't a good feeling.

"Was this all fabricated, Marcia? The whole money laundering angle you brought up last night?"

She shook her head, reached for the paper. I pulled it back. She said, "That's the truth, Jack. I don't know who the target is, and I'm not even sure if that matters now. This could be months old. It's just something that was in her possession that proves she was still being used. The thing that concerns me is that piece of paper appears to be the only thing left."

I debated whether I should tell her the reason it had survived. Glenn had kept it in a drawer. Jessie didn't know about it, neither did her killer. Whichever of them destroyed the remaining documents had no idea the one in my possession existed.

In the end, I said nothing to Marcia about it.

"Jack, please tell me what's going on."

"Who says something is going on?"

"I can see it in your face, your actions, your reactions. You are overly stressed. I know enough about you to realize that doesn't occur very often."

In truth, it happened more than it should. Sometimes I wondered how I was still alive.

She said, "Please, Jack. Level with me."

"Jessie's husband Glenn, his brother Matt, and their friend Jed were murdered last night."

41

ALESSANDRO MESSAGED A CONFIRMATION TO Vera. The hit had been successful. He fled the neighborhood, and best he could tell, no one had noticed he'd been there. At the same time, he assumed someone had seen him. Every job, that was how he operated. It kept him from doing something stupid afterward. That was how men in his position got caught, and subsequently killed. They got drunk, bragged to a bunch of guys at a bar. Or maybe he took home a stripper and let her in on his dirty secret. Or perhaps, still intoxicated from the kill, he killed again.

He had never done that.

But this time he had to.

Now he stood at the end of a quiet street, positioned behind the Impala. The trunk lid was open. A single light bulb provided enough light for him to see the contents of the trunk clearly. He removed the spare tire and pulled out the bag containing the jack. Vera had told him to look in it. So he did. He lifted an eyebrow at the contents of it. He closed the bag and brought it with him, placing it cautiously on the passenger seat. He considered strapping the seat belt over it. That'd be overkill, he told himself.

He received a text from her at that moment. It contained a one line address, number and street. Nothing else. He plugged it into the Impala's navigation system. A computerized voice spat directions back at him.

Pretty simple. Only a couple turns and a few miles to drive.

Alessandro drove to the end of the dark residential street. He made a right and headed further away from town. Everything was dark. Houses, businesses, streetlights even. The town and surrounding areas shut down in the middle of the night. He couldn't imagine how people lived like this. He would go crazy.

The navigation system said he was close. It counted down from a quarter-mile, five hundred feet, one hundred feet, turn left. He did so, and pulled into the mostly empty parking lot of a senior care facility. The entrance was in the center of the long building. Two wings extended out on either side. All of the lights were off, except for a desk light beyond the front doors. A woman sat behind the broad counter. She glanced up, her gaze meeting the headlights that shone in on her.

Alessandro took a deep breath. He'd killed plenty during his time on the job. At the very least monthly. Often weekly. Sometimes daily. He liked that the best. Continuity, he'd learned at a seminar one time, was the key to success.

He leaned over, grabbed the bag on the seat, reached inside, pulled out the explosive device and remote.

The woman stood.

Alessandro cut his headlights, leaving the parking lights on. He exited the Impala and walked up to the door. He kept his left hand behind his back, hiding the explosive. The sliding doors didn't move for him. He knocked against the glass with the knuckles of his right hand.

The woman approached. She looked concerned. She had on pink scrubs and white tennis shoes. Her black hair was pulled back tight. She looked to be early forties. A wedding ring adorned her left ring finger. She probably had kids. Worked here part-time to bring a little extra money home each month while they slept, safe at home.

He did his best to appear panicked. He bit his lip, shook his hand, shuffled from right to left and back again.

"What is it?" she called out to him from behind the glass doors.

"My father," he said. "He called me. He thinks he's dying."

She looked over her shoulder.

"Please," he said.

She puffed out her cheeks and blew the air through her lips. "OK." She reached out and grabbed something. The lock, he presumed. Her forearm turned. He heard a click. She stuck the fingers of both hands into the crack between the doors and slid them open manually.

"What's his name?" the woman said.

Alessandro didn't answer. He threw a quick punch at the woman's face. Her head snapped back. She dropped in place. He walked over her still body. The hallways were empty. Were any other workers there? He placed the explosive behind the desk. The woman rolled over on the floor. She crawled toward the door. He ran to her, grabbed her by her hair and dragged her to the desk. She flailed her arms and kicked with her legs. She tried to scream, but it sounded like her throat was clogged with her own fluids. He pressed her against the desk, hit her twice in the head and let her fall to the ground.

Alessandro didn't stay around long enough for anyone to come to her aid. Amid the whirring and beeping of machines hidden in rooms beyond the hallway entrances, he fled through the open double doors. He didn't bother to shut them. Waste of time, he figured. He got in the car, backed up, turned toward the road. He hit the highway and pressed the button on the remote, setting off the explosive.

He watched the rearview mirror. After a five second delay, a fireball erupted in the center of the building. He assumed that was only the beginning. A facility like that had oxygen tanks. He wondered what else? Additional explosions ripped through the building, sending another fireball into the air. He stopped a mile down the road. The flames rose high. The smoke higher. It'd be several minutes before a fire truck responded.

By then it would be too late.

42

MARCIA SEEMED PANICKED. SHE INSISTED THAT WE LEAVE THE house. I didn't object. Whoever did this could possibly have the resources to track me down in London. Or track Sean and his family down wherever they went.

"I don't like this, Jack." She stepped backward, out of the kitchen. "How did they know? What else do they know?"

I had the same questions. Perhaps Glenn had said something. But to who? As far as I knew, the man who killed Craig had fled. It wasn't as if Crystal River was the type of place someone could hide out for weeks on end. Everyone knew everyone. A strange face did not go unnoticed. If you murdered someone there, it'd be stupid to return.

For the moment, I had to work under the assumption that Glenn knew more than he let on. Matt and Jed were meat shields and too stupid to have anything to do with it. They were in the wrong place at the wrong time. Killing all three was an aggressive move.

I'd have done the same thing.

"Whoever's responsible is over there," I said. "Thousands of miles away."

She shook her head. "You think they don't have connections here? Didn't you listen to me last night? This has something to do with me, Jack. These people are everywhere."

"You keep telling me that, Marcia. But you're not telling me everything. What are you hiding?"

She turned and took a few steps away. Her head dropped back. Her hair cascaded down to her waistline. She wrapped her arms around her chest. I saw her fingertips curl around her triceps.

"Jessie was terminated. We had contact in the past. It had been some time. I can only assume she still had information. Perhaps someone was trying to get her to come out, reveal me for who I was." She paused, then turned around. "Who I am. The threats I've received, Jack, they say they'll out me. That will ruin my chances of a political career."

"Why kill her then? If she's dead, she can't help their case."

Marcia nodded. Her eyes glazed over. She steadied a quivering lip. "What I said is what I hope is happening. They know who I am, my past, what I did. They know she was connected to me. They killed her. She's not the first. I don't think she'll be the last. They are trying to erase every connection to me. They want to terminate me and everyone I ever came into contact with while undercover."

"Why?"

She shrugged, shook her head. "Any number of reasons. Take your pick. I know too much about things that happened, the corruption behind the scenes. I could use my position in government to bring them down."

"Who is 'them'?"

"It's a collective them, Jack."

On the one hand it made sense. On the other, it sounded like a story made up with the intent of pulling wool over my eyes. I didn't have the luxury of time to debate it.

"Did you ever meet Glenn?" I said.

She shook her head. "Like you said, he stumbled onto something. It cost him his life. I would assume that the man who killed the cop discovered this. He had to lay low for a day or two, then he returned to finish the job."

It made sense. Loose ends were all around. Time to clip and burn them off.

Her expression changed from scared to steeled. "We need to get out of this house, Jack."

"You're right," I said. "And I need to go back to Florida."

"What are you going to do there?"

"Put an end to this."

"How? You don't know who you're dealing with."

I walked up to her. "Do you?"

She didn't move, budge, or respond.

I leaned in. Our eyes were inches from each other. "If you know something, then you better tell me now."

"I don't know for sure, Jack." She blinked, stepped back. "You'll be dealing with people who operate outside of the law, but with backing from certain high ranking officials."

"That's nothing new for me, Marcia." She had described the last decade of my life. My phone rang again. "I need to get this."

She turned away and went to the bedroom.

I answered the call. It was April, and she sounded frantic. I hurried to the back door and stepped outside.

"April, calm down." The sun hovered over the trees. Bright rays stabbed at my eyes. "What happened? Are you at the murder scene?"

She took several breaths. They started ragged, then calmed down.

"I'm at the scene. It's bad. Blood everywhere. All three of them are dead. There was a struggle with Matt. In the end, two of them took a bullet to the head. Matt took several."

I pictured the scene. The guy hadn't hesitated in doing his job. He misjudged the men, though, and it nearly cost him.

"Don't tamper with anything," I said. "If there was a struggle, some of that blood could belong to the shooter."

"Jack, wait. Listen to me." She paused. Someone said something to her. She responded to them, then came back on the line. "We just received a call from dispatch. There's no easy way to say this."

"Then say it." I braced for the news that Sean, Deb, Kelly and Dad had been found murdered.

"Someone blew up your father's retirement home."

I nearly dropped the phone. Marcia had said I was in danger, but back-tracked on the statement. I told Sean to get his family and Dad out of the state because of what she had said to me. If she hadn't made it seem like the end of my life was imminent, I might not have taken that step.

"He wasn't there," I said. "He left with Sean."

"Oh, thank God." The words were breathy, part of a long, deep exhale.

"April, I need to make some calls. You keep me posted. I'll be in touch soon."

"OK."

We held the line for a moment.

"Jack?" she said.

"What?" I said.

"I love you."

I hesitated. "No, April. You love an image of me. I've told you. I'm not that man."

She started to say something else, but I ended the call before she got the second word out. Perhaps there was something between us. Or maybe, there was something to end. Either way, that required the appropriate time. This wasn't it.

I placed a call to Sasha. She answered on the first ring.

"Where the hell are you two?" she said. "We've been by her place and yours and wherever the hell you ditched the car. We found it, but not you two."

"Don't worry about that. I need you to get me a jet."

"Why?"

"Something's happened. I need to go."

"Where?"

"Home, Sasha. I'm going home again."

"Christ, Jack." She paused, groaned. "How long till you can get to the airport?"

"It'll take close to an hour."

"OK, good. That gives me enough time to arrange it."

"Thank you." She'd proven time and again I could trust her to come through for me.

"You're going to owe me big time. I'm talking porterhouse steaks."

I tried to smile. Couldn't. I ended the call and went back inside. Marcia stood in the living room. She looked worried.

"Our arrangement is over," I said.

"What?" she said.

"I'm going to Florida."

"I'm going with you."

"Not a chance in hell." I walked past her.

"Jack, I've got the skills and contacts you need for this. I know people here, there, in D.C."

"So do I."

"I've got something you don't. I can be something you can't."

I stopped, looked back at her. My hand was on the doorknob. All I had to do was turn it and walk out. I'd be done with her. Instead, I said, "What?"

"I'm the best bait you can find. Someone wants me worse than they want you. If I'm there, you'll get your man."

I let go of the knob. More than anything, I wanted to find Jessie's killer and make them suffer. Chances were he was the one wreaking havoc on the rest of town. If I was to believe Marcia's story, whoever wanted Jessie dead also wanted her dead. A tangled web, she had said. I saw it now.

I was near the center. She was stuck in the middle of it.

"Get your things. We need to head to the airport."

43

VERA SAID, "GO TO THE sheriff's office. Kill anyone that enters. Afterward, go to the airport and get on a plane to Boston."

Alessandro said, "OK."

44

I TOOK THE M4 TO the M25, London Orbital motorway. The entire stretch of motorway spanned one hundred and seventeen miles around the perimeter of the city. I had to drive just under half that distance. I elected to go south. In either direction the drive would take an hour. This kept us moving and not sitting in traffic. I held the speedometer at ninety miles per hour. The trip took just over forty-five minutes. After exiting the motorway, we had to backtrack seven miles to the airport. That took close to twenty minutes.

Sasha met us at the airport. She stood next to her Audi. I pulled up next to her. She glanced at the car, then me.

"Can't believe you ditched the car I gave you."

"You found it safe, right?"

She nodded her head.

"I should be the one upset," I said. "You gave me a car you were tracking."

"Give me a reason I shouldn't keep tabs on you."

I didn't. "If I don't make it through this, it won't matter." I followed it up with a smile.

She pressed her lips together and looked away.

Marcia exited the vehicle and joined me. She said, "I'm ready whenever you are, Jack."

"What's she doing?" Sasha said.

"Coming with me," I said.

"No way. I'm not letting you drag her along," Sasha said.

"It's her choice, not mine."

"Sasha," Marcia said. "I have to apologize. There are things you don't know about me."

"What are you talking about?" Sasha looked at me. "What is she talking about, Jack?"

I said nothing. It wasn't my place.

Marcia stepped forward. She said, "Operation Patheos."

Sasha's expression didn't change. The name appeared to mean nothing to her. She glanced at me again. "They're ready for you guys."

Marcia walked toward the jet. I stayed behind, waited until the woman neared the stairs.

"I feel like I should go with you," Sasha said.

"You've got too much to do here," I said. "Did you uncover anything on the threats against her?"

"I'm still working on it. I think I have a few leads. If they come through, this is way more than political corruption and local criminals."

I looked over her shoulder. Marcia climbed the stairs to the jet. The sky behind the plane was clear. Clouds hovered overhead.

"Do you think it has anything to do with that Operation Patheos?" I said.

"First I've ever heard of it." She paused, looked toward the jet, then back at me. "Do you?"

I nodded. Sasha hadn't uncovered the woman's background yet. Letting her figure it out on her own would uncover more than I knew. If I said anything, it would distort her view.

"Do me a favor?" I said.

"What?" she said.

"Send me any information you find. Can you make sure to do that?"

She reached into her purse and pulled out a cell phone. She held it out. "Take this."

"I have a phone."

"This is more powerful than that old piece of junk you carry. I'll be able to relay the data to you on this."

I took the phone and stuck it in my left pocket. My cell was in the right.

"Fancy pants two days in a row?" She gave me a half-smile.

I forced one in return. "I'm only wearing them so I can give them back to Sean." We stared at each other for a moment. "Can you arrange for a car?" I added.

She nodded, reached out and grabbed my arm. "Be careful, Jack."

"Always."

I jogged toward the jet and boarded. It looked like my first flight. Marcia had claimed the couch. I saw the flight crew, didn't recognize any of them. We departed soon after I took a seat. A man said it would be close to nine a.m. in Florida when we landed. I didn't want to be groggy when we touched down, so I did pushups in the aisle every half hour, and paced the length of the cabin.

Every fifteen minutes or so, I checked the phone Sasha had handed to me. If she had found something, she hadn't sent it yet. I planned to call her for an update the moment we landed. I'd have to get away from Marcia for a few minutes to do so.

The trip took just over five hours. After three Trans-Atlantic flights in a Gulfstream, I never wanted to cross on a commercial flight again. I could sit on the floor surrounded by roaming livestock and be happy about arriving in record time.

Marcia followed me to the exit. Hot, humid air blew in. I stopped, turned and told her I needed to use the restroom. She stepped aside and allowed me to pass.

Inside the cramped bathroom, I checked the phone again. Still no documents. I called Sasha on my cell. She answered right away.

"I can't get into the file," she said.

"What do you mean?" I said.

"Security."

"Don't you have the highest clearance possible?"

"I do. That's what's so frustrating. I'm stuck waiting for an answer now."

"OK. We've landed. Did you arrange a car?"

"There should be a Lincoln out there."

"No driver this time, right?"

"What?"

"Last time, the car that you had arranged had a driver waiting."

"It shouldn't have. The car should have been left for you."

"It wasn't. There was a man who insisted on driving."

She paused. "Someone screwed up, Jack."

It didn't sit right, but that was a couple days ago, and I didn't have time to worry about it now. We ended the call with promises to share information and be careful. I exited the plane. Marcia waited for me by the Lincoln's passenger side door.

I glanced around the deserted airfield and jogged toward the car. A large hangar lingered in the background. Small single prop planes lined the outer edges of the runway. Anticipation built with every step. I expected a sniper's rifle to send a sub sonic round through my skull at any moment.

"Get in," I said to Marcia from twenty feet away.

She opened her door and slid inside. I flinched at the sound of her door slamming shut.

It hit me then what had made me so uncomfortable about the driver. Sasha hadn't arranged it. Someone else had. Someone else knew that I had left England for Jessie's funeral.

What if that someone knew I'd returned again?

45

ALESSANDRO FORCED HIS WAY INTO THE SHERIFF'S OFFICE BEFORE
the sun came up. They only had a single lock on the front door. Child's play
for him. He took his time down the short, narrow hallway. He stepped past it
and saw a large square room. He passed a door on his right. He pushed it
open and saw a break room. The door closed and he continued forward.
Three cells lined the back wall. Each cell looked to be eight foot square. In
front of the cells, there were four desks. The desks were split into two
groups, butted front to front, with a five-foot space creating an aisle between
them.

At most he'd deal with four cops. Those odds did not favor him. Drop
the headcount by one or two and he'd feel better about his chances.

He settled in and waited. Always one to arrive early, he'd been through
this many times before. The element of surprise was his greatest asset. It
would benefit him once again. The cops, when they entered, would let their
guard down. They would be in the safest place they knew of. The station was
their home away from home. And they ruled the building.

Light began to filter in through the shaded windows. The room was no
longer dark. He'd have to change his approach now. The dark had provided
him with cover. The light would force him to act swiftly and decisively. He'd

have to change his tactics a bit. He could use one of the desks, but that would put him in a non-optimal position. The wall that separated the room from the hall was an option. But if there were multiple officers, he'd have to count on all of them entering at once.

He knew this was a fatal flaw in his plan. Why had Vera sent him here? It was only going to get him killed.

He called her, but received no answer. He didn't leave a message.

She wouldn't have let him out of the job, anyway.

He continued to assess various spots in the room for the advantages and disadvantages they gave him. He ruled out the desks, the wall, the drop ceiling, and the cells. In the end, he settled on the break room.

The best-case scenario involved only one cop. He could think of no second best option. Anytime he had to confront multiple armed individuals, the odds dropped.

Time passed. Six, then seven in the morning. Eight approached. He sat in a chair in front of the cells beside a window. He kept an eye on the street. He could see anyone coming from the right, left, or head on.

Shortly after nine in the morning, three cops in uniform approached the door.

Alessandro rushed to the break room. He closed the door so that it remained open a crack. His gut tightened. He didn't like the set up. If his first shot missed, he was screwed. They'd have him pinned. He'd go down.

The front door opened and shut several seconds later. Had they all come in? He stood next to the wall, his ear pressed against the break room entrance. He heard their voices. They sounded tired, defeated.

A result of his handiwork. It made him smile.

A desk chair groaned under someone's weight. A woman said something. A man chuckled. He heard the word coffee.

A hand slapped against the door. Alessandro pressed his back into the cinder block wall. The door swung open, stopping inches from his nose. By the time the door retreated, a man had walked two feet past him. Alessandro crept toward his unwitting target. He reached out with both hands. His left wrapped around the front and grabbed the guy's stubbled chin. His right grabbed the base of the man's skull. He pulled them in opposite directions. The guy's neck snapped, and he fell to the floor.

Alessandro reached down and removed the cop's Glock from its holster. He walked toward the door, stopped, listened. There was nothing to indicate that the others had heard the sound of their partner dying.

He eased the door open. Two cops, one male, one female, sat at their desks, facing him. They stared down at paperwork. They had pens in their hands, not pistols.

Alessandro whipped the door open. He aimed at the man with his right hand, the woman with his left. He fired off two simultaneous shots.

The man jerked backward, stiffened. Blood trickled from a fresh hole in his forehead. He fell off his seat.

The shot missed the woman. She dove toward the floor. He couldn't see her through the desks, so he unloaded the Glock he'd taken from the dead cop's holster. Bullets crashed against the metal frame.

He screamed. So did the woman.

Alessandro had to get out of the break room. There was no exit other than the way he entered. The woman would surely be on the phone, if she wasn't already, calling for backup. He fired off another shot, and stepped out.

The woman squeezed off a round. Thunder exploded in the room. Intense pain rose through his leg like burning acid. He fell to the ground. Blood pooled around his ankle. She fired again. It missed. He shuffled on the floor toward the cells. A mistake, he realized, but he couldn't backtrack. The second set of desks provided him some cover.

He pressed his head to the floor and saw the woman. It looked like blood stained her uniform. He stuck his arm out and fired. She screamed in pain.

"Come on out," he said. "Let's do this."

Desk drawers opened as the woman clawed her way up.

Alessandro reached behind himself, grabbed hold of the cell bars and dragged himself to his feet. He couldn't stand on his injured leg. He used the iron bars to support his weight.

They faced each other.

She leaned against her desk for support. She had blood on her shirt in two spots. He'd hit her in the shoulder and the abdomen. She held her pistol in her left hand. She'd had the pen in her right.

He smiled, knowing he had her.

Alessandro lifted his arm, squeezed the trigger and closes his eyes at the sound of his Glock firing. The sound echoed all around him.

He opened his eyes. The woman stood there, another crimson blossom forming on her thigh. His stomach burned. He looked down. She'd hit him in the gut. He looked up and saw her lift her arm again. He fired another shot. This one hit her in the chest. She collapsed. Alessandro leaned back against the bars. The pain he felt intensified. He glanced down again. She'd hit him in the abdomen a second time.

He knew enough about human anatomy to know that there was little chance he'd survive his wounds. Even if an ambulance drove through the wall at that moment, they'd take their time. He'd killed three cops, and they'd pin the fourth on him.

The weight of his body became too much for his weakened core to handle. He took a shaky breath and slid down the cell bars. The desks blocked his view of the woman. He saw the male cop's feet, but that was it.

Alessandro closed his eyes and waited for death.

46

I KEPT THE SPEEDOMETER FIXED AT EIGHTY. I DIDN'T USE THE
cruise control. A steady foot did the trick. How I managed to keep my foot
steady, I wasn't sure.

I'd tried to call April a dozen times. The phone only rang two or three
times the first few attempts. I had pictured her diverting my calls to voicemail. I hoped it was because she was busy. I figured it had been because I'd
spurned her and left her pissed off. I feared that something had happened
to her.

The last few calls rang several times before being sent to her mailbox. It
wasn't her voice on the message, either. A computer generated greeting
answered each time.

My nerves built. I'd hit redial, wait, hang up, then check the phone that
Sasha had given me. Still nothing from her. I wanted to call her, but didn't
with Marcia sitting next to me.

Marcia appeared to have no reaction to any of this. She kept her eyes
forward. I wondered what went through her head.

The minutes flew by. Before I knew it we passed the burned remains of
the senior care facility where my father had stayed. There was nothing left. A

burning pile of rubble and smoke. A few people gathered nearby. They hugged and consoled one another. Families, I presumed.

This town had never experienced so much killing. Probably not in its entire lifetime. And it all started when I came home. Except for Jessie. But there was no doubt she died because of me.

We passed the abandoned road where Craig had been executed. The Tercel was still there. Yellow police tape had been strung around it, hanging from the trees.

I tried April again. No answer. I called four-one-one, had them connect me to the sheriff's office. The line was busy.

I saw the entrance to Matt's neighborhood. Turned right. Saw the purple house that my grandfather had built with his own two hands. I imagined him turning in his grave, again.

Police tape surrounded Matt's house. April's car wasn't there, and neither were her deputies. I didn't stop. I went to the end of the street and whipped around in the tight cul-de-sac.

"Where are we going?" Marcia said.

"I guess we should go to April's house," I said.

"Wasn't the line to the sheriff's office busy?"

"Yeah."

"We should go there."

I glanced at her, surprised she offered any input. She stared at me. I thought she looked steeled and determined. I nodded and turned toward town.

Downtown Crystal River looked deserted. Typical for a Sunday morning. Though many had been to Jessie's funeral the day before, they still attended church for Sunday service.

I hopped the curb and parked the car. I left a few feet of space for pedestrians to pass through. I made it halfway to the entrance before Marcia got a foot on the ground. I stopped and turned and waited.

"Sorry," she said as she kicked off her flats and ran toward me barefoot. She held her purse in her left hand and stuck her right arm out for balance.

She might have been undercover at one time, but she'd never had the type of training I'd been through.

I yanked the door open. A cool gust blew toward me. The humid air fought it back. I entered, heard Marcia slap the door and step in behind me. This wasn't a time for manners.

We stood in the dark hallway. The office was quiet. I caught a trace of nitroglycerin and sawdust in the air. I held one arm out and ushered Marcia behind me.

I crept along the wall, the M40 drawn and in front of me. As I neared the end, I saw a door. It had three splintered bullet holes. I straightened up, looked over my shoulder, mouthed the words, "Wait here." Then I crouched and stepped around the corner. The area looked clear. I kept the pistol in front of me and sidestepped toward the bullet hole ridden door. I leaned against it. It opened. A man lay on the floor. I didn't see any blood, but he didn't appear to be breathing.

Easing back into the room, I heard a cough. I scanned and saw the desk in front of me had been shot up. I saw a man on the floor behind another desk. I went to his side. He'd been shot in the head. His lifeless eyes stared up, focused on nothing.

I heard a heavy sigh, looked back. April lay on the floor behind me.

"Jesus, April," I said.

If she knew I was there, she didn't show it. I checked her pulse. It was thready, weak, and slow. Maybe fifteen beats per minute. Whatever her eyes stared at, it was beyond this world. I moved my hand to her face. My fingertips brushed against her soft skin, and warm blood. I closed her eyes as she let out her last breath.

I heard another cough.

"Stay back there, Marcia," I said.

If whoever else was in there was in the position to do something, it would have happened already. I remained cautious. I stood and walked toward the cells. I saw a man on the floor. A pistol lay next to him. He held both hands over his stomach. Blood trickled between his fingers.

"Why?" I said.

Somehow he managed to smile. I didn't need an explanation after that.

47

SASHA STARED AT THE BALD MAN IN FRONT OF HER LIKE HE'D stepped on her puppy.

"I'm telling you, Operation Patheos does not exist now, nor did it ever exist. Someone is feeding you a bunch of crap."

"What do you know about Marcia Stanton? And I'm not talking about the company line. You're the only one who knows more than I do around here. I want to know what you know."

He got up and walked around his desk. He stuck his bald head into the hallway and then let his door fall closed. He adjusted the blinds so that no one could see in.

Sasha waited, staring out at the Thames. Two single sculls raced by. One had a full-length lead over the other.

The man sat down. He blocked her view. He cleared his throat, took off his glasses, held them to his mouth, exhaled and cleaned them. He put them back on and stared at her for a moment.

"What I'm going to tell you can't ever leave the walls of this office. Got that?"

She nodded.

He said, "Prior to five years ago, we have no information about Marcia Stanton. She's a ghost."

48

THE MAN'S EYES SHIFTED TO HIS LEFT. HE LOOKED PAST ME. HIS smile faded. He tried to speak. No words came out.

"Jack, shoot him," Marcia said.

"He's dying," I said. "And after what he did, I'd rather he suffer."

The man worked his lips open and shut. Blood trickled from the corners of his mouth. His tongue was coated in crimson. "Vera," the man said.

"Do it now, Jack!" she said.

The man shifted. He winced as he did so. He said, "Th...th...this is Jack? What are you doing with him, Vera?"

He'd regained some of his strength. Adrenaline, presumably. His hand dropped to the side and found his pistol. He didn't look at me. He kept his focus on her.

"Dammit, Alessandro."

It was Marcia speaking, but the accent was American. It sounded like what I had heard at my house in England. The voice she claimed was her half-sister's.

"You couldn't pull this off successfully," Marcia said. "And you couldn't just die."

I started to turn toward her. I caught a brief flash as I did. Gunfire ripped through the room. Instinctively, I dove toward the wall.

The bullet hit Alessandro in the face. His head jerked back and racked the cell bars. He remained motionless for a beat, then fell to the side. Blood pooled on the floor around his stomach and his head. It crept beneath the cell bars, headed in lines toward a drain in the rear of the room.

I rolled over and got into a crouching position. I rose up an inch, caught sight of her. She was close. She fired. It caught me in the left arm. I fell back again. The phone Sasha had given me vibrated against my thigh. My cell rang in the other pocket.

Marcia appeared in front of me. She aimed the pistol in my direction. I cooled my reaction. My right leg covered the M40.

"Who are you?" I said.

She shrugged. "It doesn't matter, Jack." She spoke with an American accent. She sounded like she could have grown up on the other side of the state. "Things got messed up beyond repair. This is the only way."

She lifted the gun. Her eyes watered over. She hesitated. Perhaps she felt some loyalty to me. Maybe she didn't want it to end this way. She cared.

I didn't.

I inched my hand over, grabbed the pistol under my leg, hiked it up an inch in her direction and fired. The bullet collided with her shoulder. Her right side jerked back. She didn't let go of her weapon. She swung her arm forward and fired blind. It hit the wall over my head. Shattered concrete poured down on me like sand.

I aimed and squeezed the trigger. The powerful handgun jerked after the bullet left the chamber. I almost dropped it.

It wouldn't have mattered if I did. A crimson bloom spread over her heart. She stared at me for a second. Confusion, fear, pain. Life left her eyes before she hit the floor.

I reached into my left pocket with my right hand and grabbed the phone Sasha had given me. There was a text message on it.

"Abort now! She's not who she says she is!"

I shook my head as I shoved it into the other pocket. I grabbed my cell and pulled it out. Before calling Sasha back, I glanced down at my left arm. The bullet had gone through. There might be some muscle damage, but the bone was intact. It hurt like hell to move my fingers. I'd worry about it soon enough.

Sasha answered before the phone rang once.

"Jack? Oh my God, are you OK?"

"I'm fine." I was aware I was speaking at close to the volume of a yell. "Marcia, or whatever her name is, is dead. This guy here called her Vera. Maybe you can work with that. I've got some other stuff. I'll fill you in on that later. I need an ambulance first."

"Are you hurt?"

"Flesh wound. I'll be all right."

I dialed emergency services. Then I got up and walked over to April.

She'd stopped breathing. There was no pulse. Judging by the location of her wounds, there was little that could have been done for her had she been inside the hospital when the bullets hit her.

I sat beside her, threaded one hand behind her neck and pulled her close to me. I should have never left. I thought that by doing so, I'd draw the trouble away from Crystal River. In the end, I let someone special die.

The door flung open. Heavy footsteps echoed down the short hallway. I recognized her father as he swung around the partition.

"April," he said. He looked at me, down at her. "Jack?"

I nodded. He was a shell of the man he used to be.

"What happened?" Tears streamed down his cheeks.

"It was meant for me," I said.

He stopped in front of us, fell to his knees. His head shook shoulder to shoulder. "This is my fault. This is my karma. She's paid for my sins."

I knew what he was talking about, the incident on the water with April's mother. I let it go. It was between him and his family now.

The medics came in a few minutes later. It didn't take long for them to figure out everyone but the former sheriff and I were the only ones alive. They led me out of the office, leaving April's father alone with her corpse. I wanted to look back as we left. I couldn't, though. There was a part of me that wanted to remember that goofy little girl, with teeth that stuck out too far, and freckles on her nose, asking me to dance with her one more time before I left.

That image was ruined, though. In time I'd replace it with the woman I almost spent a night with.

49

THE AMBULANCE TRANSPORTED ME TO Clearwater. It was
the closest hospital prepared to deal with a gunshot wound. I insisted that it
was only a scratch. The paramedics appreciated my bravado, but decided
against letting me walk.

Probably for the better. Infections and all.

Sean left Deb, Kelly and Dad behind and met me at the hospital. He'd
taken them to Santa Rosa Beach. They'd bought a condo there recently. No
one knew about it. Not his office. Not even Dad.

"So the threat's over?" Sean said.

"Yeah, for you it is."

"What about you?"

I shook my head. "I don't know, Sean. My life is…complicated. There's so
much in my past. There are people out there who might never stop trying to
find me."

"So what'll you do?"

I ignored the question. I didn't have an answer for it.

The doctor entered the room with my discharge papers. There had been
no substantial damage to my arm. The stitches would need to come out in a
couple weeks, but that could be done anywhere.

Stares were cast my way as we walked through the hospital. I glanced down. My shirt was half white, half crimson. My arm was bandaged. They wanted to check my head, but I refused. They noted that on the paperwork. Did it matter? Not really.

"Where to?" Sean said when we got inside the Suburban.

"I need a shower and a change of clothes. I suppose the airport after that."

"Not planning on staying around?"

"I think it's best that I don't."

Thirty minutes later, we approached Crystal River. Sean bypassed the downtown area. He'd heard that the Tampa Bay media had found its way up the coast and they were reporting on all of the recent carnage.

Fifteen minutes later Sean put on a pot of coffee and I was in the shower. The amount of information I had to process was too great to deal with at that moment. The lives that had been taken would haunt me. The worst part of it was that I had no idea what I had done to Marcia, or whatever her name was, to draw her ire. How had she gone from wanting me to protect her, to trying to kill me? Had it been planned from the beginning? Or was it all one big coincidence?

I had a hard time believing that anything in my life could be classified as such.

The water in the shower turned from red to pink to clear over the course of ten minutes. I cut the water, toweled off and put on a pair of Sean's khaki cargo pants and a t-shirt. Flip-flops completed the ensemble. It'd make me look like a tourist later on, but at least I'd be comfortable on the plane.

Downstairs, we each drank a cup of coffee. I took mine black. Sean added cream and a sugar substitute. I tried to tell him those things were poison. He wouldn't listen.

After that, we left. He turned onto Suncoast, headed south. We neared town. Sean looked at me.

"Want to go visit mom?"

"Sure." There were others there, too.

The church lot was empty. Services had ended for the day. We got out of the Suburban and headed toward the graveyard.

"You go ahead, Sean. I'll catch up."

He walked one way, and I another. I found Jessie's freshly dug grave. Hers was the only grave in the row. That'd change soon.

I knelt next to the turned earth.

"Jessie, I don't know if you're around or can hear this. If you are, you're probably laughing because you of all people know I'm the least likely to do something like this. I want to say I'm sorry. I'm sorry for leaving when we were kids. I'm sorry for not sticking it out when things got tough. I'm sorry for dragging you into the Keller situation. I'm sorry for letting you go again. There's so much I would change if I could go back."

A breeze blew in from the gulf. It felt cool and tasted salty. I glanced up, out over the water.

"You were one of the most amazing women I ever knew, Jess. I guess I'll see you around, someday."

I rose and brushed the grass and dirt off my pants. Sean stood at the other end of the cemetery. I headed his way, walking in between two rows of graves.

We stood next to each other, staring at Mom's grave.

"When's the last time you visited her?" he said.

"The day of her funeral," I said.

He nodded. We both knew he was aware of that.

"Miss her?" he said.

"Of course," I said.

"What do you miss most?"

"The homemade pizza she used to make. It was better than any of that crap we used to get in Clearwater and Tampa."

Sean smiled, nodded. "Very true." We were silent for a moment, then he added, "Want to go visit her?"

I followed his gaze toward Molly's grave. It had been over a decade since I stood before it. The guilt ate away at me. Not for failing to visit, but for coming up short when she needed me most. I watched the man take her away and did nothing to stop him.

Perhaps Sean read my thoughts, because he said, "It's not your fault, Jack. It never was. You were twelve for Christ's sake. What could you have done?"

"I could have stopped him, Sean. I could have taken a knife and plunged it into the guy's stomach and yanked it up until he split into two."

Sean took a step back and turned toward me. "Is that why you live the life you do? Is it some kind of way of avenging her death?"

I hadn't ever thought of it in those terms. I didn't want to start now. "Come on, let's go say hi."

We stood at Molly's grave for five minutes. Neither of us spoke. I said a lot in my head, though. I recounted my life up to this point, and I asked her to be with me until I returned.

It was a somber walk back to the Suburban. The mood didn't lighten during the drive to Tampa. I had him stop at a bank in Clearwater. I had a safe deposit box there with an identity I had never used.

When we reached the airport, the path forked in two directions.

"Want me to come in with you?" Sean said.

I pointed toward the drop-off lane. "Go back to your family, Sean."

He pulled up to the curb and placed the shifter in park.

"Jack, do you think it's..." He looked up at the ceiling, then back at me. "Safe?"

"Stay out of town for a few days. Hell, a week. If you don't hear from me by then, go home."

I opened the door and slid off the leather seat. My feet hit the ground. I took a step away, flicked the door shut, and didn't look back.

Inside the airport, I used my cell to purchase a plane ticket. I had nothing to check in, so I found my way to the gate, scanned the code on my phone and went through security. I ordered a double espresso at the Starbucks placed at the entrance to the terminal where my flight would later depart from. The girl behind the counter lifted an eyebrow and asked if I was sure. I smiled politely and nodded.

I finished my coffee, then located my gate. I didn't stop there, instead continuing on until I reached an empty stretch of seats. Using the phone Sasha had given me, I gave her a call.

"Jack," she said. "I've been wondering when you would call."

"I had a few people to visit before I left town."

"Oh, are they doing OK?"

"You could say that."

She said nothing for a moment. Neither did I. We both tried to speak at the same time.

"You go ahead," I said.

"You're on a secure line?" she said.

"The phone you gave me."

"Good enough. OK, where to start? Marcia was not Marcia at all. She wasn't Vera either. We're not sure who she really is, or was, yet. She never worked in MI5. We think she might have been CIA at one time. Again, that's something we're chasing down. We have our friends over there working on that now."

"Any idea what this has to do with me?"

"Well, perhaps. We did a lot of digging, tracing her cell phone records. Most of the calls were to me, or other legitimate numbers. But there were a ton of texts and calls that went to a, I don't know, I guess some kind of server. This server basically squashes the trace. She then rerouted her calls to their destination. That's how it has been explained to me, at least. I'm guessing those calls went to the guy in the sheriff's office."

An old contact of mine had a similar system. He had explained it in a similar fashion.

"OK, makes sense. But that has nothing to do with me."

"Tell me what she told you, Jack."

I leaned back. My head touched the window. The glass felt cold. I stared at the plain ceiling and recalled everything I could remember.

"She said she worked undercover. One of her investigations brought her in touch with Jessie. It was around that time her cover was blown. She returned to England, started a law practice, started going after bigwigs and built a name for herself. Politics, so forth, you know that."

"Right," Sasha said. "And that's about the time we pick up on her.

Nothing before, though. Obviously, outside of the contacts required, she had the education. Who knows from where, though?"

I took a deep breath, exhaled, said, "So, again, what's—"

"I know, I know. This is tricky, because I don't want to worry you too much. There's a threat, but it's not enough for us to deem it credible. At least, not anymore."

"Against me?"

"In a roundabout way, Jack. Your friend, Jessie, she saw Marcia on the tele or in the paper or online, whatever, right? She recognized her and knew that the woman was not who she claimed to be. She saw that as her chance to break free. She reached out, said she could offer the woman up, plus a handful of documents in exchange for whoever controlled her letting her go from their grasp."

"Does this have something to do with that FATF task force?"

"That's irrelevant, actually. Your name on that piece of paper wasn't."

"Why was it there?"

She sighed. "I hate to say this, but we can't be one hundred percent sure. That truth behind that died with Jessie and possibly Marcia."

"So how did Marcia find out about Jessie's plan to out her?"

"We can only presume the answer to that. Currently, we think that—"

"You think?"

"Yes, we *think* that whoever Jessie told notified Marcia. It's very much a possibility that Marcia and that person still worked together."

"Still? As in this person might be out there?"

"Yes." Sasha exhaled heavily. "Again, this is all based on presumption."

"So, what you're telling me is we don't know anything."

"Pretty much."

"How did this woman fool every intelligence agency out there? Think about it, Sasha. She worked for someone over here and managed to escape from them. She builds a reputation over there, including a top-secret persona within MI5, but prior to five years ago Marcia Stanton didn't exist."

Sasha said nothing.

"So either she or the person she still worked with had some high-level contacts or the ability to hack into and manipulate what should be the most encrypted databases in the world."

"See, lots of presumptions."

"Am I crazy in saying that this sounds like one huge coincidence? I don't know, a big web that we were all drawn into somehow? This woman wants Jessie dead. Makes it happen. I go down there. She pieces it together, realizes that I have to go because I'm too close to figuring it out. In the end, it's me or her."

"Jack, that's about as plausible as anything we've come up with. Like I said, we'll continue to work on it. If we come up with something, you'll be the first to know."

I said nothing. Someone who could make things happen was out there. They might know my name, and they might have reason to make something happen to me. I studied the faces that passed by. Any one of them could be a murderer. Most people had no idea how close they came to a stone cold killer on a daily basis.

"Anyway," Sasha said. "I can get you out on a flight this evening. I'll pick you up and get you back to your flat."

"I'm not going back," I said.

"What are you talking about, Jack?"

"I quit."

"You can't quit."

"Then I'm taking leave."

"You...why?"

"Personal reasons."

"What about Mia?"

"Erin is understanding. She'll work something out."

A voice came over the intercom and announced boarding had commenced for my flight. Since I had a first-class ticket, I rose and walked toward the gate.

"Jack, think this through please."

"I have. I'm done."

"Are you at the airport?"

"I am."

"Where are you going?"

"I'm going home, Sasha."

I hung up and tossed both phones in the first trashcan I came across.

50

NEON LIGHTS REFLECTED IN POOLS OF WATER THAT GATHERED IN the middle of the street. The storm hit hard and fast. By the time I found cover, the rain had soaked me. At that point, I had no reason to seek shelter. I walked through the rain and let it wash over me.

The cab could have dropped me off in front of the apartment building. Something about the night air in the city made me want to walk. After all, it's hard to pass up a gorgeous night in New York City.

When the rain stopped, I stared up at the sky. City lights bounced off low, racing clouds. Thunder rumbled, but it headed away. Although, it could have been a truck running over a pothole.

My apartment building loomed up ahead. I turned my eye to the street. The wet sidewalk shimmered from a combination of oil runoff and overhead lights. Since I couldn't look up and see a sky full of stars, the illuminated concrete would have to do.

I looked up when the entrance was a dozen steps away. I hadn't been there in months, but I knew the moment my left foot hit how many more I had to go.

The old man who worked the door at night watched me. It appeared that he failed to recognize me. Then his eyes lit up, he smiled, and nodded.

"What do ya say, Mr. Jack? Haven't seen you around here in quite some time."

I had never heard him talk to anyone else like that. Perhaps I didn't come off as stiff as the rest of the building's inhabitants.

"How's it going, Willie?" I said. "Anyone been by to see me?"

At least a half-dozen people knew I lived here. A couple were friends. A couple weren't. I never knew when someone showed up what the outcome would be.

"Nah, you haven't had a visitor in months. Shoot, at least since before you went and disappeared. Where you been, anyway?"

I stuck my hands in my pockets and shrugged. "Here and there. You know how it is."

"That's the truth. All right, get yourself out of this muggy New York air."

I smiled. This was nothing compared to Florida. I pulled my hand from my pocket with a twenty tucked in my palm. I reached out. Willie met me halfway. He winked after the exchange.

They'd done away with the carpet and installed tile while I'd been gone. It looked like marble. I doubted it was. Probably something cheaper, able to withstand another seventy years. The furniture was the same. Someone had told me it was the original from way back in the forties. The rest of the building had been remodeled over the years, but they kept a few things original, like the furniture and some of the light fixtures and mirrors. My apartment was modern. That was one of the things I liked about the place. Old and new at the same time.

Gold-plated doors parted in the middle. I stepped onto the elevator and pressed the button labeled twenty-eight. Second from the top. After a minute or so, the doors reopened. I stepped into the hall. The lights were always on, never too bright. The carpet on the floor was muted. There were four apartments on the floor. I'd been there seven years and had never spoken with one of my neighbors. It was rare any of us were in the hallway at the same time. If I encountered them in the elevator, I pretended to get a phone call, or looked at a newspaper or a magazine if I had one.

My apartment had an electronic access panel. They weren't crazy about me installing it, but in the end they let me. I reached out and entered the eight-digit code. I held my breath while opening the door. Anticipation built. I half expected an explosion.

But nothing happened.

A puff of fragranced air blew out. I never canceled the cleaning service. Apparently, they'd been coming the entire time.

The door swung open quietly and effortlessly. I stepped inside. I had expected an inch or two of dust to coat everything. There was none. The place was clean and organized. I went into the kitchen, pulled open the refrigerator door. They had dumped all the expired food. The only thing in there was a twelve pack.

Of water.

I shrugged and turned and grabbed the phone off the wall. A three-tone beep greeted me. Messages were waiting. I dialed into the mailbox. Turned out at least ten people thought I was worthy of receiving a message. Half of those were solicitors. Four others were wrong numbers.

The last message had been left from a Florida area code. I straightened up. My finger hovered over the play button before pressing.

"Jack, hi. It's Jessie. I know it must be strange that I'm calling you after all these years. I'm not trying to reenter your life or anything like that. It's just, well, I'm in trouble. The big kind. And I have reason to believe you are, too. Look, I need you to call me. We need to meet. This woman, she's a politician in England. She's not who she says she is, though. I know her secret. She's gone crazy. I think she's trying to have me killed. There's more to it than that. A lot more. On top of that, I have some information that has to do with you, Jack, and it's not good. I'm sorry I'm telling you all this in a voicemail. We need to meet. Take down my number and call me as soon as you can."

The message had been left over a week ago. Whatever information she had, died with her. Of course, it could have been nothing more than I already knew. That was what I made myself believe as I erased the message and hung up the phone.

Jessie, April, and several others were gone. Would Jessie have died if I had arrived a week earlier? Would the others have lived had I never shown up at all? There was no way to answer the questions that pervaded.

And I never wanted to think about any of it again.

(EPILOGUE - NOBLE JUDGMENT: CHAPTER 1)

Those who knew well the man sitting at the head of the table called him Butch. He let his subordinates call him by his last name, Monaco. Even at age sixty-three he was tall and straight and lean and lanky. A smooth scar a centimeter in width ran the length of his cheek from the corner of his mouth to the spot where his earlobe met his head. The reminder stood out most when his skin was tanned, like now. When asked, he'd always told different versions of over a dozen stories. A single version of one of those stories contained the truth. Only Butch knew which. Despite the danger that plagued his life for so long, he had aged well. Aside from a few wrinkles around his eyes and his mouth, he looked much the same as he did the last time he held a secret meeting in Aspen, Colorado.

He couldn't say the same for the five men he knew in the room. They'd gone bald, or had bellies that hung over their guts, or sprouted double chins, or had faces that looked like scuffed leather. Taken as a whole, the description described one of the men to a tee. The rest were some variation. He let three of those men call him Butch. Two addressed him as Monaco.

The other five men at the table were unknown. And chances were that the last time he held a meeting around that same table in that same room, those five guys were in high school or college. Perhaps they'd had some experience since then. Maybe not. At least not the kind Butch accepted. It didn't matter, because he needed ten men in the room for the meeting and the other five original members of the group were dead. Some from natural causes. The others, not so much.

Butch Monaco looked at every man in turn. The blank stares returned to him said more than words ever could. None of them wanted to be there that day. Hell, even Butch had a knot in his stomach. Up till this point, the purpose of the meeting had been left unstated. Too many words led to too many trails which led to people in Butch's position being sentenced to life in prison or death by firing squad, if you lived in the right state. The rest got the chair or an lethal dose injected into them. They go to sleep, never to wake. And if he were honest with himself, he'd admit that every man in the room deserved it.

So the meeting had been arranged in a private manner. The only guy Butch trusted, Waldron, went man to man, speaking in a code that only twelve people knew. He found all of them, minus one, Goetz, who had disappeared four years ago and hadn't been heard from since.

Like the previous meeting in Aspen, there would be no documentation. Nothing would be recorded. And every man in the room would deny ever having been in Colorado that day. What need was there? They all knew that it had to be done, and they were the only ones who could sanction it.

And what was the purpose of the meeting Butch Monaco held that day? The organization they had formed over twenty years ago had to be shut down.

And to do so, secrets had to be eliminated. The men who held those secrets, at least the ones outside of the room, had to die.

Butch drummed the fingers of his right hand on the table, tips to pads to knuckle, growing in intensity. Chatter died down like the tail end of rolling thunder. When all eyes were on him, Butch took a sip from his glass of water, then set it down near the edge of the table. Condensation ringed the bottom. Enough vibration, and it might carry the glass over the side.

Rising, Butch addressed the group. "In 1991, eleven of us met in this same exact room. That meeting, like today's, was unprecedented, unsanctioned, unrecorded, and never happened."

The five men who had been there twenty-two years ago smiled.

The others glanced around the room. Two shrugged. One lifted an eyebrow. The other two remained stoic. They all knew the outcome. None of them knew the story of how it started.

Butch continued. "We all know what we did that day. We might describe it in different ways, depending on who we're speaking with. I'm sure there are those who consider us prognosticators, considering that we were ahead of the rest of Washington and every intelligence agency in so many ways. I know I consider us the original Homeland Security. A decade ahead of our time."

A man named Davinski chuckled. Butch cut right through him with a cross look. Davinski brought a fist up and coughed into it. His cheeks puffed out and his face turned red.

"What we created, our own police force that could operate anywhere, anytime, and without scrutiny, was a beautiful thing twenty some years ago. Hell, most people, even high ranking, never even heard of our baby. We dodged some bullets, of course, but for the most part, over two long decades, it operated flawlessly. Then, a few months ago some intelligence fell into the wrong hands. Possibly through the aide of someone in this organization. We know of at least one agent who was working for the other side. She's dead now. But there could be more. On its own, this is not the issue, for we've dealt with such things in the past. This group has been great at policing itself, and we've used them for it. But this time, it goes too high. It is above all of you. Above me. Someone, and I can't name who, has ordered this thing shut down, or it will be us who'll pay the price."

The man seated at the opposite end of the table lifted his hand in the air. Butch stared him down for a few seconds. Said, "Name?"

The guy rose. "Ballard, sir. Joe Ballard."

"You've got a comment, or a question?"

Ballard ran his right hand through his short black hair. Flecks of silver caught the sunlight coming in through the panoramic window behind him. "What if one of us were to object to what you're proposing?"

"Then you won't leave Aspen alive."

The guy straightened, held his left hand out in front, fingers splayed. "So you're saying that—"

"Shut up, Ballard, and listen to me. There is no choice here. We are not taking a vote. And what's more, you don't have a say in this thing. The SIS is being shut down, and all members, current and former are to be eliminated. That clear?"

Ballard said, "Crystal, sir."

Butch waited for the guy to sit back down. Then he picked up a folder on the table to his right. Inside were a dozen copies of the same information. He handed five to his right, six to his left. The men each kept one and passed the rest down.

"First, these are to be handed back to me in a minute."

"What's the point then?" Davinski said.

"The point is that I want you all to look over this list and tell me if you object to any of the names on it."

"There's gotta be fifty names here."

Butch hiked his shoulders an inch, and said, "And?"

Davinski had no response. His gaze, like the gazes of all the men in the room, shifted to the paper. Their eyes moved right to left repeatedly as they read the names to themselves. Butch felt his stomach tighten even more. He knew the five men who had been in the original meeting would not speak up. This was part of the weeding out process. Any man who objected could be a man who might leak what they planned to do. And a guy who would do that needed to be dealt with immediately.

At the other end of the table, one man lifted his hand.

"Yeah, Ballard?" Butch said.

"I know a name on here."

"Who?"

"Jack Noble."

"And do you object to Mr. Noble being on that list?"

Ballard looked down at the paper. The guy fidgeted, tapping his thumb against the table. He glanced up at Butch.

"Well?" Butch said.

"No. I knew him from the Marines is all. I have no objection to him being on this list."

The End

Jack Noble's story will continue in Noble Judgment (Jack Noble #9). Continue to read an excerpt, or visit https://ltryan.com/pb for purchasing information.

Sign up for L.T. Ryan's new release newsletter and be the first to find out when new Jack Noble novels are published. To sign up, simply fill out the form on the following page:

http://ltryan.com/newsletter/

As a thank you for signing up, you'll receive a complimentary digital copy of *The First Deception* with bonus short story *The Recruit*.

If you enjoyed reading *Never Go Home*, I would appreciate it if you would help others enjoy this book, too. How?

Lend it. Share with a friend or donate to your local library.

Recommend it. Please help other readers find this book by recommending it to friends, readers' groups and discussion boards.

Review it. Please tell other readers why you liked this book by reviewing it at Amazon or Goodreads. Your opinion goes a long way in helping others decide if a book is for them. Also, a review doesn't have to be a big old report. Amazon requires 20 words to publish a review. If you do write a review, please send me an email at contact@ltryan.com so I can thank you with a personal email.

ALSO BY L.T. RYAN

Visit https://ltryan.com/pb for paperback purchasing information.

The Jack Noble Series

The Recruit (Short Story)

The First Deception (Prequel 1)

Noble Beginnings (Jack Noble #1)

A Deadly Distance (Jack Noble #2)

Thin Line (Jack Noble #3)

Noble Intentions (Jack Noble #4)

When Dead in Greece (Jack Noble #5)

Noble Retribution (Jack Noble #6)

Noble Betrayal (Jack Noble #7)

Never Go Home (Jack Noble #8)

Beyond Betrayal (Clarissa Abbot)

Noble Judgment (Jack Noble #9)

Never Cry Mercy (Jack Noble #10)

Deadline (Jack Noble #11)

End Game (Jack Noble #12)

Noble Ultimatum (Jack Noble #13) - Spring 2021

Bear Logan Series

Ripple Effect

Blowback

Take Down

Deep State

Rachel Hatch Series

Drift

Downburst

Fever Burn

Smoke Signal

Firewalk - December 2020

Whitewater - March 2021

Mitch Tanner Series

The Depth of Darkness

Into The Darkness

Deliver Us From Darkness - coming Summer 2021

Cassie Quinn Series

Path of Bones

Untitled - February, 2021

Blake Brier Series

Unmasked

Unleashed - January, 2021

Untitled - April, 2021

Affliction Z Series

NOBLE JUDGMENT: CHAPTER 2

New York City.

THREE MEN MADE the trek from Queens to Brooklyn to lower Manhattan in a black BMW 750i on a humid and cloudy Tuesday morning. They crossed the river by way of the Williamsburg Bridge. While suspended over water, one made a remark that he saw at least a dozen heads bobbing below, racing in the currents and heading toward sea. They were former friends of his. Guys that had remained loyal to the Old Man after his passing. And more importantly, guys who'd refused to accept Charles DeCosta as the new leader of their organization. Charles gave them time to come around, the ones he deemed worth keeping around, at least. But time, finite in this world of crime, had run out.

So the three men in the luxury vehicle had acted the part of good soldiers and captains and performed their jobs and arranged the executions, because there was no other way to refer to it when friends kill friends, though the three men tried, and had the bodies disposed of in a rather conspicuous manner.

Twenty-four hands. Same number of feet. A dozen heads. And the left-over bodies. All cast into the river in various locations with no attempt at concealing the task. Charles didn't care if the remains washed ashore, got tangled up in fishing nets and crab pots, or if they found their way to the Atlantic. He gave little regard to the idea that a group of kids might hook into a decapitated head, reeling it in and coming face-to-face with a ghost. Or that a group of old women on their morning walk might stumble over the ass-up headless body of a criminal.

So long as the act achieved the intended effect.

Fear begets more fear, which in turn creates allegiance.

Charles's thinking, at least.

The deepening of the new boss's maniacal nature had coincided with his rise to power. From a street hustler to a private mechanic for Feng, the Old Man and notorious gangster that led the organization. From driving Feng around town to becoming the Old Man's most trusted adviser. And when the Old Man was assassinated in broad daylight outside a Queens restaurant, Charles returned to New York from Europe, where he had headed up overseas operations, and stepped into position to claim control over the organization.

He met with resistance. More than two dozen, a third of them captains, disagreed. The most vocal were dealt with immediately. The rest fell into line, for a while, at least. Murmurs of dissent made their way through the compound, through Queens, bypassing Brooklyn, and finding their way to Lower Manhattan where they were whispered into Charles's ear.

So he formed the plan that required a mass assassination. Kill to keep the peace, he said.

None of the men in the BMW wanted to think about the screams and pleads of dying. Men they had laughed with and hustled with and killed with. For simply killing wasn't enough for Charles. The bastards had to suffer. If things had gone the other way, they would have done the same to Charles before casting him into the Atlantic after fitting him with concrete pants and shoes.

The transition from the bridge to Delancey Street erased the thoughts from their collective memory. For a while, anyway.

"Who's calling the overgrown bastard?" the driver said. He forced a laugh to cover up the remark, but none of the men in the car bought it.

"I'll do it," the guy in the backseat said, pulling his cell from his pocket.

CHARLES STOOD WITH his back to the reinforced steel door that separated his office from the rest of the complex. Designed to stop a .50 caliber round, the door provided him with a sense of security. A false one considering his only other way out was down, but he found solace behind the door. If someone reached it, Charles knew his chances of getting out alive were closer to zero. But at least he'd have the opportunity to take a few of the assailants out with him.

He glanced back at the three silent men seated on the opposite side of his dominating mahogany desk.

Two bodyguards remained outside the office any time Charles was present. Near them sat two assistants who handled Charles's day-to-day schedule. One for legit activities. The other for all things related to the organization. A wall separated the bodyguards and assistants from the receptionist who sat behind a counter, with a headset on, underneath an oval sign labeled *CDC Industries, INC.*

The place had to look legitimate for a crime boss to work out of it. Not that it fooled anyone. Charles took notice of the stares in the lobby. He felt the judgmental thoughts in the elevator. Women would stop short and allow the doors to close before stepping on if he was the only one inside it.

The top floor looked down on West 3rd Street, and offered an unblocked view of the fountain in the center of Washington Square Park. Charles had grown accustomed to staring down at the park while mulling over important, and not so important, decisions. Even on a humid mid-July morning, the place teemed with activity. The high-powered binoculars perched on the ledge allowed him to watch the women as they jogged or roller-skated along the walkways. Stress relief. Nothing more. So far.

Looking to the northeast, Broadway stretched to 14th Street. With a brief smile, Charles recalled how he longed to perform there when he was a kid. His mother had taken him to see *Fiddler on the Roof* when he was eight or nine. He even took two weeks of dance lessons, but quit when his friends found out and turned on him. The secret wish didn't die, though. But when he filled out and his size offered easier and more immediate ways to make a buck, Charles gave up on his dreams of fame under the lights and embraced the criminal life. A couple bucks here and there grew into a hundred a pop. Before long, he had more money than he knew what to do with. His favorite theater was a benefactor of that wealth. Anonymously, of course.

Stretching his arms overhead and directing his gaze to a spot just over the city horizon, Charles contemplated why the Old Man never moved to a proper office. Even when Charles had urged Feng to do it, the old bastard stubbornly refused. The compound served a purpose. No denying that. It made a great base of operation, and housed several of the underlings at any given time. But as a place to bring in guests and conduct business?

Not anymore. Not a chance.

Another mistake Charles refused to duplicate was Feng's inability to delegate. The Old Man's refusal to do so until the end led to a near-Civil War within the organization. It also resulted in the Old Man's assassination. The geezer could've retired four or five years back, enjoyed time with this granddaughter. Instead, the little girl witnessed Feng's brains exiting his cranium at high velocity.

To appease those in the organization on the fence about Charles's over-seeing the operation, he promised to avenge the Old Man's death. He didn't care if he ever did. Killing off two-dozen dissenters would be enough to get everyone in line. The timing had to be right. And finally, it was.

So now he had the office, where he spent most of his time, and the compound, where he only made brief appearances. There were people Charles trusted, and those were the ones who remained in charge in Queens. He also had snitches on call should his captains turn on him. Loyalty, as far as he was concerned, did not exist. Charles and the Old Man had turned on each other. And over what? Something to do with a woman and Jack Noble?

No, even the concept of loyalty only got one so far. If a concept could be packaged into something similar, then his group would be considered as loyal as they came. Which meant a quarter to a third were scamming and skimming off the top. To be expected, though. Charles did it when he was coming up. He presumed Feng did as well. Didn't mean he had to accept it. He'd already decided that would be the next order of business.

From the compound, Charles's captains oversaw day-to-day activities. From the high-rise, Charles worked on broadening and expanding his empire. Opportunities existed that Feng never bothered to investigate. The money the Old Man had, which now belonged to Charles, meant a chance to move into businesses other than drugs and racketeering and selling secrets. And now that things had been handled and he expected operations to run smoothly here on out, that was precisely what he planned to do.

Charles reached for the binoculars. He followed two women, one brunette, the other blond, as they jogged through the park, honing in until their brightly colored running shorts disappeared behind the thick leafy cover. His gaze lifted over the tops of the trees, down the shimmering, hazy corridor of 5th Avenue. His eyes switched focus from the cityscape to the reflection of the three men seated behind him.

"Which of you thought this would be a good idea?" Charles turned, folded his forearms across the top of his expensive high-backed leather chair. It swiveled to the left until his weight settled.

The first guy that spoke drew Charles's wrath.

"Shut up," he said before the guy managed a second syllable. "All three of you are lucky I brought you down here and didn't have you dismembered and dissolved in the compound basement."

The looks on the faces of the men were as varied as they were. Each had come up in Feng's organization in a different manner. None of that mattered, though. They remained loyal to Charles when others hadn't. They carried out his wishes exactly as requested. Until the final slaughter.

"Didn't I say," Charles said, "that Mikey C. was off-limits? He was the only one from the old regime, from back when I was a damn grease monkey working in the garage, who remained neutral in the face of change. He had ties with groups outside our organization that wouldn't talk to me. Now we lost him, we lost them, and we lost a lot of damn money."

None of the three men spoke.

"I said don't touch him!" Charles kicked his chair, sending it to the left. It toppled over on its side. Caster wheels spun without resistance. "But now his body is torn into pieces and floating in the damn river."

Sunlight shone against the sweaty foreheads of the men across from him. One snuck a peek toward the office door, presumably in a failed attempt to locate Charles's bodyguards.

"We didn't know he was gonna be there," the guy named Paolo Almeida said. "I mean, once we started, he came out from a back room where I guess he was banging some whore. Charles, man, he saw what we was doing. He reached for his piece. I had no choice." The guy closed his eyes and flinched, having given up the critical information Charles searched for.

Charles leaned back against the window, massive arms crossed. "You two, out."

Paolo remained seated while the other two captains rose and exited the office.

"What are you thinking right now?" Charles said.

"I'm wishing I'd kissed my wife before I left today."

"You're single."

Paolo shrugged. "Figure of speech."

Charles smirked. "Well in that case, if you had one, probably woulda been a good idea."

"Look, I'm telling the truth. It was me or him. I had no choice."

"Yes, you did." Charles pushed off the window and planted his thick knuckles on the desk and leaned over it. "You could have known who the hell was in the damn house before going in, guns blazing."

Paolo said nothing. Better that way. Every word he uttered dug another six inches in his eventual grave.

"So what should I do with you?" He didn't wait for the man to answer. "Death is too simple an answer. It lacks the punch I'm looking for. Maybe a demotion. You know, knock you down a peg or six. You're young enough to hustle on the street. Of course, you won't have any protection if you get picked up."

"And I'll rat your ass out first chance I get."

"Oh, hotheaded Paolo. The moment you arrived from Brazil or Argentina or wherever the fuck you're from, I knew you'd be a problem."

Charles smiled at the guy while an internal switch flipped. Rage rose up within him like angry bile. Still smiling, he reached out, grabbed the back of Paolo's head and slammed it against the edge of the desk. Cartilage met solid mahogany. The desk won. Paolo choked on the blood that flooded his mouth and throat. Another round of head-meets-desk split Paolo's forehead and sent him to the floor.

With his heart racing and his breath rapid and uneven, Charles rounded his desk. A pool of blood seeped into the twenty thousand dollar rug. He slammed his foot into Paolo's midsection, cursing at the spreading tide of crimson, then he proceeded toward the door.

"You two," he said, aiming a finger in the direction of the men who had accompanied Paolo. "Get him off my floor. Clean him up, take him upstate, and get rid of him. Use the express elevator straight to the garage. Anyone asks, he slipped in the bathroom and hit the urinal."

NOBLE JUDGMENT: CHAPTER 3

New York City.

TWO WOMEN. ONE blonde, the other brunette. Skimpy outfits. Did they run for exercise? Or for attention? The blonde glanced over, then back, smiling as she passed. The diamonds on her wedding ring glinted in the sunlight.

Jack Noble returned a complimentary nod as he stayed far to the right of the Washington Square fountain. In part to stay out of view should someone be watching from above. Also to seek shelter from the heat. But not even the cover of the trees could provide respite from the mid-July humidity. Even at nine in the morning. Didn't bother the kids at the playground, although few things did. They raced past, sidestepping adults without taking their eyes off one another.

The sight brought images of Mia to the forefront of Jack's mind. He hadn't seen his daughter since he left London to deal with a matter in his hometown of Crystal River, Florida. Things there hadn't gone as planned. Once again, his past had resurfaced, as it always did. And as much as he wanted to be near his daughter, her safety was paramount.

So Jack came back to the closest thing he had to a home.

But there wasn't much left for him in New York. The properties he co-owned with his former partner Riley "Bear" Logan were all up for sale or sold. It had been Jack's idea. Bear followed through with it. The properties were a waste at this point anyway. They sat unused, and would remain that way if the duo hung onto them. Better Bear have the money to set aside for his and Mandy's futures, than the condos and apartments go to waste.

Bear had kept another promise Jack forced upon the big man. He and Mandy had disappeared. Calls to his main forwarding number were met with a fast busy signal. The line was gone. All other numbers Jack tried received a message indicating the same.

Better this way. At least, Jack convinced himself of it. Anyone connected with him met an untimely and painful ending. Somehow, Bear had managed to survive for close to twenty years as Jack's partner, first in the military, then in business. The odds weren't in the big man's favor if he remained in that capacity.

At the northeast corner of the park, Jack crossed Washington Square North and continued along the busy sidewalks of University Place until he reached 11th. He'd made the same walk four other times in the past month. Each time, his knocks went unanswered. Had they gone unheard? All he wanted was proof that Clarissa was OK. The last time he'd seen her, she'd saved his life by stopping a rogue SIS agent from filling him with bullets.

Since then, she'd been a ghost.

Perhaps that meant it was time to accept his duty to her was done. He'd protected her long enough. She obviously could make her own way now.

From 11th, Jack made his way to the Upper East Side. An eccentric millionaire had reached out to him through a private channel and showed interest in securing Jack's services as head of security for the duration of the man's stay in New York. The call came as little surprise. He'd fielded several over the past month after gaining a reputation in some circles. The reason? He'd prevented the assassination of a rising political star in London. In retrospect, it would have been best for all involved had she died. Eventually, she did. Regardless, Jack's status in the wake of the event offered new prospects. This one, being close to home, intrigued him.

He didn't need the money. Even after turning ninety percent of his assets over to Bear, his bank accounts provided enough to live on for years to come. But Jack wasn't ready for retirement. Yet. And rather than eat up his accounts, he figured a better plan would be to add to them while he still had the ability. Short-term security gigs would provide an opportunity to do just that. Plus, they had the added benefit of giving him something to do every day. He expected his senses to dull over time due to age. Little could be done to prevent that. Maybe slow the decline down. But there was no need to accelerate the process by sitting around on a barstool all day.

Upon entering the millionaire's condo building, the phone in Jack's pocket buzzed. He'd acted on a whim and purchased a smart phone. It had gigs of memory, and multiple gigahertz of processing, and cloud capabilities. At first none of that meant anything to him. The phone had nearly ended up in the trashcan on more than one occasion. But he took the time to figure it out. The devices, he figured, were here to stay. No point fighting them.

A man the color of coal and the size of a box-truck entered the lobby. He had a dark t-shirt on that said, "Yeah, I'm That Guy." Jack figured he got asked the question a lot. The man gestured with his head for Jack to follow, so he did. They took the hallway to the left and entered a small windowless room.

"I'm sure you know how this works," the guy said.

"I'll save you the trouble." Jack reached behind and retrieved his Beretta. He released the magazine and set it and the pistol on the table, grip facing the other man.

"Appreciate that, but it ain't gonna keep my hands off of you."

Jack didn't resist the man's attempt. Wasn't like he was going to find anything. Hands ran roughshod up and down Jack's torso, legs, ankles. Finally, the guy stepped back and opened the door.

"Let's go."

They took the elevator to the top floor and walked the length of the building where they came to a stop in front of the last door. The man made Jack wait in the hallway. Murmurs escaped through the gap between the door and the floor. They were too low to decipher. After a few minutes, the guy returned and waved Jack inside the condo. The drawn curtains, perhaps purple in color and made from velvet, blocked out all the light. One dim bulb illuminated the room. A flash of orange shone from the corner. Jack didn't recognize the face behind the cigarette.

The guy took a step forward. Curly silver hair with traces of black adorned a chiseled face.

"Ah, Mr.-"

Jack held out his hand and said, "No names."

The guy nodded. "No problem."

"Can we get some light in here?"

"I'd prefer not." He paused a moment. "Took a bullet to the head twenty-five years ago, eyes haven't been the same since. I've got special glasses to help when outside, but I don't like wearing them inside the house."

Jack's eyes adjusted. He made out the scar on the man's right cheek, between ear and eye. Maybe a remnant from the bullet that affected his tolerance for light.

"So what happened? Mugged? That why I'm here?"

Laughing, the man stepped forward again. His frame was slender, but muscular. "Twenty five years ago I was a SEAL. Do the math."

"Panama."

Nodding, he said, "At least I wasn't one of the unfortunate twenty-three souls who perished there. Anyway, what about you?"

"Panama? I was in eighth grade. I was ready to go, but they wouldn't take me."

The guy's smile widened. "No, not Panama. Military?"

"You invited me here, figured you knew that already." Jack paused to allow the man to rebut. He didn't. Jack continued. "Eschewed college to join the Marines. Selected for a special assignment early on for some new program they were testing."

"With the CIA."

Jack shrugged and continued. "Did that for a couple years before the whole thing fell apart. They threw a lot of money at me to get me to retire early. I took it. Considered making it a permanent situation. Problem was, being a drunk in the Keys didn't pay all that well, so I hopped on board the government wagon again and worked for another agency. Couple years there, then went into business for myself. Picked up the security gig for that politician by accident after working with British Intelligence a few months back."

"And I heard you did an excellent job."

"I suppose." Jack glanced around in an attempt to locate the large man who'd escorted him through the building. "Then again, she's dead."

"Not your fault, from what I hear."

"Don't believe everything you're told."

The man fidgeted with an envelope and said nothing.

"What's this all about?" Jack said. "You obviously have the skills and contacts to take care of yourself. You're not some eccentric that's being stalked or extorted or living in fear of his own shadow. So why me? Why here? Why now?"

The envelope disappeared behind the man's body. "Perhaps you are right. Maybe I don't need your services right now."

For a moment, Jack's gut tensed, and he had the feeling that mortars were incoming. "Was it something I said?"

The guy said nothing.

"What's in the envelope?"

"Down payment, that's all." He brought his hands around, empty. "Seems we won't be needing it."

"The hell is this all about?"

The guy lifted his hand and snapped. "Martellus, please escort our guest out."

The big black man crossed the room. Each step reverberated through the floorboards. Sensing he had a few seconds left in the condo, Jack spoke up.

"Never got your name."

"You don't need it," the older man said.

"Why'd you bring me here?"

The big man's hands wrapped around Jack's shoulders. He didn't budge.

"Easy way or hard way, man. Either way, I get paid the same," the man said.

"Why?" Jack said.

The older man turned away and went into the next room without saying a word. The door shut behind him, sending a slight gust toward the windows and ruffling the dark drapes.

"Last chance of easy way," the guy said.

Jack broke free of the man's grasp and started toward the door. "I can find my own way out."

"You want your piece?"

Jack stopped, turned, held out his hands.

"Elevator," the guy said.

A minute later, the bronze-plated doors opened up to an empty lobby. The big man didn't get out. He handed Jack his Beretta, then tossed the magazine halfway across the room. By the time Jack reached it, the elevator had started its ascent to the upper floor.

Not quite sure what to make of the meeting, Jack exited the building and walked north one block. Heat reflected off the concrete surrounding him. The temperature had risen ten degrees since he stepped foot inside the building. The humidity was close to maxed out. Despite that, the sidewalk was packed, and the park across the street too. The meeting played over again in his mind. What had the man wanted with him? Maybe he'd built a team of some sort, security or mercenary. Not much difference these days. The guy had some interest in Jack, but apparently not enough to extend an offer. What had he said to discourage the guy?

As soon as a break in traffic presented itself, Jack jogged across 5th Avenue. A curb marked the crossover from asphalt to concrete. He imagined a sniper rifle protruding from a window in the condo, aimed at his back and tracking every move. The cover of the trees on the opposite sidewalk failed to provide the security he needed. So he hopped the solid fence and cut across Central Park, always moving forward, resisting the urge to look behind.

Click Here to Purchase *Noble Judgment*

ABOUT THE AUTHOR

L.T. Ryan is a *USA Today* and international bestselling author. The new age of publishing offered L.T. the opportunity to blend his passions for creating, marketing, and technology to reach audiences with his popular Jack Noble series.

Living in central Virginia with his wife, the youngest of his three daughters, and their three dogs, L.T. enjoys staring out his window at the trees and mountains while he should be writing, as well as reading, hiking, running, and playing with gadgets. See what he's up to at http://ltryan.com.

Social Medial Links:

- Facebook (L.T. Ryan): https://www.facebook.com/LTRyanAuthor

- Facebook (Jack Noble Page): https://www.facebook.com/JackNobleBooks/

- Twitter: https://twitter.com/LTRyanWrites

- Goodreads: http://www.goodreads.com/author/show/6151659.L_T_Ryan

Printed in Great Britain
by Amazon